WARLORD RISING

WARLORD RISING

THE GREAT INSURRECTION™ BOOK TWO

DAVID BEERS
MICHAEL ANDERLE

DISRUPTIVE IMAGINATION®

This book is a work of fiction.
All of the characters, organizations, and events portrayed in this novel
are either products of the author's imagination or are used fictitiously.
Sometimes both.

LMBPN Publishing
PMB 196, 2540 South Maryland Pkwy
Las Vegas, NV 89109

First US edition 2021
eBook ISBN: 978-1-64971-370-4
Print ISBN: 978-1-64971-371-1

THE WARLORD RISING TEAM

Thanks to our Beta Readers

Kelly O'Donnell, John Ashmore, Rachel Beckford

Thanks to our JIT Readers

Wendy L Bonell
Diane L. Smith
Angel LaVey
Jackey Hankard-Brodie

Editor

SkyHunter Editing Team

DEDICATION

For my brother, Danny.

— David

To Family, Friends and
Those Who Love
to Read.
May We All Enjoy Grace
to Live the Life We Are
Called.

— Michael

THE WRITTEN HISTORY OF THE GREAT INSURRECTION

We lost a lot of people in our escape from Pluto. Even now, I worry the gods may not ever let us wash the blood from our hands. I think about the thousands and thousands of lives wasted and wonder whether Prometheus could have been born any other way?

Perhaps it is as the myths say. Fire made him, or at least without the flames, humanity would have never known him.

There will be time at the end to remember the lost lives. For now, we trudge onward. For now, we live in this new world Prometheus has given us and hope we don't burn too much of it to ash.

Where was I?

Yes, the AllMother, unconscious and on a strange planet. Her children hunted from all sides.

And Prometheus in the middle of it.

CHAPTER ONE

"The Commonwealth's hand grips our solar system, but it reaches far, and when it swings, it swings the might of suns."

–Aurelius de Finita, First Imperial Ascendant

Primus Veena de Ragnimus had thought she knew the glory of the Commonwealth. She had thought she understood the scope and breadth of its rule.

Six months after the destruction of Pluto, she realized she'd been a child in her understanding. Perhaps she'd even been in the womb, so little had she known about the universe around her.

As Veena looked back on the past six months, she was hesitant to say she understood or knew anything about the universe. What she knew for sure, and perhaps the only thing that couldn't be doubted, was that she stood on a dreadnought and commanded the group of pilots in front of her. Less sure but something she had to trust was that three other dreadnoughts sailed on either side of her ship, also listening to her commands.

From there, Veena's confidence in the universe faded.

Over the past six months, she'd gone from thinking that portals were only theoretical constructions to traveling through the Commonwealth's apparent network of them. The Ascendant had made it known that at most of these portals, Commonwealth dreadnoughts waited. The Commonwealth had spent a thousand years figuring out ways to ship its force across the universe.

Veena, Ares, and Hel—the three of them had left Earth, the Solar System, and the Milky Way. They were now hunting down the Titan who should have burned on Pluto, and they had very simple instructions.

Kill or capture Alistair Kane. That, or never return to Earth.

That was where she was—in the middle of a galaxy she didn't know, listening to her AI's instructions and hoping the arrogant child or the psychopathic woman didn't kill her as they hunted down this man.

Veena stood on the bridge of her ship, staring at panels that showed her the outside world. They were traveling in the fourth dimension, though they could only do so for brief periods before their human bodies began taking damage. Very soon now, she would command them to drop back to the third dimension. They probably had one more fourth dimension jump left in them, then they would finish it out where the human body was best suited.

"Show me the planet," she said.

A pilot pulled up the planet without turning away from her post. Her eyes were static-gray since she was harmonized with the dreadnought.

The planet they wanted was Phoenix in the Mayall galaxy. Veena also learned that while the Commonwealth didn't control other parts of the universe, they had spies throughout it. When the Ascendant asked questions in this galaxy, answers came back swiftly. The portal opened on this planet, and indeed, a large number of refugees had come through.

Veena looked at the planet on her panels. It was a massive thing, larger than any planet inside Earth's Solar System, yet its atmosphere was unlike anything Veena had ever imagined, let alone seen. She stared at it now, almost unable to believe such a thing could exist. Fire wrapped around the planet, its atmosphere made of continual explosions and the resulting flames. Veena had looked up the science behind such an uninhabitable planet and come to understand that the humans who'd arrived here nearly a thousand years ago had created this.

Their terraforming wasn't to make the world more habitable, but less so. For what reason? To stop the exact thing that was now about to happen: they wanted any invaders to have to consider the cost of their incursion.

Which was what Veena had been doing since realizing what her fleet was flying into. Their ships would be damaged. The atmosphere was too hot for the shields to hold up during the entire descent, not to mention the heavier gravity they would encounter due to the planet's mass. The AI would navigate around most of the explosions, but Veena knew it couldn't do it perfectly before reaching the surface. That meant death.

In the end, though, the cost didn't matter. The Fallen Titan was on that planet, and Veena had no choice but to go down there and get him. Once they were closer, they'd make contact with the sub-surface-dwelling people. Hopefully, those creatures would give Kane up, but if not, the Commonwealth would invade.

There would be no more fire rains. Veena had made her decision. She would no longer risk portals or any other new magic the Subversives might show her. Boots on the ground would ensure his death or capture.

Veena could not fail, not if she wanted to ever see her home again.

Ares stalked through the ship like a restless cat. While Veena spent most of her time on the bridge, Ares couldn't stop moving.

He thought as he walked the ship, and those ruminations were starting to bother him. If he ever let anyone know what he was thinking, he imagined they'd have called him obsessive. Perhaps they would have been right. Obsessive or not, he couldn't make the thoughts stop.

That was why he came to the War Room. It was a one-hundred-meter-square space near the top of the ship where the Titans trained. However, whenever Ares entered, anyone else using the space left. Ares didn't know if he had changed since his encounter with Alistair, not yet at least, but those around him acted as if he had.

He didn't even need to look at whoever was in the War Room. They simply exited, which was what he wanted.

The War Room was a surprisingly efficient and reactive piece of equipment. Until shipping out on this dreadnought, Ares had preferred practicing against real people, yet these machines were more advanced. They were preparing him in a way he hadn't thought possible.

That was what he wanted more than anything in this universe: to be prepared the next time he saw Alistair. The *mutant*.

Ares waited for the two young Titans to exit the War Room, then he walked to the middle of it. "Three enemies."

The walls opened on three sides of him and three black poles floated out, hovering above the floor. Three stick-like arms emerged from each pole, and laser strands flowed from the ends of those arms.

"Difficulty level?" the War Room's AI asked.

"Deadly," Ares responded as he pulled his Whip from his belt. He could pick from multiple difficulty levels, but he'd seen Alistair move against the insectoid back on the other dreadnought. The man had always been lethal, but now he was something else, almost otherworldly. Ares honestly wondered if he could defeat him in a one-on-one match. He'd studied the images from the portal, watching as Alistair destroyed ten Titans in MechSuits.

They're not me, he thought. *A mutant versus me in a Mech-Suit will be no contest. Not even him.*

"Battle commencing," the room's AI alerted.

The three black poles came at him. They surrounded him, then started circling. The AI was learning his strengths and weaknesses, adapting to him with each battle.

The first machine came at him, all three arms vertically twirling their Whips. Ares didn't take the bait but glanced over his left shoulder. The machine behind him was coming from above, spinning, the lasers moving horizontally.

Ares dropped to the floor, and the weapons barely missed his head. He swung his Whip at the pole but it jumped backward, floating through the air as if he were moving in slow motion. The third machine slid horizontally to the floor, its laser sticking up straight in the air.

Ares pushed off the floor with his left arm and leg, flipping himself into the air with tremendous strength. He twirled, his Whip reaching out to lash the machine, then hit the ground and rolled twice to create more space.

"One enemy down," the War Room alerted.

Ares bounced to his feet, and the remaining machines formed a triangle with his body. They were more cautious now that one of their number was down.

"Person entering," the War Room instructed. "Standing down."

The lasers died and the black poles floated to the ground, their stick arms folding in.

"Bravo, bravo." The new voice came before the person had entered. Ares didn't need to see who it was. Only one person on this dreadnought would dare interrupt his session. "I honestly didn't think you'd be able to take down three, but here you are with one dead already. It took you over a day to get past two of them."

Hel entered the room on Ares' right side. Ares looked at

the floor, his Whip remaining unfurled. "Why are you interrupting me?"

She turned to face him full on. "Just wanted to say how proud I am of your dedication. You badly want to kill this man, don't you?"

Ares didn't know everything about the woman, but he had heard enough rumors to understand that her reactivation would send shockwaves through the Commonwealth hierarchy. He had hardly spoken to her since boarding the ship, and he'd hoped to keep it that way. "A Titan practices," he responded. "Regardless of where he or she is. It's our duty to keep our skills keen."

"You're pushing yourself, Titan. You're not simply keeping things keen. You want to improve."

Ares turned and raised his head to look at her. She was twenty years his senior but shockingly beautiful. Her hair was short and black as space, curling around her chin. Her body was thin but muscular.

"A Titan's duty is to improve if there is room for it."

The woman smirked. "Did he show you that you had room for it?"

"Is your Whip as sharp as your tongue?" Ares shot back. "Because if it is, perhaps you can show me, assassin."

He knew Hel had never been a Titan. She might be the only human not in their order to be granted a Whip. Her talents weren't only in her Whipmanship, though. He'd heard the rumors.

"Maybe one day," she responded, "though I'm not sure it's in your best interests."

Ares shut his Whip down. He didn't see hers, but that

didn't mean the bitch didn't have it. Still, he was tired of this banter. "Is there anything else?"

She shook her head. "No. Just a bit of congratulation. I hope to see you defeat four soon." She bowed slightly. "One People. One Purpose. Good day, Titan."

The assassin left the room, and Ares stared after her. The reason she'd come was simple: so he would know she was watching him. She had somehow known he was there, which meant the Ascendant had given her authority neither he nor Veena possessed.

In the Ascendant's eyes, she was more powerful than him.

Ares didn't move and didn't show any emotion. He kept his mask on and thought about what he must do to regain the respect due to him. The answer wasn't hard. He had to push himself, and when the time came, he had to kill his mentor.

He heard his father's voice in the recesses of his mind.

Your obligation to the Commonwealth is paramount. Your family's rise in the Commonwealth is paramount.

Hel vi Thraxus had misgivings about both of the soldiers she'd been matched with. She knew the former Titan they were chasing. Once, long ago, she'd tested him. She didn't know the people flying with her.

So Hel had spent time learning about those she now served with. Hel thought both Veena and Ares were soft, but for different reasons. She also thought Alistair Kane was soft, but in a different way. His softness centered around his wife.

Hel spent a lot of time understanding those she hunted. She didn't think Veena or the young Titan understood that was what they were doing. Veena, the Primus of the First Fleet, only wanted to make up for her failure; that was her weakness. Ares? He was seeking something greater than forgiveness, glory, and another failure might sacrifice his legacy. For him, it was a balancing act between being great and being nothing.

Both of them were wrong, but that was why the Ascendant had summoned Hel. Veena and Ares weren't here for glory or forgiveness. They had come to catch prey, to hunt, and to consume. That was what predators did, and not for external reasons like the ones these two had concocted. Predators did it because they were born to.

Hel had no plans to let these two return to the Commonwealth with her. She wasn't sure how the Ascendant would feel about losing two Primuses, but then again, he had to know she would kill his prizes.

Hel couldn't help it. She was a predator. Some might call her a psychopath, but she shrugged such things off. She'd learned long ago that most people didn't think like her, and the ones who did hid it.

She didn't. The difference between her and other predators? She was better at it. That was why the Imperial Ascendant had never been able to kill her. He knew, or maybe his orb of ghosts did, that one day she would be needed—the secret weapon the Commonwealth had to hide, lest it blow up unexpectedly.

She wasn't hidden anymore, though. She was out in the

open, and she could smell her prey. He sat on a planet just a bit in front of her. Fire guarded him, but she could still smell him sitting beneath the earth.

Alistair Kane didn't know his personal Grim Reaper was on the way.

But he would very soon.

His time was almost up, as a Titan, a revolutionary, a whatever. The predator didn't care. He was only prey now.

CHAPTER TWO

"The future is already writ. We must only go forth, brothers and sisters, since fate paved our way long before we were born."

–The AllSeer, originally of de Finita lineage.

Location unknown.

Ajax had no surname. He had no family lineage like the Earthborn. No house to call his own. Ajax came from only one lineage, that of the true inheritors of the universe. He did not think of himself as human, nor did any of the AllSeer's children.

They were not mutants, as the Earthborn disdainfully called them.

They were simply superior in every way. The AllSeer had created them, given life to Ajax and all his brothers and sisters, and led them across galaxies. Across an entire universe.

He had nearly led them to victory, and Ajax was here to see that the AllSeer's vision reached fruition.

The AllMother was only a few million kilometers away. Ajax could no longer feel her, but he knew what had happened to her. She was weak now, not the woman of might she had been when Ajax was younger.

All these years we have chased you, he thought from his ship, *and they seemed endless. The AllSeer was right, though. They were not meant to be endless. Indeed, we are nearly finished.*

Ajax didn't know how much the Earthborn knew of their quest, nor did he care what they thought of it. Humans had lived as long as they had because the AllSeer allowed it. Once he had the AllMother, that would no longer be true.

Ajax didn't know what the AllMother had told her people, but again, he didn't care. They would be ended very soon.

Ajax currently sat in a strange room, having ventured to a strange land. He was alone right now, though his fleet hovered above the planet his people had just thoroughly searched. Ajax was not stupid; he knew he hadn't done this alone, but through the AllSeer, all things were possible.

The room he occupied belonged to the planet's royalty; he didn't know who, nor did he care. The planet had given him almost everything he wanted almost immediately. It was better to have the AllSeer as a friend than an enemy, and people in this star system understood that. It was the new solar systems Ajax ventured into, the ones that weren't aware of his master's power, that had problems.

The AllSeer offered blood or wealth, and he only made the offer once.

There was a knock on the door.

"Enter," Ajax commanded.

A Myrmidon slave opened the door and meekly took a few steps in. "The search of the planet is nearly finished. Your brothers believe the governments are telling the truth. None have escaped here, and they believe the AllMother to still be on the world next to this one. The world with the Terram."

Ajax looked at his nails, carefully studying them with his red eyes. "Is there any word on the Commonwealth's fleet?"

The slave didn't look up from the floor. "They are continuing their journey toward the same planet."

"How far out are they?" The slave had better have answers for Ajax. He didn't know the lower one's name, but he'd seen him before. He would have answers because he knew what would happen otherwise.

"Three weeks, sire."

Ajax nodded, putting his hand on his lap and finally looking at the slave. "Ready my brothers and sisters. We go to the AllMother."

"Yes, sire." The slave exited the room, leaving Ajax alone once again.

The AllSeer's plans had been wise, but for so very long, many in the universe had thought him mad. Insane. Now that his plans had nearly come to fruition, those who harbored such heretical notions would pay for their crimes.

The AllMother knew the AllSeer was wise. That was

why she had run for so many long years. Why she had eventually gone to hide in the Commonwealth's Solar System.

No longer, Mother. The time for weakness was over. The time for might had arrived.

Ajax and his fleet flew toward what they thought was their destiny. They went toward humanity, toward the AllMother and a man they knew almost nothing about.

A man named Prometheus.

CHAPTER THREE

"I dream my painting, and I paint my dream."

–Van Gogh

The dreams kept coming. Theos, the mutant who had changed Alistair, advised him that they were a possibility, but he hadn't told him how intense or frequent they would be.

Every time Alistair slept, they came for him—lucid dreams, some of the past, some of the future. He didn't know what caused him to go back and forth through time, nor did he enjoy them all.

Now he was in the past, at the age of sixteen. Alistair remembered the feeling from when he entered the Academy. Fear. His name was Alistair Kane, not Alistair *de* Kane. He had no house to speak of. His father had died when he was young, one of the few deaths caused by hazardous jobs. His mother? She'd wanted him to go to university, off-world if possible. The best universities were on Mars, and she thought it might be feasible if he tested well enough.

Then he took the test. He knew it had been graded instantly, and the Commonwealth's bureaucracy most likely decided the rest of his life just as quickly, all from one test: where he would move, what he would do, the last two years of his schooling planned out. He only needed to go home and wait, and the Commonwealth would send him a notification.

One People. One Purpose.

That was not what happened, though, and Alistair saw it plainly now.

He'd been in his apartment, bored out of his mind since the school term was done until he received his notification.

The holovid alerted him to a visitor, a Commonwealth official it said in the dream. Alistair looked at the message, not understanding what it meant. He blinked, then stood up slowly. His mother wasn't home yet; she was still at work.

"Turn off," he told the holovid as he turned to look out his apartment window. He watched as the vehicle rose to his apartment level. He didn't give the GLASS wall permission to open. Whoever was inside the vehicle had all the permission they needed simply by being who they were.

The platform rolled out to the taxi, and the windshields shot up.

Alistair was tall for sixteen, but the man who stepped

out of the taxi was a mountain: all muscle, a chin like granite, something you might see in a clichéd holovid. He walked into the apartment as if he lived there, and Alistair thought the same thing as he had all those years ago.

This man has never felt fear. It's as strange to him as flying is to a fish.

"*Salve*, son," the mountain said. "You are Alistair Kane, correct?"

Alistair swallowed and nodded. "Yes, sir. Can I help you?" He didn't know what the hell to say. He didn't know why this mountain was in his home or what he wanted.

The mountain extended his hand. Alistair did the same. It was an old act, the Shaking of Hands, only done in the rarest of circumstances now. Alistair might have done it twice in his whole life, but it showed grave respect. The man's hand enveloped Alistair's; he could probably have crushed every bone in it if he wanted to.

"It's an honor, son," the mountain said as he pumped Alistair's hand.

When they finally quit the ancient ritual, Alistair looked up at the man. "I'm sorry, good sir, but I don't understand what's happening right now. My mother won't be home for a few standard hours yet. Is there something I can do for you?"

Alistair had never thought what came next could happen. The mountain reached into his vest and pulled out a sheet of *paper*. Alistair couldn't remember the last time he'd seen one. Only the most important messages were put on paper. The man handed it to him.

It was thrice-folded.

Alistair stared at it, feeling the smooth material under his thumb. "What is this?"

"You're being invited to attend the Academy, Alistair Kane. That is your formal letter of invitation."

Alistair shook his head, not wanting to open it. Tears were in his eyes, but he didn't believe what this man was saying. The Academy was the stuff of myth for people of his heritage. Sure, anyone could get in; that was the whole point, that the strongest rose to the top. But in reality? Alistair had never even heard of anyone of his heritage being allotted a spot.

"It's not possible," he whispered, not wanting to unfold the paper.

"Son, the offer ends tomorrow at midnight," the mountain said. "You'd be a fool not to take it, and given your test scores, you'd be a strong addition to the Commonwealth."

Alistair had looked up at the mountain, still not understanding what he meant. Alistair didn't know the man's name, though he would later.

In this lucid dream, Alistair wondered what would have happened if he'd said no. If he'd told the mountain to go frag himself, how much different would his life have been?

He could change it, at least in this dream. He could say he was perfectly fine going to college on Mars. If his test scores were good enough for the Academy, they would be good enough for that distant planet.

There would have been no Luna, though. He wouldn't be on this distant, strange planet, alone for the most part, facing death every moment he breathed air.

But he wouldn't have known Luna.

So he let the dream version of him do the same thing he had done.

"You're serious?"

"Son, you got a perfect score on the aptitude test; I've never been more serious about anything in my life. I'll see you next week."

He had, and Alistair's life had never been the same.

CHAPTER FOUR

*"Humans think we are the last in evolution's lineage.
That we are its greatest creation. We are but stewards of
the universe, and poor ones at that."*

–The AllMother, former lineage of de Finita

"We don't have any choice. All the rest of this talk, every bit
of it, is just that: talk. We have to leave this planet, and we
have to run." Thoreaux paced as he spoke. His head was
down, and stress rippled through every word.

Servia was relaxed, sitting on a thin cushion on the
floor. Her legs were crossed beneath her. "How do you
propose we get the fifteen thousand people who followed
us here off-planet? Unless I'm missing something, Thoreaux, I don't see dreadnoughts that can carry them."

Thoreaux shook his head. "Don't see dreadnoughts? Do

I need to show you the holovid of the dreadnoughts that are coming? The amplification we used yesterday won't be needed today, believe that. They're closer, and the Terram aren't going to let their world be destroyed." He stopped pacing and pointed at the ceiling. "All those flames up there are to prevent exactly what is happening now. They don't want war with the Commonwealth, and they've protected us for too long as it is. To ask them to do any more than they already have would be immoral."

Servia looked at Alistair, one eyebrow raised. "Did you know that trying to save your people makes you immoral, Prometheus?"

Alistair wasn't looking at either of them. He sat on a ledge carved into the wall, leaning forward and stroking Obs' neck. The drathe was looking at his owner. The animal was a special breed of beast, able to understand a seemingly inexhaustible number of languages. He even understood the Terram's strange, guttural speech.

Alistair hadn't asked for the responsibility of deciding for thousands. He was a soldier, bred to kill in battle and lead other soldiers, but not an entire people. Even so, he couldn't shirk this duty. The people looking at him awaited a decision, and he had no choice but to give them one.

The Fallen Titan didn't look up. "Thoreaux, how far would you have us run? How long?"

"Until the AllMother is safe. Until she can tell us what she wants us to do. It's not only the Commonwealth coming, Pro, and you know that. The AllSeer is coming too. You heard the Terram today. They've spotted stealthed Myrmidon ships. The Myrmidons don't care about you.

They don't care about me or her either. They only want the AllMother."

"They've wanted her since before either of us was born," Servia shot back. "But they still don't have her. The goal was never to run. The goal was to overthrow the Commonwealth." She looked at Alistair. "Has that goal changed? Are we now refugees who will run forever?"

Alistair listened to them bicker like children. It was their usual form of communication. Obs sighed and laid on the floor. "Even the animal grows tired of you two arguing."

It was the portal that had given them away. Alistair didn't know it at the time, but the power it took to use such a machine could be detected by the right instruments. He didn't know if the Commonwealth had those instruments or simply a network of spies, but he imagined the AllSeer had been able to determine when they landed here, especially after the Terram showed Alistair the technology their ships used. It wasn't a StealthBlanket like the Commonwealth used, but something different and more advanced.

"The goal hasn't changed," Alistair finally said. "We're here, all of us, to overthrow the Commonwealth. But Servia is right. The Terram don't have the ships to get all of our people off-planet, and I won't leave them here while we run and hide. The AllMother's strength is her people, and I won't leave them stranded as refugees. Hell, I don't know if the Terram would keep them. We're definitely wearing out our welcome."

Thoreaux stepped forward. Obs raised his head and let a low rumble emanate from his throat. The man ignored him. "Then what do we do, Pro? Saying we'll stand and fight isn't an option."

"Have we heard from Relm?" Thoreaux asked Servia.

"He and Faitrin are due back in the next couple of days. I asked that their communications remain minimal because I don't know who above can hear us."

Alistair had sent Relm and Faitrin, the former Commonwealth pilot, to a neighboring planet. The Terram had lent them one of their ships, though they weren't happy about it. As a whole, they were a grumpy group, but Alistair figured living beneath the ground would do that to people.

Alistair had sent them because there were rumors that the Myrmidons had already blocked that planet as an exit. "So, we don't know yet if we can jump there. Are they on their way back?"

Servia nodded. "They should be, but again, we're keeping communication to a minimum."

This was a precarious situation, to say the least. Portal politics were denying Alistair's group the use of the Terram's portal. They wouldn't let him send even *some* of his people to another world while he figured out how to defend against the forces coming here. "I need to hear what they have to say before we make a decision. They'll be here before the Commonwealth."

He looked up to meet Thoreaux's eyes. "I'm not going to let her die."

Thoreaux held his gaze for a few moments, then left the room without another word.

Alistair sighed and leaned back against the rock wall. Servia stood, then sat down in front of Obs. She stroked his neck while she spoke. "Thoreaux trusts you. He's just not the best at handling his emotions. The AllMother is the only family he has left, and he's scared to lose her. You're making the right decision here. He knows it. He just doesn't know how to deal with the fact that she might die."

Alistair didn't look at her. He kept his eyes on the rock ceiling. "How are *you* dealing with it?"

"Only slightly better than him. I just don't let everyone see my emotions." She paused for a second as the drathe rolled over on his back, giving her his belly. "How about you? Not Prometheus, but Alistair. How are you handling it?"

He shook his head. "I don't know. I need her to live because she should make these decisions, not me."

Servia stood up, grinning. "You keep talking like that and she'll never come back, Prometheus. Whatever you think about her, she's wiser than you can imagine. She saw all this coming, and you stepping into your role as our leader was paramount to her designs. Keep doubting yourself, and she might just disappear entirely."

Servia winked, then left him with his animal. He looked down at Obs. "Any time you want to eat them, feel free."

The drathe gave a bark. It wasn't one of agreement.

***

"It ain't the best news, broth."

Twenty-four hours had passed since Alistair's last meeting with what he considered his council. Relm and Faitrin had arrived faster than anyone figured, and now the two of them sat in front of Alistair, Thoreaux, and Servia. The room was the closest thing the Terram had to a meeting room. It was carved into the ground, like all their rooms, though this one was circular.

Obs had left Alistair's feet and padded over to sit at Relm's. The drathe seemed to have a soft spot for the soldier, and to Alistair, that meant he could trust Relm with his life.

He looked at his council and knew he had to trust all of them with his life, including Faitrin. If he was ever to make it back to his wife, these people would help him accomplish it.

"Let's hear it," Thoreaux said. "What's the news?"

"The Myrmidons have shut down the neighboring planet, and the governments appear to be acquiescing to their demands."

Alistair spoke up. "What do you mean, they're acquiescing to their demands? An entire planet is simply bending to this group?"

Relm shrugged and scratched the drathe's ears. "This is a weird part of the universe, broth. I thought the same, but we met some folks who felt it was easier to bend to Achilles' cause."

Faitrin rolled her eyes. "That's what he's taken to calling the AllSeer."

"Fuck him. If he didn't want to be called Achilles, he should have never taken that stupid Myrmidon name for his troops, should he?" He changed his tone for the drathe at the end, sounding like he was talking to a child.

"You know he understands everything you say, right?" Servia asked.

"I know he does, don't you?" he asked Obs in the same childlike voice. He looked up, still stroking the animal, who seemed to take no umbrage at the change in tone. "Anyway, before Faitrin here rudely interrupted me, I was saying it seems this Achilles character is known out here, and the governments don't want to challenge him."

Alistair's eyes narrowed. "How many soldiers did he have on the planet?"

CHAPTER FIVE

"My father was a cruel man. He, of all the de Finita bloodline, deserved to rule. What he did to my sister and me was cruel but in some ways necessary. The rest of the Imperial Ascendants are shadows to his greatness, and what I do, I do in his name."

–The AllSeer

Ajax knelt with his hood removed. His head was bowed, and his skull was marked with pale scars like dried riverbeds from attacks long ago from friend and foe alike. Most of those who had given him the decorations were now dead, most of them by his hand.

Without looking up, he spoke. "We are on our way to her. Based on all evidence, Master, she is still there beneath the ground."

"Very good, Ajax." The voice that spoke sounded like

DAVID BEERS & MICHAEL ANDERLE

two pieces of sandpaper scraping one another. "It is important that she be taken alive. I fear some of our brothers are full of bloodlust after having searched for so long. It is important that they understand she is to be brought to me alive."

"Yes, Master. I understand."

"I have no doubt that you do," the gravelly voice responded. "Go forth and conquer."

A click sounded from above, and Ajax knew his master was gone. He raised his head to the place where his master had been standing moments before in holovid form. The Commonwealth used primitive chambers, but the Superior had long ago surpassed such things. His master could appear wherever he pleased.

The comm in his ear switched on, knowing Ajax wanted to speak to the First Slave. "How far away is the Commonwealth?"

The First Slave's voice came back immediately. "One week out, once they drop out of the fourth dimension."

"They have not gone to the fifth dimension, correct?"

"Yes, master," the slave answered.

That meant they hadn't brought any of the modified persons. There were only humans on that ship, and the Superior would reach Phoenix first at their current pace. "Remain in the fifth dimension even once we arrive."

The comm went dead, Ajax not waiting for the slave's response. Humanity did not have the strength to rule their own star system, let alone the universe. The fifth dimension was denied to them, but even the Superior's slaves had been engineered to survive such travel.

Ajax rose to his feet.

It was almost over.

He closed his eyes and took a deep breath. All the years. All the sacrifices. Even the dead who piled higher than Ajax had ever imagined possible, bodies on bodies, forever and ever it sometimes seemed, all of it culminated in what came next. All of it was finally for something.

He let his breath out and opened his red eyes.

A few more days and the AllMother's reign would end. Then the AllSeer's would begin in earnest.

CHAPTER SIX

"Cruelty is an animal trait. The prophets, the Jesuses, Buddhas, and Muhammeds, will be remembered until humanity is extinguished. Did they promote cruelty or love?"

–The AllMother

"We need to capture one of them."

The others in the room looked at Alistair like he'd asked them to kill a child.

Even Thoreaux looked confused, though he was the only person who understood why Alistair would ask such a thing.

"Pro," Relm said, "just so I'm clear here, you mean a Myrmidon, right? You want to capture one of *them*?"

The group occupied the circular meeting room. The

same people as before were present: Faitrin, Relm, Servia, and Thoreaux.

"That's right," Alistair responded. "I want to capture one of those things."

Servia raised a finger from her lap. "May I ask why?"

"It's the first step in figuring out what we need to do."

"How's that?" Servia asked.

"Do you know where the AllSeer sits on his throne? Do you know how great his empire is? Do you understand his technology?" Alistair was silent for a second as he studied Servia. There was no need for an answer; they both knew that. "The truth is," he continued, "we know next to nothing about those creatures. For whatever reason, the AllMother has kept that information to herself. We need to know as much as possible as quickly as possible. The only way to do that is to get one of them here beneath the ground and make them talk."

Relm nodded, though his face said he didn't have much faith in this plan. "That's all well and good, broth, but how do you propose we do that? As far as I know, they're in the fifth dimension right now, and I've got an inkling they don't plan on sending just one of them down here to talk to us."

Alistair looked at the pilot. "Faitrin, do you think you can fly one of their ships?"

Her eyebrows raised over her pale blue eyes. "I've never seen one, so I have no idea, to be honest with you. If I can harmonize with it? Maybe—"

"Or maybe it would fry her brain," Servia interrupted.

This was the first time she had pushed back on one of Alistair's decisions.

Relm rubbed his jaw roughly, his hand scraping across his beard. "What's your plan, Pro? I think we should hear that first before we all start shutting it down."

Alistair leaned back, grinning. His plan was suicide, and he knew it. "Well, remember when we got Faitrin off her ship? It's basically the same, only instead of smashing into it, we take off from this planet and let them capture us. Then, when we're on the ship, we kill as many as it takes until we subdue one. If we can't put him on our ship, we let Faitrin pilot the Myrmidon vessel back. That's the plan."

Servia laughed, both eyebrows raised and disbelief in her eyes. "Prometheus, why not just pull your Whip out and cut us down here? Wouldn't that be a lot easier than this insanity you're proposing? The result will be the same, and think of all the time we'd save."

Alistair ignored her and looked at Thoreaux. Alistair had told the group *one* of the reasons for bringing the Myrmidon down, but not the other. Not the more important one. Thoreaux knew, even though Alistair hadn't told him the plan until just now. "What do you think?"

"I think we'll probably die," Thoreaux replied. "Is there no other way?"

"That's why it's going to work." Alistair's eyes were alight with hope. "Because no one has ever attempted this. No one would attempt it. These creatures are used to landing on planets and having kings bow to them. They'll take our ship as a legitimate escape attempt, and by the time they realize what we're doing, their throats will be slit."

He looked at Relm. "You scared to get a little Myrmidon

blood on your hands? And you, Faitrin, do you not think you can handle their ships?"

Servia spoke before anyone else had a chance. "I see you're ignoring my concerns."

Alistair nodded. "Yeah, this time you're wrong, so I'm ignoring you."

"Does 'wrong' mean I disagree with you?"

Alistair smirked. "Most of the time, yes." His face grew serious. "Do you have another way, Servia? If you do, I'll hear it now. If not, I see no other way to get the information we need. You didn't want us to flee, and we're not doing that."

Servia studied him for long seconds, the room silent, then turned her gaze on Relm and Faitrin. Her eyes were narrow and her face as solemn as Alistair had ever seen it. Finally, she looked at Thoreaux. "You told him?"

So she knows, Alistair thought. He figured she probably did, but he hadn't known for sure. His mind had been elsewhere, too busy with this plan to ask Thoreaux.

"I did," Thoreaux answered.

"Told him what?" Faitrin interjected. "If we're heading to our death, I think it's fair we know why."

"I'm gonna agree with her on this one," Relm said. "What's the deal?"

Alistair sighed and leaned back against the wall. He hadn't wanted to explain it all, not up front.

But why? he asked himself.

The answer was simple: it had been a secret before. No one had known about this or about the AllMother's gifts, only those extremely close to her—Servia and Thoreaux, and perhaps their parents before them.

And now that you lead, what will you do, Allie? his wife's voice chimed in, playfully mocking him. *Will you lead like the old woman, or will you do something different? Perhaps something more? What would she have you do?*

"Pluto paging Prometheus," Relm said. "You here?"

Alistair blinked and pulled himself away from his wife's voice. "You're right. I should have told you. Both the Commonwealth and our movement shroud so much in darkness that sometimes when the light wants to shine through, we won't let it."

He stood up, put his hands on his hips, and looked at the floor. "I wasn't trying to lie to any of you. Until me, no one besides Thoreaux and Servia knew this. For some reason, I thought that secrecy was necessary," he said to the two across from him. "It's not, and I won't do it as long as I lead here."

He glanced first to his right at Thoreaux, who nodded. Alistair turned to Servia next and received another slight nod. They agreed, and that was important. He couldn't unilaterally make every decision, not if he wanted people to follow him to their possible deaths.

"There's a chance," he continued, "that if we bring a Myrmidon back, we can wake the AllMother up. There's also a chance that it will kill her. From what I understand, there is no other way we know of. She has to be put in front of one of those beasts. He paused for a few moments, then said, "Otherwise, she's too old now to wake up on her own. That's what we think. This could give her the jump-start she needs."

"Or kill her?" Faitrin asked.

"Yes. Or kill her."

"Well," Relm said, "Faitrin here hasn't met the AllMother yet, and if we're talkin' truth, that's unacceptable. The only way I can see to have the two of them meet is to go get one of those big dumb bastards in space, so I'm in."

Servia chuckled. She was looking down at the floor.

"Faitrin?" Alistair asked. "What about you? Want to help?"

"I'm going to have to start getting hazard pay," the pilot responded, "but yeah, I'm in. How many people are we taking on this little adventure?"

"The four of us and Brenyo, our old commander." Alistair looked at Servia. "You'll stay. If this is a suicide mission like everyone says, you'll lead when we don't return."

There was no humor on Servia's face. "How will I know if you're not going to make it back?"

"This shouldn't take more than a few hours. We shoot up out of the atmosphere, get captured, and take control of the ship. If we're not back after six standard hours, you'll know we're not coming. I trust you'll make the best decisions for our people."

Was that the first time he'd used such language? *Our* people? Perhaps. It would have been unthinkable for him a year ago, yet now he was bonded to them. Not just those in this room, but the legions that depended on him.

To make the right choices. To keep them safe unless danger meant their dream might finally reach fruition. Above all, to keep that dream alive. To give it a chance.

That dream and Alistair's own of seeing Luna once more. For better or worse, they were tied together now.

"I'll do it, Prometheus," Servia answered.

Alistair stretched his arms out to the sides and groaned. "Okay. Let's go cheat death once again, ladies and gents."

Alistair was on one knee, and four others were in the same position before him.

The ship they would use was twenty yards to their right.

Each of them wore SkinSuits with the hoods off. Each held a knife in their right hand, their left hands empty.

"I do not kill for glory," Alistair said. "I do not kill for malice. I kill because it is right. Because if I do not kill, those who seek to harm me and those I love will do so."

The four in front of him echoed his words, whispering them as one.

Alistair didn't look up but cut the circular wound on his left arm. The others followed his lead and the room stayed silent, no one gasping or showing signs of pain.

Alistair continued the Titan ritual, which was as much his as it belonged to those seeking to kill him.

"I do not fear the enemy. I do not fear death. I only fear living without protecting those I love. I only fear cowardice and hiding from my duty."

The others repeated the words after him as their blood dripped down their arms to the floor.

"As this blood flows, so will I. I bleed now so that I will not later. I bleed now so that those who sow harm against me know that blood does not frighten me."

They echoed his words.

"I bleed now because it is this blood that will conquer anyone in my path. See it and fear. See it and die."

"See it and die," came the finish.

Alistair placed his knife on the floor and, with his right hand, wiped the blood from the wound, which he brought up beneath his right eye and smeared a red line. He then dipped his hand in the dastardly paint again and smeared another line under his left eye.

He looked at those in front of him, the four who would follow him to their deaths if he demanded it. Each of them stared back with red lines across their faces.

"You are the finest warriors I've ever served with. If we go to our deaths, we go with honor. We live with honor, so it is our right to die with honor. If we must die, we will bring our enemies to meet the gods with us, yes?"

"YES!" the four roared, everyone standing up at the same time.

"Let's go get us a Myrmidon," Alistair said.

The ship was small, only slightly larger than a corvette, and of a design Alistair had never seen. The Terram's technology was slightly different than Earth's, leading to a slightly different spacecraft.

Faitrin had no problem flying it, though. She harmonized with it as well as she had with the Earth-made ships. She sat in her seat silently, her eyes static-gray.

Alistair was at the very back of the ship, his SkinSuit covering his body.

They'd broken the fiery atmosphere about ten minutes

ago. It was a magnificent feat of engineering, what the Terram had done to protect themselves. It had ended up altering their bodies; living underground for generations had shortened their bones and overall height.

Now Alistair was in space's cold embrace, awaiting an even deadlier hug.

"Any sighting?" he said quietly.

"Thoreaux," Faitrin answered. "Have you seen their ships before?"

In front of Alistair, Thoreaux shook his head. "No. They say if you see their ships, it's the last thing you'll see."

"Why?" Alistair asked. "Why does it matter if he's seen them?"

"Because something is showing up here that I've never seen before."

Alistair leaned forward and looked out the ship's screens. "I don't see anything. What are you talking about?"

"Exactly," Faitrin said, and for the first time, he thought he heard fear in her voice. "I think a ship just dropped out of an upper dimension, but you normally see a flash of light when that happens. They have a stealth device like I've never seen if it cloaks them when they enter and leave dimensions."

"How far away is the ship?" Alistair asked.

"Hard to say, but I'm guessing two thousand kilometers."

"Does it know you can see them?" he asked.

Silence answered Alistair's question.

"Faitrin? You hear me?" He knew a pilot could sometimes get lost when harmonized.

"It doesn't matter if they know. They don't care. They're taking control of the ship."

More silence followed as everyone tried to understand what that meant. To take control of a ship this small from a thousand kilometers away? It wasn't only unheard of, it was impossible.

"Fait," Relm said, "I'm not trying to tell you your business, but that don't make too much sense, sister. You wanna run that by me one more time?"

"Are you still harmonized?" Alistair asked before she could answer.

"Yes, I am. That's how I know what they're doing. The ship is being directed to them. I've lost control over it."

Alistair stood and walked to the front. "You're sure this isn't just Terram technology, something different about *this* ship?"

Faitrin didn't turn to look at him but kept her gray eyes on the screens in front of her. "It's not the damned technology, Pro. They're fucking pulling us to them, and we're accelerating."

"Can you get us out of it?" he asked.

"I'm trying," she replied through gritted teeth.

Alistair turned to Thoreaux. "Do you have any idea what this is?"

He couldn't see his second's face due to the hood covering it. Thoreaux shook his head. "All I know are the myths that their technology is far beyond what we understand. The times I have seen them, they were already on-planet."

"You sound calm, broth," Relm said from his side.

"Especially given that some kind of tractor beam is pulling us into a psychopath's ship."

Alistair heard a rare smile in Thoreaux's voice. "We've got Prometheus. We'll be all right. Just be ready for a fight."

Alistair looked at Faitrin. "How long 'til they board us?"

"At current acceleration, two standard hours."

"Then you've got two hours to understand what the hell they're doing so we can reverse it once we get one of those bastards under our control. Is it possible for you to get a peek into their ship? Are you able to harmonize with them, given that they're taking us over?"

The pilot was quiet for a few seconds, and Alistair said nothing. He knew she was trying to figure out if she could do what he asked.

"I think so. Somewhat, at least. It's impossible for them to keep me completely out, though they can hamper how well I harmonize. What do you want?"

"Everything. Anything. Ship's layout. If you can get into the security system, I want to know how many there are. I want to know where they're clustered. As we get closer, I want to know where they're moving to. I want to know where their fucking bathrooms are, if possible, and how many people are in them."

"I'll do what I can," the pilot responded.

"Tell us as you get the info." Alistair looked at the remainder of his small crew. "The rest of us are going to strategize using the information she gives us." He glanced at Relm. "You scared?"

"Only time I'm scared, broth, is when Servia gets pissed at me. Thoreaux is right. We've got Prometheus; no reason to worry." Relm looked at the other four sitting with him, then back at Alistair. "*Ave* Prometheus!" he shouted in the tight enclosure.

The other three were quiet for a moment, then all said as one, "*Ave* Prometheus!"

Alistair straightened, realizing what they were saying. The word "*ave*" was from one of the greatest Earth regimes to ever exist, Rome. Loosely translated, those here were saying, "Hail Prometheus!"

He blinked, once, then twice, recognizing they were in some small way elevating him as close as they could to the gods.

When Alistair spoke, it was in a whisper. "Let's prepare."

CHAPTER SEVEN

"The AllMother's plan has always relied on humanity.
Mine never has. That is the difference."

–The AllSeer

"My gods," Thoreaux whispered. "My gods, is this real?"

Alistair said nothing but felt the same about what he now saw. Their tiny ship was facing something not of their species. Something not *human*.

"What powers it?" he asked those in the room, not expecting an answer.

"I've never heard of an energy source like this," Brenyo answered. His voice contained awe.

Have I made a mistake? Alistair thought. *Have I just killed us all and destroyed any chance of seeing Luna?*

StealthBlankets didn't operate like this, and Alistair didn't need an engineer to tell him that. A blanket reflected the surrounding space, regardless of how far it had to go to find something, so if you were in outer space, the blanket would show blackness and stars. You could see through it when you got close, or at least see that it wasn't *real*.

That was not what Alistair was looking at. This was something very, very different.

The Myrmidon ship was long but not very wide—a stretched-out oval almost the shape of a missile. Alistair could see through it but not inside it. The ship had somehow turned transparent, but everything encapsulated in its walls looked the same. The only time he *could* see the ship was when static rippled over the outside, which occurred every standard half-hour or so. It looked almost like lightning that moved from one end to the other, and Alistair could see the actual outside of the ship.

"Anything else, Faitrin?" he asked in a whisper.

The pilot shook her head.

She'd given them a basic layout of the ship and tried her best to understand the count of the enemies inside. The number was one hundred to five hundred, which was such a large range that no one bothered pointing it out.

"Thoreaux, anything else you can give us?" Alistair asked.

Thoreaux shook his head but remained silent. This was all they had and all they were going to get.

"Remember. We've already bled. It is their turn to bleed."

Silence ensued for a few moments as they neared the ship, but no doors opened on the outside. It appeared as if they were going to slam into the ship, killing all of them.

No, Alistair thought. *I couldn't have misjudged that badly. Something is going to happen. They will believe the AllMother is here. They don't want her dead, or else they wouldn't have tried to take her off Pluto.*

He saw Brenyo's Adam's apple move beneath his Skin-Suit as the warrior swallowed. They were all thinking the same as he was: that the beam pulling them would crush them against the ship. They were all scared, but no one said anything.

Someone gasped when their ship finally touched the enemy's, but there was no sound of metal crunching. The air did not rip out, and no one flew out into space. They simply began passing through the outer barrier of this strange ship very slowly.

Then Alistair understood what was different. He only knew of one *thing* that allowed for osmosis, and it was...

"The ship is *alive*," he whispered in awe. "It's like our insectoids but much more advanced."

"Broth," Relm said from up front, "I hope you're even more badass than I think you are. We're going to need it."

Alistair said nothing.

Inside the black SkinSuit, he was changing.

Odin was dead.

Alistair moved to the back of the man's mind.

Prometheus stepped forward.

The ship finished its slow movement through the outer shell of the Myrmidon's vessel, and as it did, the panels that showed the outside world died.

The ship still had power, though Faitrin had no control over it. The Myrmidons decided what parts of the ship would remain operational, and they wanted the inhabitants to be blind.

Alistair stood facing the door at the back. "Assume they can see inside here, they know we don't have the AllMother. Perhaps they'll try to capture us, but I doubt it. It doesn't matter what we do. We kill until we have control of this ship or we've captured one of them and have a way to escape. Faitrin, you ready?"

"Not much choice," she answered. "Just keep me safe."

It was a wild plan, and Alistair couldn't know if it would work. They'd made it in the last five minutes as the ship submerged inside this one. Alistair had come to realize that somehow this thing was an organism of its own. The Whip in his hand was sentient, though not to the degree of this spaceship.

It'll work, he thought. *It has to.*

The door to the ship flashed open with a whoosh.

A red-eyed monster stood in front of Prometheus, holding one of those weapons with a laser on either side of the hilt.

The Fallen Titan rushed forward. He appeared to expend no effort, just displayed a speed no human should have.

The Myrmidon's eyes grew wide as a dull understanding washed over him. It was clear he'd thought those inside this ship would be easily subdued.

When Prometheus fell on him, the realization that he'd been wrong and this was vastly different than he'd expected it.

The Myrmidon tried to raise his weapon and thwart the attack, but it was too late. Prometheus dropped low, still rushing forward. His Whip formed a sword and sliced through the man's waist.

The enemy remained standing for a moment, eyes still wide, his mouth slightly open. Then his legs gave out. They collapsed and sent his upper torso spilling across the deck.

Relm yelled from inside the ship, "Hey, Pro, we maybe could have used him, no?"

Prometheus realized what he'd done. He couldn't turn back time, though. He'd have to check his instinct to kill if they came across another lone enemy.

He didn't look behind him, just walked out of the ship as his Whip extended into three tentacles. He scanned the area but heard no sirens and saw no movement. Faitrin had given them a basic map of this place, so he knew where he needed to take the team.

"Let's go," he called over his shoulder.

The four moved around the body, leaving boot prints in the pooling blood.

Prometheus looked down at his feet. The deck, indeed the entire ship, was *spongy*. His feet sank slightly into the deck, and it had a slight bounce to it. He didn't understand what it meant or what this flying thing could *do*, and he didn't have time to consider it.

"We should assume that whatever this thing is, it's allowing them to track us. Assume they're going to know our every move," he told those circled around him. They were in a small bay with no other ships. The bay doors that led farther into the ship stood open. Relm wouldn't need to blast through anything. Apparently the Myrmidons weren't worried about what this group might do.

They walked through the doors, and once on the other side, listened as they shut behind them.

Relm looked over his shoulder. "I don't like the fuckin' looks of that."

"Eyes forward," Prometheus commanded. There was no backward, not until they had one of those creatures in tow.

They went forward, the spongy floor remaining constant. Right, left, another right. They saw only walls that looked Earth-made but weren't. He didn't know how long they hustled through the strange ship, but Prometheus finally brought them to a stop. "They're changing the layout of the ship. We should be there by now."

"That's not..." Thoreaux's voice trailed off. Everyone knew he meant to finish the sentence with "possible," but nothing they'd seen in here should exist.

Yet, it did.

"This ain't good, broth," Relm said. He looked over his shoulder at the way they had come. "You think if we turned and went back, we'd be able to find our ship?"

Prometheus' eyes were narrow as he peered down the endless hall before him. "I doubt it." He faced the four of them. He'd underestimated this enemy, perhaps worse than anyone he'd ever faced.

What are they expecting us to do? he thought. They know we're here, yet they're leaving us alone.

The schematics Faitrin had found showed two square structures that rose from the floor. She thought someone had been standing at each one and that they were some kind of control mechanisms. Faitrin said she didn't think they were pilots, at least not in the normal sense. They weren't like her.

They had been heading to the north square, but they should have arrived.

"What do you want to do?" Thoreaux asked.

Alistair looked at Faitrin. "Can you try to harmonize from here?"

"I'm not sure." She looked at the walls. "I suppose you mean *through* them because they're alive, or whatever you want to call it."

"Yeah," he answered. "These hallways aren't taking us where we want to go, and I don't think they ever will. If you can harmonize from here, maybe we can find out what the hell is going on."

She sighed and shrugged. "I'll give it a try."

Alistair understood the basics of harmonizing, though he'd never be able to do it. Pilots weren't considered mutants by the Earthborn, though technically they were. Certainly, they'd been modified, but it had become a necessity for space travel, so humanity looked past it.

A pilot harmonized with a ship, the wiring in their brains able to detect the AI and other technical pieces. Once modified, the pilot could never be unmodified, but it came with guaranteed employment for the rest of their life.

This ship was like nothing Alistair had ever seen or even thought possible. Maybe Faitrin's brain wouldn't recognize the codes here. Maybe there was no AI.

Maybe they were fucked.

"I don't sense anything," she told the group as she stood staring at the wall. "Normally I would as soon as I was within the vicinity of a ship. Even if I don't have the codes to control it, I can still sense it."

They'd been hoping those alien squares were the place she'd connect.

Faitrin raised her hand and placed it on the wall. Her eyes immediately started graying over, showing that she was harmonizing.

"Oh, my gods," she whispered. "Oh, dear gods."

Prometheus' Whip extended farther from the hilt, sensing his apprehension. "What is it?"

"Run," Faitrin said without looking away from the wall. Her eyes remained full of static. "Just run."

"Don't move," Prometheus commanded.

"He's here. He sees us," Faitrin said in a raspy whisper.

"Who?" Prometheus asked. "You've got to tell us more."

Before she could answer, the walls started fading. Prometheus blinked twice, not believing his eyes, yet the walls continued disappearing until Faitrin's hand touched only air and her eyes were cold Plutonian blue once again.

The five of them stood in the same bay they had arrived in. Their ship remained in the same spot. They'd never left. They had only thought they had. The Myrmidon's appearance was the only thing that had actually happened, and its body still lay on the ship's ramp.

"Are you what she prophesied?"

The words came from the bay walls, the ceiling, and even the floor. The substance, whatever this ship was made of, vibrated as the words filled the air. There weren't any speakers; rather, the ship was speaking.

"Who are you?" Prometheus asked. His Whip was ready, but there was nothing to kill.

"The one not seen," the ship replied. "The one who sees all. Are you him? The one she prophesied would come? Has she finally found you?"

"Show yourself," Prometheus demanded. His group tightened around him, their backs to each other as they formed a circle to fend off whatever might come.

Prometheus saw it immediately: a black shadow twenty yards away against a far wall. The outline was human-like but huge, massive in a way none of the other Myrmidons had been. Huge like Prometheus imagined the gods might be, a hulking black mass that...

How is any of this possible? he wondered again.

"I take many forms." The voice came from the shadow now. "I promise you, Prophesied One, you do not want to see any form other than this. Do you know yet what she wants you to do for her? Why she picked you from your obscure nothing of a life?"

Prometheus didn't answer. His pulse remained steady despite the seemingly insurmountable odds. He was trying to figure out what to do. The plan was gone, and he had no other ideas.

"Pro," Thoreaux said from his six, "we've got more company."

He turned his head slightly over his shoulder. A line of Myrmidons was walking in, and each had their laser weapon alight. At least twenty had entered so far, encircling the bay, with more coming.

"What do you want us to do?" Thoreaux asked.

"Hold." Prometheus didn't even need to turn his head to see them. They had made their way across the bay and stood behind the black shadow.

"You are smart for your species," the shadow's deep voice proclaimed. "You correctly assumed we would think you were trying to escape with the AllMother. Intelligence without knowledge ends in despair, though, as you now see. We are not of you, Prophesied One. Your modifications are nothing compared to us. Your technology is little more than Stone Age to what we possess. You are alive right now because I allow it. Now tell me, why did you come here?"

"Thoreaux," Alistair said into his comm, his hood masking his voice to the outside world. "Are you ready to fight?"

"I'd rather die than listen to this creature speak anymore."

"Relm, Brenyo, you two ready as well? Faitrin?"

"*Ave* Prometheus," was the response from all three.

He knew one thing. When you stood before the devil, you didn't discuss terms.

"Answer me, Prophesied One," the shadow commanded.

"I came for this," Prometheus said to the room at large. He raised his red Whip high, then slammed it onto the deck. Sparks didn't fly, but rather a viscous black substance exploded from it. Prometheus leapt forward as the liquid rained down around him.

He aimed for the shadow, and his Whip slashed through it. The black form broke into a thousand pieces and streaked into the air, leaving Prometheus standing where it had been.

He didn't slow but flashed to the Myrmidons against the wall. His Whip raked through three of them before they'd even realized what was happening. Their stomachs opened, and their guts splashed on the deck.

He heard MechPulses from behind him, his team aiming at the Myrmidons against the wall. He didn't turn to look but kept going forward. There were far too many enemies here for him to slow down for even a second. A mutant came from his right and swung a laser at Prometheus' neck. The speed and force were unreal.

He dropped just in time, flicking his Whip at the creature as he did. It wrapped around the Myrmidon's knee, leaving him with one less leg when Prometheus pulled it back.

It wasn't bloodlust that possessed his mind but a calm, intense focus. He lost track of everything but the need to kill and the realization that if he stopped for any reason, his enemies would end him. Blood, entrails, and body parts littered the deck, as well as the black goop from the ship when his Whip made contact. He heard screams, pulses, and grunts from across the room and could only hope that his team hadn't died yet.

A Myrmidon charged him, laser up. Alistair's Whip turned into a sword, and the two slammed into each other. The Myrmidon bared his teeth, growling and shoving the former Titan with all his might. Prometheus felt the mutant's strength, a power unknown on Earth. He wasn't sure he could best him, and he saw more coming from his side.

The sound of MechPulses filled the bay.

Black liquid oozed from the walls where the shots had missed.

Three huge mutants were convening on Prometheus,

and he saw his death. These weren't Titans but something alien, creatures barely of human lineage anymore.

He closed his eyes, the gods now seconds away from greeting him in their immortal realm. He thought back to his trainer Linc. He thought back to his words.

You can only master one form. To try both is to die.

Prometheus did what he shouldn't, and what no man had done before, at least not successfully. He combined two forms, the Sanctum and the Edge. There was no name for what he did, only action.

His Whip lost its sword shape and wrapped around the laser. Prometheus' legs dipped slightly, and he pushed himself off the floor. His modifications made it possible. Even in a MechSuit, he couldn't have been so elegant. He propelled himself into the air and somersaulted over the giant. His Whip immediately knew what to do; it unwrapped from the laser and turned on the creature. Nothing separated it from the Myrmidon as Prometheus flipped over him.

The moment Prometheus touched the deck, the Whip plunged into the creature's heart. He dropped, and his Whip sliced from the Myrmidon's heart through his shoulder and out the other side.

"ENOUGH."

It was the shadow's voice. Alistair's suit was covered in blood. He looked at the deck, his Whip hanging at his side, then up. Everyone in the room was staring at him.

Even Relm had lowered his MechPulse, unable to help it, having never witnessed anything that superhuman.

Prometheus rose to his feet and surveyed the damage around him. Where he had moved across the bay, the dead were legion. Fallen soldiers missing limbs and heads, torsos ripped through, Blood flowed across the bay. He located his crew and saw that the four of them still had their backs to each other in the middle of the room. There were dead surrounding them too, but not as many. The Myrmidons had focused their attention on him for the most part, seeing him as the largest threat and consequently saving the lives of those who followed him.

Hearing their master's command, the Myrmidons stopped moving toward Prometheus. They slowly backed against the wall in the same places they had been before. Half their brethren were lying on the floor, either dead or dying.

"Well done, Prophesied One," the shadow said. Prometheus saw the massive black entity across the room. "You did not come here to defeat us; that much is clear. I know the one you serve is not well. I know she is in danger, and I assume you understand my connection to her, yes?"

Prometheus was backing up, trying to get closer to his friends. He saw no way out of this. He couldn't kill them all, and his crew had been lucky, nothing else. If the Myrmidons had focused on them instead of Alistair, they'd most likely be dead.

The shadow continued talking like none of this bothered him, his dead warriors or the enemies circled together on this ship. "I don't think you know the endgame here, though. She does, your precious AllMother. She hopes to avoid her fate, but that can no more be done than stopping the universe's expanse. We are trapped by our fate. We are slaves to it. Even you, Prophesied One."

The shadow started to float across the room. Where there should have been feet, the shadow darted out and pulled back in like black strikes of electricity. It stopped about five meters short of where Prometheus stood.

"Do you know how long it has been since I last spoke to my sister?"

Prometheus had no answer for this creature.

"A long time, Prophesied One," the shadow answered, his voice almost a whisper. "I wasn't sure at first why you had come, but now I understand. Go on, take one of my children. They will give you no trouble. Bring him to your AllMother and summon her back to this reality. She will not escape her fate, no matter how much she wishes to." The shadow waved a black arm, and as if commanded by name, one of the Myrmidons stepped away from the wall and moved toward the group.

He knelt and placed his weapon on the deck.

"Take him," the shadow said. "Bring him to her." The shadow floated closer to Alistair as if it were studying him. "Do you consider your fate, Prophesied One? Do you consider fate at all? I know yours, as I know your little friends' here. All of your fates are tied to mine, as is that of the one you serve." It paused, letting silence drape the room. The Myrmidon remained on both knees, looking at the deck. The monstrous creature was cowed by this shadow's mere wave. "Go. Take my child. I will see you again, Prophesied One. Things will be different then, I promise."

CHAPTER EIGHT

"Maybe it was a mistake to alter my children. I try not to dwell on the past since it's too late to stop what may already be in motion."

–The First Imperial Ascendant, Aurelius de Finita, found in his personal journals after his death

The flight back to Phoenix was made in complete silence. No one wanted to speak around the Myrmidon, although the creature acted almost as if he was in a coma. Alistair remained directly behind him, his Whip floating inches from the thing's massive neck. It was human-like in shape and form, but Alistair couldn't consider it a person. It was bigger than he, much larger, and if he had learned anything from that strange ship, it was that he knew next to nothing about the Myrmidons or their leader.

Their small ship finally made its way through the fiery atmosphere and beneath the surface.

There were Terram waiting, as was Servia. The Myrmidon exited the ship first, Alistair directly behind him with his deadly Whip close to the creature's neck.

The three Terram flashed short-range weapons at the creature, yelling in the guttural language Alistair still didn't understand.

Thoreaux stepped between the weapons and the Myrmidon. He spoke to them, likely trying to explain what in the hell was going on, though Alistair would never know for certain.

Servia remained a few meters back from the giant Myrmidon. "I was beginning to think you weren't going to make it."

Alistair let out a long sigh. His body was tired, though he knew there was a long way to go before he could rest. "Yeah. We almost didn't. It's a story, to say the least. Where's Obs?"

"Not a hundred percent sure." Servia stepped a bit closer to inspect the hulk. "He'll know you're here, though, so I imagine he'll be along soon. He seemed a bit pissed you didn't let him go on your little adventure."

"Yeah, well, he wouldn't have enjoyed himself, I promise that."

The rest of the crew lumbered off the ship while Servia's eyes narrowed. "Is he alive? I mean, I can see he's standing up, but there doesn't seem to be much going on inside." She waved her hand in front of his face, but the creature's eyes didn't react to the movement.

The Terram had calmed some, but they still pointed

their weapons at the newcomer. The Myrmidon paid them no notice. Thoreaux turned back to Alistair. "We need to talk before we put him in front of her."

Alistair had figured this was coming and agreed. That dark figure had changed things, though he didn't know exactly how. He nodded at his second.

"The Terram have a place we can keep him," Thoreaux continued.

"Relm." Alistair looked over his shoulder. "You mind finding Obs, then watching this guy until after we talk?"

"Not a problem, broth. Where's that big animal anyway? Faitrin, you coming?"

"I'm going to sit this one out," she responded. She had seemed off since touching the false walls in the Myrmidons' ships. Alistair knew he would have to talk to her soon. He wanted to know what she'd seen and how badly it had affected her. She'd been strong up until this point and had witnessed innumerable deaths, but this had been different.

"Oh, my gods." "Oh, dear gods." Those had been the words she'd whispered.

"Pro, you here?" Thoreaux asked, snapping Alistair back to reality.

He shook his head. "Yeah, sorry. Relm, go ahead and take him to the room. Obs will probably find me in a minute or two, and I'll send him your way."

"Yessir. On it." Relm looked at Faitrin. "I'll stop by later, but let me know if you need anything."

The pilot nodded but didn't say anything. Her eyes were distant, which concerned Alistair even more.

Relm pushed his pulse into the Myrmidon's back.

"Come on, you oversized cow. Give me any trouble, and I promise you won't ever have to put pants on again. Thoreaux, is one of them going to lead me to the room?"

Thoreaux said something to the Terram. The one on the left shook his head angrily but started walking toward the bay's exit. The second one followed after a hard look at Thoreaux.

He turned to Alistair. "They aren't happy about this."

"They knew what the hell we were doing when we took the ship. Now they're mad?"

Thoreaux shrugged. "It's different, I guess, when the creature is standing in front of them."

Faitrin walked away without saying anything, heading in the opposite direction from Relm and the Terram. Alistair gave the Myrmidon one last look before locking his eyes on Faitrin. "Any idea what she saw?"

Thoreaux pursed his lips. "Maybe, but now's not the time. We've got to talk about what the hell just happened."

"And I'm gonna need someone to fill me in," Servia said. "Because none of this makes a lot of sense."

Alistair's hood had retracted to his neck long ago, and he rubbed his hand through his hair. It was growing long. "Things have changed, and I don't think anyone knows what it means. Come and let's talk. Time is short. Much shorter than any of us thought."

"A shadow?"

Servia's expression was one of confusion. She didn't

understand what they were saying, and Alistair couldn't blame her. He hardly understood it, and he'd been there.

"Either of you ever heard the term 'magic?'" he asked.

Thoreaux's eyes narrowed, and Servia shook her head.

Alistair nodded and looked at his feet. He was sitting on one of the Terram's ledges. He would be glad to be rid of the rock benches and beds. He didn't know how these people had lived on them for so long. Or perhaps, even as a Titan, Earth's comforts had spoiled him.

"Magic was something that humans used to believe in a long time ago. Even after we stopped believing in it, there were still stories about it. Magic? Well, it was how humans explained things they didn't, or couldn't, understand. The ships we have today? They would have been magic to early humanity. Something impossible, but here all the same. Ancient superstition."

He paused, remembering the shadow. How it had exploded when he'd attacked it.

"That's what it all felt like—magic, because I don't understand it. The AllSeer, or whatever his name is, was there, yet not there. That ship bled, Servia. Not red blood like ours, but it bled all the same. When I struck it with my Whip, there weren't sparks or even burn marks. There was this weird black blood instead."

He looked at Thoreaux.

"They gave us this Myrmidon to put in front of her. The AllSeer knew why we were there. He knows too much, and I'm not sure how. What do you think we should do, Thoreaux?"

His second was quiet for a few seconds, then he stood up.

"Damn it," Servia complained. "Can't you just sit like a normal person?"

Thoreaux ignored her. "If we put that thing in front of her, the AllSeer will be on the other side of him. Magic or science, it doesn't matter what we call it. It'll be him on the other side; that Myrmidon is just an empty vessel at this point, and the moment he's in front of the AllMother, the AllSeer will fill him. When we made this plan, we didn't know he was on the other side."

"Does that change anything?" Alistair asked. "Regardless of who comes through that Myrmidon, we're putting them together in hopes of jumpstarting the AllMother, right?"

Thoreaux stopped walking and looked at Alistair with his eyebrows raised. "Yeah, I think it changes things plenty. Having the AllSeer in front of her right now versus one of his minions? You saw what that creature can do."

Servia spoke up. "So you don't want to put the Myrmidon in front of her? That's what you're saying?"

He started pacing again, looking at his feet as he did. "I don't know. It's dangerous. We might lose her."

"If we don't," Alistair whispered, "we've already lost her. We don't have her right now."

Silence fell across the group. Alistair needed time to think. "I hear your points, Thoreaux. I need a bit of time to myself. Not long. An hour or so, and I'll have my decision made. Can we get someone to relieve Relm? He's going to need some rest. Tell Obs to come here as well. I'd like to see him."

Thoreaux nodded, and Servia stood. They would accept his decision, whatever it was. They wouldn't argue with him on this. His leadership was intact; now he just had to make sure his decision was the right one.

To do that, he had to talk to Faitrin. He had to know what she saw. What had made her say, "Oh, my gods."

CHAPTER NINE

"If there are gods who created this vast expanse of space, it is clear they respect only one thing: strength."

–The AllSeer

Alistair found his best pilot in a small alcove. Obs was lying outside the little room, and he lifted his head as his master arrived. Alistair squatted and stroked the drathe's head. "Sorry, buddy. You didn't want to be on that trip anyway."

The drathe licked his hand, showing that all had been forgiven. Alistair nodded into the alcove. "How's she doing?"

Obs whined quietly, which confirmed what Alistair was thinking. The drathe was at least as attentive as humans, most likely more so. Something was wrong with Faitrin.

Alistair stood and stepped into the room. The pilot was lying on her back across one of the ledges carved into the wall. Her eyes were open, and her arms were folded over her stomach. She didn't look at Alistair. "Did you send the drathe?"

He shook his head. "Nope. He came after he got done guarding the Myrmidon of his own accord." Obs was still sitting outside, his head between his massive paws. "He's guarding you now, I guess. Wants to make sure you get the rest you need."

"Then he wouldn't have let you in," the pilot responded. Alistair couldn't tell if she was being sarcastic or serious.

He stepped farther into the red rock room and sat down on the far end of the ledge. "We need to talk about what happened up there, and we don't have a lot of time. I need to know what you saw when you touched those walls. It wasn't just the falseness of them, or that I was there, was it? There was something else?"

Faitrin didn't move; she just kept staring at the ceiling above. "Yeah, I suppose there was, Pro."

"I have to decide very soon whether to put that creature in front of the AllMother. It may be our only chance to bring her back, but if it's too dangerous, it could kill her. If that black thing that was in the spaceship is too dangerous, I can't risk it." He turned his head to look at her. "What did you see?"

Faitrin blinked a few times rapidly as if to dispel what she saw inside her head. At first, Alistair didn't think she was going to tell him, and when she started talking, he wished she would stop.

"I didn't connect to that ship, Pro. It connected to me. I've never had that happen before, and as long as I live, I never want it to happen again. You were right, though; the ship is alive. Maybe like you and me, or maybe it was different, I can't be sure. But when I touched those walls, they weren't real, and yet they were. The ship wanted to show me their world, the one he comes from. The dark one. The shadow."

She fell silent and Alistair said nothing, giving her space to speak when she was ready. He knew she wasn't done.

"I didn't ever think we could defeat the Commonwealth, Pro," Faitrin said after long moments of silence. "We're a rag-tag bunch of desperados going against an empire, but I wanted to be on the right side of history. Maybe not the one that would be written, but still, the right side. When I saw you, I thought there was a chance. A next-to-nothing chance, but still a chance."

She shook her head. Her face was calm, her eyes still on the ceiling.

"There's no chance of defeating that thing or the monsters he's bred. Their world isn't like anything I've ever seen. It's not like this strange place, and certainly not like Earth. The power is insurmountable, Pro." She tilted her head and met his eyes. "There's no hope. Not if we try to fight them. There's only death. He will have the AllMother, and anything else he wants."

Alistair could see the woman's fear. It was plain on her face; she was not trying to hide it. "Do you know what he wants?"

She laid her head back down on the rock ledge. "Everything? The universe? I don't know, Pro. If you're wanting to know whether to put the Myrmidon in front of her, it doesn't matter. He's coming, and he will have her. And the Commonwealth? He will have that too."

Alistair stood up. He looked at the doorway and saw Obs standing there. The animal had heard what she said, but his face was expressionless. With his back to Faitrin, Alistair looked partway over his shoulder. "Are you giving up, or are you still with me?"

"I'm with you, Pro," the pilot responded. "Just don't ask me questions you don't want the answers to."

Alistair left the room. His mind was made up, now more than ever. He'd put the Myrmidon in front of the AllMother. He wasn't backing down from the Commonwealth or this new foe. He would see his wife again or die trying, and those who followed him would either have that same determination or fall by the wayside.

The shadow might have his magic, his *fate* as he termed it.

Alistair had something else.

Love.

Faitrin listened as Alistair's footfalls faded in the distance. When he was gone, she looked at the doorway and saw that the drathe had resumed his watch over her.

Good animal, she thought.

Faitrin rarely thought of herself as needing to be watched over, but right now, she didn't want to be alone. She wanted to close her eyes, to sleep, but she didn't want to see the things that had been shown to her.

The things she hadn't told Alistair about. How could she? What good would it do?

He had never asked her why she had decided to join his

crusade, and she appreciated that. The question he asked before leaving the room was perhaps the most aggressive he'd ever been.

Her answer was true, even if she had hidden some of the things that disastrous ship had shown her. She would follow Alistair Kane—Prometheus—until her death.

Faitrin joked that she was owed something, and when the time came she would collect it, but that wasn't what kept her here. It wasn't what had made her give up her life, and perhaps those of her family.

It was him.

What she saw in that man when he attacked the Commonwealth ship was the only reason she had joined this lost cause. He had fought with an insane lack of care, and that was the only way to defeat such overwhelming odds.

Faitrin had kept back some of what she had seen because it wouldn't matter. Alistair Kane would never quit. She saw it in him, and she thought he was finally seeing it in himself, too.

Most humans didn't understand that about pilots. Their alterations allowed them to harmonize with ships, but they also gave them a certain predisposition to understand humanity. It was true, even if rarely discussed.

Unaltered humans thought pilots could only harmonize with ships, not that they had an ability to harmonize with humanity. And if they did understand that? Well, pilots didn't want to find out, not after what they had seen happen with the physically altered mutants.

Faitrin lay on her rock ledge, wanting to sleep but scared of what she'd see. The pilot had thought they would lose this war against the Commonwealth, but she now understood their chances were zero. Less than zero, if such was possible.

Yet, her hero would go forth.

And she would follow. Perhaps she would never have a restful sleep again, but she would follow.

Until death, the pilot was with him.

CHAPTER TEN

"When I set my might in motion, nothing will stop it. Not even my own will."

–The AllSeer

The pilot had seen something never before witnessed by a human. The Superiors, as the Myrmidons thought of themselves, considered other altered merely humans.

Only those born in the image of the AllSeer were Superior. Everyone else, regardless of species or evolution or human alteration, was inferior.

The fact that the pilot had seen the distant planet, the homeworld as the Superior thought of it, was lost on her. She didn't know that the images given her were things never seen by outside eyes.

The Homeworld was now in a state of mass production. Centuries before, the AllSeer had understood that such production would drain the homeworld of its resources before the time was near.

So for long years, the Superiors remained dormant. They staged search parties to look for the AllMother, but back then, she had been strong. It was a different kind of strength than the AllSeer possessed, but strength all the same. He hunted her, but he knew the time was not yet right.

The hunt had mainly been to keep tabs on his sister.

To make sure she wasn't too close to her goal.

The pilot had been allowed to see the AllSeer's power in all its glory. A machine that would not stop, indeed, that could not stop now, even if the AllSeer wished it to be so.

He had thought the Prophesied One was ridiculous, a dream of his long-lost sister's that would never come to fruition. He thought the Prophesied One was simply her hope of having a combatant who could fight him, yet even as the AllSeer aged, she kept on looking for this man.

The moment the Terram ship was captured, the AllSeer understood she had found her man. The Prophesied One.

He didn't know if she was right, only that he knew of no one else who would have had the gall to attempt what he had. This new man thought differently than the AllMother. He was altered, that was clear, even if not in the lineage of the AllSeer.

So for the first time, the AllSeer had shown a human his power. He wanted them to know how far his hand stretched and how mighty his rule was. He wanted this Prophesied One to know, and even if he couldn't see for himself, the AllSeer wanted it to infect his people.

To spread like a cancer.

THE WRITTEN HISTORY OF THE GREAT INSURRECTION

Now, so close to the end of this Insurrection, it's easy to see the lines that connected all the different players. It's easy to see where this started and where it will end, if not who will come out on top.

I need to take a moment inside this history and discuss the decision Prometheus had to make when putting a Myrmidon next to the AllMother. Some decisions he made were consequential. Combining the Sanctum and Edge forms into one fighting style was one such. Certainly, it put him a step above those he fought, and against the Myrmidons, even Prometheus needed an edge. Their strength and speed were practically alien. The decision could have killed him. As his trainer said, it had never been done before. One only became a Wielder, a master of the craft, over one form, not both. To attempt both would result in death if the enemy was a skilled practitioner.

Even that decision wasn't as consequential as Prometheus' decision to pair the two: the AllMother, and for all intents and purposes, the AllSeer.

He'd seen the truth behind the Myrmidons' strength, or been told of it. He had experienced the AllSeer in a way that was hard to explain. He heard my arguments against it that she was too weak and too old to face one of them, especially given the strength I'd just seen.

Prometheus saw all that, yet his belief, his force of will never faltered. Something was changing in the man, and I felt it. So did Servia and the rest who served him. Some called it madness. Some still do. Perhaps they're right, and he is insane. A lot of people have died due to the change in him.

And yet, he hasn't quit. He hasn't stopped believing that we will win this. I don't know when the change began, from a man who thought the entire endeavor was futile to someone possessed with an intensity I'd never seen before.

I don't know if everyone inside our endeavor understands where it comes from. It's not something he talks about often, if ever, even to me, his most trusted confidant. I've only heard it a few times.

Those who call it madness don't understand what drives Prometheus. It isn't what drove the AllMother: freedom from the Commonwealth's ironfisted rule of a species. It isn't what drove the mythical Prometheus, bringing fire to humanity.

His drive is to see his wife again.

His drive is to hold her in his arms. Perhaps to whisper in her ear. To hear her laugh. To make love.

I can't say if that's better or worse than what propelled the AllMother. I can say, though, that it's human. In some ways, I understand it.

Love propels him across galaxies. In truth, across a universe.

Is it madness? Probably.

Does that make it any less incredible? No, not in the slightest.

Few things change the course of human history. Love might be the greatest of them.

CHAPTER ELEVEN

"She and I? We are one and the same, even if she doesn't want to admit it."

–The AllSeer

Thoreaux made his arguments, but in the end, he knew Alistair was right. The group had a strong leader, military strategy, and heart, but what they were missing, the AllMother held.

Knowledge. Understanding of this new part of the universe. Perhaps a way out of the coming annihilation.

Thoreaux did not want to put the AllMother next to a Myrmidon, especially not after seeing that shadow creature. *Magic.* Maybe the term was right. This creature used methods and materials Thoreaux could not possibly understand.

Perhaps putting the AllMother in front of him would kill her.

Yet, Thoreaux would do what she'd wanted. He'd trust this new leader.

He and Alistair stood in her room. Her Terram nurse had left shortly after they entered. For all the Terram's grumpiness and even anger, they took good care of the AllMother. Thoreaux would forever be in their debt for such selflessness.

"Do you want a word with her?" Alistair asked. "Before we get started?"

"Yes, please," Thoreaux responded.

Alistair nodded, then stepped forward and knelt in front of the AllMother's face. "We're doing everything we can to bring you back. I need you to be strong for what comes next. Everyone who serves you says you're the strongest person they know. Prove them right, old woman. Prove them right, AllMother."

He stood and left the room without saying anything to Thoreaux. There would be only four people in the room when this took place: the two of them, the AllMother, and the dreaded Myrmidon. The fewer people, the fewer possibilities for fuck-ups. Servia said she understood, but Thoreaux could tell she was worried.

Thoreaux walked over to the woman who had replaced both his parents. He went down on both knees and gently ran his hands through her gray hair. The Terram had washed and cut it to keep it from growing ugly while she was unconscious.

"It's me, Mother," he whispered above her face. "It's been nearly seven months since you saved Alistair's life.

You were right about him, but you already knew that, didn't you? The doubt I showed just revealed my stupidity. If anyone can lead us to victory, it's that man."

He grew quiet and continued stroking her head. Her eyes remained closed, her face still. She looked at peace.

"I know you hear us somehow. I believe you know what's coming, and I'm sorry we're doing it. Nobody knows what else to do, though, and we need to hear your thoughts. Alistair is strong, but he knows his limitations, and he can't figure this one out. Probably that was one of the reasons you picked him."

He leaned down and gently kissed the old woman on her forehead. He stayed close as he spoke. "I love you, Mother. Survive this and come back to us. We need you. *I* need you."

Thoreaux looked at her for another few seconds before nodding and standing up. He stepped out of the room and saw Obs five meters away. "Go get him. Tell him I'm ready."

The drathe padded over to where Thoreaux stood and licked his hand, then pushed his large body against Thoreaux's leg. The message was clear: *I'm here for you.*

"Thanks, Obs. Go get your master. Let's bring her back."

The drathe barked and trotted down the hall.

Please be right about this, Pro, Thoreaux thought. *Please.*

The Myrmidon had not moved in the hours since they reached this planet. He didn't request water or to use the bathroom. He simply stared forward as if his brain didn't work.

Relm had had a smart idea earlier and had wrapped a blindfold around his eyes in case someone on the other side was looking out. The Myrmidon hadn't moved while it was done. It was as if he didn't notice.

Now the huge creature was strapped to a chair, one of the very few the Terram possessed. Alistair had no illusions about this creature's strength. If he wanted to, he could simply stand up and destroy his restraints. That was why Alistair stood behind him, his Whip wrapped around the Myrmidon's neck. It wasn't touching him, but he could feel the laser's heat.

A single movement and his head would roll across the rock floor.

Thoreaux stood in the doorway, Obs five meters outside. Alistair had tried telling the drathe to leave, but the damn thing was obstinate.

Alistair looked at Thoreaux. "So, how do we do this?"

Thoreaux started to shrug, but the voice that came from the Myrmidon made him stop and stare.

"Remove the cloth blinding me." His voice was deep but had no inflection of fear or anger.

Alistair's Whip tightened, singing the creature's neck. The Myrmidon didn't flinch.

Alistair looked at Thoreaux, and his second shrugged. The Myrmidon said nothing else, and after a moment, Alistair reached up with his free hand and pulled the cloth loose.

It fell to the floor, and the Myrmidon finally made the slightest of movements. His eyes fell on the AllMother.

You are old, Sister. Much older than I am. Isn't it a weird thing for us to be born as twins, but now you are nearly dead, and my power is growing?

The AllMother heard his voice, even so deep in the darkness. It was a voice she knew she would have to hear again, one she'd grown up next to and watched turn evil.

The AllMother had known she wasn't dead, but she'd doubted she would ever live again. She'd thought she would remain deep in the dark until her body gave out, whether in a year or a hundred. Her mind would never recover.

I know you hear me, Sister. Your Prophesied One lives by the mantra "no risk, no reward," I think. He has brought me to you in hopes that our connection will pull you out. I am, as always, the only one who can reach this far down. Not even our mother had that ability, did she?

Their mother.

She had been the only temperate influence on their father, but even she hadn't been enough. Not in the end. In the end, she'd lost her mind. They all had.

So many memories, and so many of them dark. Had she wanted rest? Was that why she'd stayed this deep for so long? Would they not let her rest?

No, Sister. No rest. You and I are not finished. Only the two of us understand what is to come, don't we? Your Prophesied One and my idea of fate. Now we will see who was right. Come out of the darkness. I'm waiting for you. I've been waiting for so very long.

She heard her brother's words. As always, they were

manipulative and full of half-truths. They were what he wanted her to hear, no more, no less.

But his words also brought some full truths, didn't they?

She was needed, and not just by her brother. They had brought him here because he needed her.

The AllMother only wanted to rest, to let her body fall away and then float to wherever the gods brought her.

Let us finish this.

Come back from the deep.

Come to me, Sister.

I must drag you back from this darkness one last time so you and I can walk to our fate together.

She didn't respond to him. She would not give such a creature that satisfaction. If they were ever face to face again, she might speak. Otherwise, let him talk to himself.

It was her children she thought about as he called her, their special twin relationship allowing him inside her deep darkness. He could call her out of it. He could lend her the strength she needed to come back. That was their bond, perhaps stronger than anyone else's in this universe, due in part to what their father had done to them.

She wouldn't come out for him. The AllMother thought she might be able to die because Alistair Kane had been found. Yet, it was truly *him* who was calling her. He was asking her to come back, using this abhorrent tool to do it.

Because that was the only way he could reach her.

One last time. Once more, old girl. Get them a bit closer to the finish line.

Her brother chuckled on a distant planet, and his laughter echoed in her darkness.

Whatever you must tell yourself, sister. Just come to me. I have waited long enough.

Alistair watched the AllMother's face twitching, the first time he'd seen movement out of her since she collapsed in the hallway. Thoreaux stepped forward, but Alistair stilled him by raising a hand.

Her face continued twitching for a few minutes. It wasn't a pretty thing to view. She seemed to be alternating between pain and concentration. Something was happening inside her, and that was what all this had been for.

To make something happen.

Three things happened at once, so quickly Alistair didn't have time to react.

The AllMother opened her eyes and stared straight up at the ceiling.

The Myrmidon's nose started bleeding, a single red trickle running over his lips. He stood up, though he made no aggressive move toward anyone.

The third and final action was Alistair tightening his Whip around the Myrmidon's neck. It decapitated him with a cruel sizzle, and both his body and head fell to the ground.

No one paid any attention to the dead monster. Thoreaux rushed through the blood spreading across the floor and grabbed the AllMother.

Alistair stepped forward, his foot landing right in the creature's blood. His breath caught in his throat. Had he doubted it would work? Or had he come to think of this woman almost as a myth, having known her for such a short time?

Here she was in the flesh, conscious, and as Thoreaux cradled her head, she looked at Alistair.

"You had better have a good reason for waking me up, young man."

CHAPTER TWELVE

"In my darkest moments, I sometimes wonder if it won't be strength that beats us but faith. Strength we have no shortage of, but do we have the needed faith?"

–First Imperial Ascendant, Aurelius de Finita

They needed days to reorient the AllMother. They had hours at most.

The old woman's mind appeared to be on point, though Alistair studied her carefully. Servia and Thoreaux were concerned about the pace he was setting, but neither said anything aloud. It was on their faces and in the way they hovered over her. The old woman's muscles had atrophied quite a bit, despite the Terram's attempts to keep her strong. She would need an oxygen chamber as soon as they could get to one.

"I'm not going to break, Servia," the old woman scolded at one point.

Servia ignored her as if she hadn't said anything.

After coming to understand how many of her children died on Pluto, she was quiet for a long time. She sat in a hoverchair and said nothing. Her eyes were dry and her jaw set, but the weight of the news was clear.

Perhaps regret too, Alistair thought but did not say. He understood why she had done it—to showcase him—but all he had done was make them refugees.

"Have there been other attacks on our moons? Back in our Solar System?" the AllMother asked.

Thoreaux answered. "We're not sure, but we doubt it. The attack on Pluto would have taxed their propaganda efforts. More warfare most likely wouldn't have been accepted. We don't have contact, though. To get word through the portals takes a long time, and it's dangerous for all involved."

She blinked, nodding. Alistair found himself taking a backseat in the explanations. It was still very strange, her being back. He had been the final word for six months, but now he didn't know where he stood. He doubted he would ever have the relationship Servia and Thoreaux did with her, and right now, the movement didn't need him.

They needed her.

So Alistair was quiet.

"And now we are surrounded, is that right? By the Myrmidons? And the Commonwealth is on its way?"

"That's about right," Servia answered. "We were sorta hoping you might be able to help us out of this mess because it's not looking great."

Alistair spoke, one question burning through him. "What does he want with you? The AllSeer."

The AllMother met his eyes but didn't say anything.

"I thought he wanted to kill you, but that's not it, is it? He doesn't want you dead, does he?" Alistair asked.

She shook her head. "No. At least not how you would think of death. He doesn't want that."

That same realization had dawned on Thoreaux and Servia. Alistair still didn't understand why she hadn't been honest with everyone, but apparently, the entire movement had thought the Myrmidons wanted to kill her.

It was only now that they understood the AllSeer wanted something different. Something perhaps even more sinister.

"What is it?" Thoreaux asked.

The AllMother was quiet for more moments, and Alistair thought she was weighing whether she wanted to tell them something.

Why wouldn't she? he wondered. What was there to keep from us at this point?

"I'm no longer strong enough to face him," she eventually said, though it sounded more like an admission to herself. "He can't get hold of me. You all must understand that. If there's a chance that he or his minions can get me, it is your duty to kill me. If I can end my own life, I will, but you all must understand that in your bones. My brother cannot—*must not*— capture me alive."

She paused and looked at the wall.

"Perhaps not even dead, but I don't know how deep his madness has grown." She switched her eyes back to Alistair. "It is deep, though. Deeper than I thought possible."

"Why does he want you?" Alistair pressed.

"Later." She waved the question away with her right hand. "Understand that he cannot have me under any circumstances, and we can move on for now. There are more important matters. How far away is the Commonwealth?"

Servia reported the newest information. "They dropped out of the fourth dimension around the same time you came back to us. They're a little way off yet, but we're expecting a transmission from them at any time."

"And the Myrmidons?"

Thoreaux shook his head. "It's impossible to say. At least one of their ships is in the third dimension and floating a few standard hours from this planet. The rest could be hovering over the planet in the fifth dimension. We have virtually no knowledge regarding what they're capable of."

The AllMother nodded. "And the portals?"

Servia picked up the conversation. "No one is letting us come through, and the Terram won't violate the Portal Governance by sending us away. We've put them in a really tough position, Mother."

Again the nod with the set jaw. Alistair respected the old woman. She'd been woken from a coma hours ago and was now taking in information like an AI. There was no fear in her, not that he could see. No doubt, either.

And then she asked him something that pissed him off.

"What do you think we should do?"

Alistair's eyebrows rose, and he leaned forward. Obs gave a small whine from his place at his master's feet. He hadn't expected the question either. "Me? It was my bright idea to attack an infinitely more powerful warship with a handful of people and then put that psychopath in front of you. I'm stumbling blindly here, depending on luck more than anything else. I did all that so you could tell us how to get out of here."

She nodded, her eyes not wandering from his. "You risked a lot for me, and here I am looking at you, newly born Prometheus, asking what you would have us do?"

He could have throttled the old woman right then. He took a deep breath and steadied himself. "Are you playing games?" His voice was level, not showing anger, but the question was real. There was no time for games. Lives hung in the balance of the decisions made here, and each passing second meant they were closer to death.

Alistair saw surprise on Servia's and Thoreaux's faces. Perhaps no one had spoken to their leader like this before, and they couldn't imagine speaking that way themselves.

There was nothing on the AllMother's face besides earnestness. "I'm not playing games. I woke up two hours ago, and you look at me as if I can somehow wave my hand and make this all go away. I have thoughts, but I'd like to hear yours. I imagine they're more relevant than mine."

Alistair sank back against the wall, staring at the woman. His thoughts? He had none. Two forces were colliding on a world that didn't want them here, and he'd put all his hope on her.

When things couldn't get worse, one of those damn Terram walked into their little room. Obs raised his head and sniffed the air.

The Terram spoke in that guttural language Alistair would never understand.

Obs gave a low growl when the Terram finished speaking and turned to look at his master.

All the other eyes fell on Alistair as well.

Thoreaux told him what the squat, thick man had said. "The Commonwealth is sending demands."

Servia had never seen this room before, and she was sure Thoreaux hadn't either. Certainly, Alistair hadn't because the Terram trusted him least of all, especially since he didn't speak their language.

Only the AllMother looked like she'd been here, showing no surprise, though Servia believed that could just as easily be her natural countenance. At her age, after everything she'd seen, not much surprised her anymore.

The Terram, despite living underground, continued to amaze Servia with their technological prowess. In many ways, they were more advanced than the Commonwealth. They simply lacked the huge population.

What of the AllSeer? part of her mind whispered. *Apparently, he's even more powerful than these people.*

She hadn't been with Thoreaux and Alistair, but what they'd said afterward had frightened her. Servia was young, but she thought she knew much of the universe.

What Thoreaux had relayed showed her she knew very little, and that scared her more.

She pushed the thoughts from her head. This wasn't the time to consider that creature and his minions. The Commonwealth had arrived, and they were enough to deal with.

Servia stood to the right of the AllMother's hoverchair. Thoreaux was to its left, and Alistair stood in front of them all. She couldn't see his face, but she wondered if he was marveling at this room like she was.

The walls were the same rock as the rest of their underground labyrinth, but the inside of the room was a technological marvel. A large holovid rested in the middle, showing the Commonwealth's fleet. The colors were striking as if somehow the satellites capturing the images were able to define different parts of the ship.

Servia didn't know what the colors, which ranged from white to red, meant. A heat map overlaid the ships to show where most people were located.

The Terram were hustling and bustling around the room, hardly paying attention to Servia or anyone else in her group. Screens hung in a circle around the holovid, though they were unlike anything Servia had ever seen. They appeared to be holoscreens since there was nothing physically there, but they allowed information to scroll up and down. More, the information and objects on these screens could be moved by touch, and Servia watched as a Terram grabbed a three-dimensional orb, carried it around the armada's holovid, and placed it in the air next to some streaming words.

This was obviously an information hub, and it was readily apparent that the Terram were anxious. Nervous energy floated in the air as surely as the holovids.

As Servia watched, Alistair walked to within two meters of the screens. One of the Terram turned her head and barked something Alistair wouldn't understand that meant, "Keep back."

Even after the six months here, the size difference between Alistair and the natives struck Servia. She didn't think he truly understood how large he was. At two-and-a-half meters, these smaller men and women were a little over half his size. They were all extremely strong, but Alistair looked as if he could wipe out four of them with a sweep of his arm.

"I'm going to need some translation here," Alistair said without turning around. "I don't think that one there was saying anything nice."

Thoreaux stepped forward while Servia stayed behind, her hand on the AllMother's shoulder. She didn't want to leave her, not even for a second. Servia wore the face of a person who usually felt disdainful mirth at the world, but in truth, she felt great guilt for not being by the AllMother's side when she fell. They had sent her with a stranger, and while she followed and respected Alistair, she felt she should have been next to the woman she loved so much.

"She said to stay back," Thoreaux told him, then spoke in the Terram language, asking them what the message was saying.

No one answered at first; the Terram were rushing around and studying the fleet. Finally, someone on the other side yelled something.

"They said to come over there." Thoreaux pointed at the wall, meaning they should follow that until they reached the Terram. Alistair nodded, and Thoreaux led.

Servia's hand still rested on the AllMother's shoulder. The AllMother laid her hand over it, and she looked down.

The old woman's eyes were following the two men. "Let's go. I'd like to hear what is said."

"Yes, Mother."

The hoverchair moved around the edge of the room, and Servia followed it. She was glad to see the AllMother wanting to be involved, but she didn't want her to overextend herself. No one had any idea of the true state of her health right now.

The AllMother parked the chair against the wall, and Servia remained next to her. The AllMother was letting Alistair lead, and Servia wasn't going to leave her side. Not yet, anyway.

The words were spoken quietly. They couldn't even hear the Terram's guttural language.

Servia looked down at the AllMother, but she was staring forward, her eyes focused intensely on Alistair. She hadn't asked Servia or Thoreaux what they thought of him since awakening. She didn't care about their opinion of the man she'd picked to save them. Her confidence was total.

A few minutes passed. The Terram pointed at the holovid a few times and at words that seemed to be floating through the air. Servia couldn't read the Terram's language, but she knew the AllMother could.

"What's it say?" she asked.

The AllMother shook her head. Her eyes narrowed as she focused on the words. They were going to wait until Alistair told them.

Finally, he turned, looking like a giant next to the smaller Terram. The Terram didn't turn, just kept touching the floating words and objects.

Alistair came to them and Thoreaux followed, and they formed a small circle.

"What's the word?" Servia asked.

Alistair's face was severe. "Pretty simple message. If the Terram give me up, the Commonwealth will leave the planet. If they don't, everyone here dies."

"Would they use nuclear warfare again?"

Alistair shook his head. "I don't know, and I don't think it matters. The Terram aren't going to let that happen. That's what we were told as well. The Commonwealth is giving them forty-eight standard hours, and they're giving us twenty-four." Alistair looked at the ground and paused for a few seconds. "After that, they'll force me out."

Servia found herself looking at the AllMother like she'd done so many other times in her life. Depending on the old woman for advice, for strategy, for leadership.

The AllMother was only looking at Alistair, though. "What do you want to do?"

Servia knew Alistair wasn't a man for rash decisions. Only in the field of battle did he not think, letting his instincts and body guide him. When it came to strategy, Alistair needed time.

That was what he said.

"I need time. I need to think."

What he didn't do was look at the AllMother and ask what she thought.

He didn't wait for any of them to say anything, either. Alistair turned and left the room that showed an armada which would shortly come kill them all.

Servia and Thoreaux looked at the AllMother. She was still staring forward, her face showing no concern. She seemed more interested in the floating words. "Thoreaux," the old woman said, "do you think you could ask the Terram how they do that?"

Servia ignored the question. "What do you think we should do?"

The AllMother didn't look up but leaned forward and stared more intently at a triangular object that had been tossed from one part of the room to another. "You just heard him, Servia," she said, sounding irritated. "He needs some time, and then he'll tell us. Now, Thoreaux, will you go ask them how they're doing all this? I find it fascinating."

Servia looked up, eyebrows raised. Thoreaux was staring at her, looking like her mirror image.

"Go now," the AllMother instructed. "I'm getting tired, and I'd like an answer before I fall asleep here in this chair." She pointed a bony finger at one of the Terram. "There. Ask him. He doesn't look busy."

Skin pale, eyes wide, Thoreaux went to ask a question no one in the room was concerned about besides the AllMother.

Servia would have laughed if the death of all they knew wasn't two days away.

CHAPTER THIRTEEN

"I am not the end, but only the beginning."

–The AllMother

The AllMother didn't think of herself by that name, despite that being what thousands and thousands of people knew her as. That had been a strategic plan because when all this started, she knew she had to be larger than life. She had to be mythic, a person who would bring people to her cause.

All of that had been long ago. Only a few creatures in the galaxy were still alive to remember it.

Back then, before she created her own legend, she'd been known as Alexandria de Finita, and she'd gone by Alex. A thousand years later, the old woman barely hanging onto life still thought of herself as Alex.

She'd never shared that name with anyone, not since she'd started this crusade. Even Servia and Thoreaux, her closest children now, knew her only as the AllMother.

Maybe one day she'd be able to tell them her name, but

not today.

After she forced Thoreaux to ask the silly question, she'd requested they take her back to her room. The same one she'd spent six months in, being waited on as an invalid.

She moved from the hoverchair to the rock bed and sat there for a moment, then stood up very slowly. Her legs were weak and wobbly, but she had to start rebuilding her strength. She did this exercise twice before her body became too heavy and she collapsed on the bed.

That's enough for today, she thought, then lay down on the bed and stared up at a ceiling she'd only seen once before.

Alex hadn't told them what her brother had wanted with her. She'd said they could focus on it later, but now she was questioning that decision. For so long, she had shrouded her life in darkness, allowing the myth to grow. It felt strange now that she was passing the mantle and giving up that secrecy.

Is that the real reason? Or am I hiding the reason even from myself?

Alex had told them the most important part—that she couldn't be captured by the AllSeer. Even their names had been similar, such was their connection that crossed galaxies.

I have to tell them. Or at least, him, she thought. *If I want him to lead, I can't keep things from him. I can't hide this any longer.*

And yet, as Alex looked up at the rock ceiling, she wasn't sure she could tell him.

Why not? She continued with her self-questioning. For

many years, she'd had no one to turn to, no one to ask her these questions, so her mind became its own sounding board.

The answer to her question—to "Why not?"—was very simple.

She was scared because the truth was that frightening. The truth could collapse the universe as they knew it. It had always been so, ever since her father decided to become more powerful than evolution.

Alex had been running from that truth and amassing her army in the hope that she could somehow change what her brother called fate.

Her entire life was built around stopping him, despite the Commonwealth thinking they were the final target. The de Finita bloodline was vain, unable to comprehend that they were not the rulers of the universe, both the current Imperial Ascendant and the AllSeer.

What about you, old woman? she asked herself. You who think your plans can subvert these other men, those with your blood running through their veins? Are you so different?

Alexandria de Finita closed her eyes. She had to decide when to tell Alistair the truth, and then she had to trust that his decisions would be the right ones.

Alex had told those beneath her to trust her. Now she had to trust the man she'd picked to save the universe.

As the AllMother thought alone deep beneath the ground, Alistair had decided to do something he'd refrained from since arriving. The Terram had changed their atmosphere, but that didn't mean they didn't want to walk above ground sometimes.

There were tunnels above ground that connected different spots of their subterranean world. Very few were allowed up in the tunnels because if any part of the technological marvels broke or cracked, the intense heat from above could ravage those beneath the surface.

Most Terram never stepped above the surface.

Alistair knew how to get to one of the entrances; he just didn't know if he would be allowed through. His lack of language skills limited everything he knew about these people. What he did know came from the small amount of information Thoreaux and Servia had given him. But even they didn't know too much about the Terram.

"They're reclusive, if the fire in the sky didn't give you any idea about that," Thoreaux had joked.

Alistair doubted he would be allowed up to the tunnels, but he wanted to try. He might only have two days left to live, and he'd like to walk among flames before that came to pass.

Obs padded along at his side, the huge drathe easily keeping pace. The drathe knew what was coming, the decision to be made, but Alistair could feel no nervousness from the beast. He gave off no anxiety, just a serene sense of calm as if his master, and therefore he, hadn't been given a death sentence.

The elevator and hatch were in the hallway ahead. A Terram sentry sat on a stone stool that had been carved into the wall.

He stood as he saw Alistair and the drathe coming. He

held no weapons, nothing that could stop someone who wanted to get up, but then, Alistair knew he didn't need to. This Terram had to grant passage to anyone wanting to get to the tunnel.

Alistair just didn't know how he did it.

The Terram waited until Alistair was two meters from him before speaking. It was the guttural language that Alistair didn't understand, though this man sounded weary, as if he was speaking to a drunk at closing time. *Go home. You know there's no more to drink. Come on, cut me a break, buddy.*

Alistair didn't know what to say, but looking at the Terram's resigned and tired face, he decided truth might be his best way. "Do you know who I am?"

The Terram nodded. Of course, he knew who Alistair was: the man who had brought an army to their world, the mutant with red eyes and a body made for killing.

"You know I might not have long left here? Not here." Alistair kicked the ground to show he meant this world. "But in the universe."

He didn't know how fast word traveled through these underground people, but perhaps someone tasked with guarding such an important part of their world would have heard.

The Terram said nothing, only nodded.

"Could I see it?" He quickly glanced at the hatch just beyond and above the man. "It's just the drathe and me. No one else. And I won't be long."

The Terram said something—a short sentence.

"I don't understand. I only speak Common and a little bit of Old English."

The Terram shook his head while looking at the

ground. Alistair didn't think that was a no, but the Terram's disbelief that he was speaking to someone so dumb.

After a long pause, the Terram started speaking again. His words were slow, and they sounded hard for the man to form, but Alistair could just make them out. "Can... you...sthop...dem?"

The Terram looked up. Obs was looking at Alistair too.

Can you stop them?

The Commonwealth, the AllSeer, or both? Alistair doubted if it mattered. The Terram's meaning was clear.

Alistair opened his mouth to say something, probably a hesitation or an *I don't know*, but then he saw Luna's face.

And heard her voice in his head.

Do you give up so easily, Allie?

Alistair blinked and cleared her voice and her image from his mind, though not the meaning. He nodded at the Terram. "I can stop them; I just need to think. I was hoping to walk up there while I did."

The Terram stared at him for what felt like forever. It was the same judging look he'd seen from time to time on Thoreaux's face. Disbelief that anything could stop the forces outside of oneself, that they were too numerous and too massive, and yet, hope that he might be able to.

Finally, the Terram nodded and moved to the side. Alistair understood that he meant for him to board the elevator. Alistair moved forward and stepped onto a circular piece of metal that was raised about an inch off the ground. Obs came next, his massive body taking up more than half the space.

The Terram motioned for Alistair and the drathe to

step farther back. When they did, the Terram also stepped aboard the elevator. Immediately, as if it had sensed the Terram's arrival, glass shields shot up around the circular platform.

Obs jumped closer, hitting the back of Alistair's knees and causing him to have to put his hands on the glass to keep from hitting it face-first.

The Terram chuckled as a blue light inside the glass slowly moved down, scanning the inhabitants of the elevator. The light turned red as it moved across Alistair and Obs, but green when it hit the Terram.

It reached the bottom and died as the elevator started ascending, which simply meant the metal platform moved up through the newly created tunnel. The hatch was about five meters above them, and it looked like they might be crushed. Alistair's head came within a few millimeters of hitting it. He actually ducked.

The hatch opened as quickly as the glass walls had shot up around them.

The Terram looked over his shoulder and chuckled at the hunched Alistair. He shook his head and turned forward as the elevator stopped.

Alistair was about to say something smart to the Terram, but as his eyes focused on the new surroundings, all thought fled from his mind. His body automatically straightened, but he wasn't consciously controlling it. He wasn't consciously doing anything. All he could do was stare.

They stood inside a tunnel that was about twice as tall as Alistair. Outside, the fire grew like plants in a jungle. Alistair moved his head from one side of the tunnel to the other, starting on his left and circling around to stop on his right.

There was nothing else to see, nothing besides the glorious flames and explosions. "How is this possible?" he asked no one.

No answer came either. Even Obs couldn't pull his eyes from the glorious yellow and orange wind blowing the fire over the protective shields around them. The drathe stepped slowly forward until his nose nearly touched the tunnel walls.

The Terram watched Alistair, the first time he'd shown anything but weary annoyance. He appeared almost happy, looking at the Earthborn staring in wonder at his people's creation.

Alistair slowly brought his head down to look at the tunnel before him. He felt no extra heat; the world here was the same temperature as beneath the ground, yet if he were to move a millimeter outside this tunnel, his life would be forfeit.

"Obs," he whispered.

The drathe didn't move or make any noise.

Alistair snapped his fingers as he stared at the tunnel. The floor was smooth and white. Alistair had no idea what type of material they used. Three rods of some type of metal ran through the capsule, encircling them on the left, the right, and one up top.

One more finger-snap broke the drathe from his trance. He backed up slowly and went to Alistair's side. Alistair looked over his shoulder at the Terram. "You mind if we walk?"

The Terram nodded and motioned with his hand for

them to go forward.

Alistair started walking as his eyes stayed on the miracle outside the tunnel.

The Terram had built this, terraformed their world into a death trap for most who tried to enter, all to remain protected from the Commonwealth. To live their lives here peacefully.

The amount of work it had taken and the sheer genius struck Alistair as he walked beneath the transparent safe-guards. The guard's question earlier meant more too. Could Alistair stop them?

Because the universe, despite how far away these Terram had moved, lived in fear of the tyrannical govern-ment, the one Alistair had fought most of his life for but was now coming to understand how wrong it was. If people had to dig tunnels under the world and light their skies on fire to avoid their rule, those rulers should be cast down.

Alistair reached down and touched the drathe's neck. Obs licked his hand but quickly went back to looking at the wonders around him. Alistair could hear the Terram walking behind him, his footfalls soft on the white floor.

How do I stop them, Luna? he asked the creation his mind had made. *How can I possibly stop them with the resources I have?*

His wife didn't answer him.

He walked on, the fire above burning eternally.

For two hours Alistair walked, knowing that each moment he spent here was a moment closer to his death or the deaths of everyone on this planet. His mind went through countless options and permutations, but nothing seemed feasible. Everything he came up with ended with him dead or the movement in tatters.

And then his wife spoke.

I don't think conventional warfare is going to work here, honey.

Then what will? he asked silently, knowing he was speaking to himself.

The answer came, full and complete. Wild, risky, but a way out.

Why not give them both what they want?

The AllMother Alex was lying on her back, staring into the darkness when she felt two entities moving toward her. The abilities her father had given her so long ago, the mutations, were weaker now, very much so. As a younger woman, Alex would have felt them the moment their minds decided to come this way. Where she was now weak, she had once been strong.

Alex knew who it was before they arrived: Alistair and his drathe, the creature that would never leave his master's side. Indeed, he would fight to his death if it meant Alistair would live.

It must be a sign, she thought. For a drathe to connect to an Earthborn from so far away.

Perhaps wishful thinking, or perhaps a sign, but either way, the Fallen Titan had finished thinking. He'd come to a decision, and Alex wasn't sure how to feel about him delivering the message in the middle of the night while everyone else slept.

The near-giant stopped in the entry, the drathe having stepped inside but paused.

"I'm awake," Alex said.

"I thought you might be," Alistair whispered. "Can we come in?"

"Obs appears to have already taken that liberty," she responded.

"He doesn't like letting me enter rooms he hasn't been in first." The warrior fell silent for a second. "Can you see us?"

"No." Alex knew the drathe and Alistair could see in darkness where most couldn't. She, on the other hand, was like the rest in that regard.

"I imagine you didn't hear us, either. So you felt us?" he asked.

Alex nodded, knowing he would be able to see the movement.

"Go on, boy," he whispered to the drathe, and the animal padded into the room. He walked over to the ledge Alex slept on, found her hand, and lightly licked it.

Alex let him for a second before stroking his head.

Alistair stepped into the room, his presence large in such a small area. Alex knew he didn't fully understand his strength yet. Only during battle did he seem to have any inkling of what he could do. *Soon*, she thought. *Soon he would come to see the truth of it, same as I do.*

Alistair sat down on the floor and leaned against the wall. He pulled his knees toward his chest and draped his muscular arms over them.

"Why have you come at night while everyone else

sleeps? What do you wish to tell me that you don't want others to know?"

The fallen Titan was quiet for a moment. "They're protective of you in a way I'm not sure I ever will be. Servia, Thoreaux. You are their mother, and I think we both know you'll never be that to me. It's not an indictment on either of us, it's the truth."

Alex nodded in the darkness. "In some ways, it's necessary."

She felt him nodding on the other side of the room. "If I were to tell them this...well, they barely wanted to go along with me bringing a Myrmidon here to see you." He sighed. "What I'm proposing could cause an out and out mutiny."

Alex said nothing, and in the silence, Alistair spoke up again.

"Can you read my mind?"

"Probably," Alex responded. "But I wouldn't. It's not what I would call ethical."

He chuckled. "Looking into someone's mind is unethical, yet you called me from another planet to lead your movement, despite all those in this movement I had killed."

"Does it weigh on you? The evil you did?"

There was no chuckle this time, just silence like that inside a coffin.

"One man's honor is another man's evil," he whispered in the darkness. "No one I care about has ever called what I did evil. Not until now. They gave me badges and medals. They cheered me."

He grew quiet again. Alex gave him space.

When he spoke, she thought he was talking to her, but

she wasn't sure. "I haven't had time for much to weigh on me in the last six months. It's been a whirlwind, and I've been consumed with protection and survival. Will it weigh on me, though? That I killed your children? That I thought the person I served was a god when he was closer to a demon? Yeah. I think at some point, I'm going to have to face that. It's not something I'm looking forward to, but I don't think I can run from my past forever."

"Maybe you'll be forgiven if you do some good now."

Another deep chuckle. "Who does the forgiving? You, AllMother?"

"No. I think forgiveness comes from ourselves. The gods are too busy for that. Now tell me, Titan, what is this plan you hide from your subordinates?"

In the darkness, his voice changed. The pensive sadness was gone, the leader returned. "We can't stop either of these forces. The Terram will force us off this world and then everyone dies, or they force me off and the AllSeer comes for you just the same. We have to change the dynamics of this battlefield, and the only way I see to do that is to give both forces what they want."

Alex said nothing as her mind deduced his final plan. "What do you propose?"

"To launch us both toward the Commonwealth. They want me. The AllSeer wants you. If we're both on the Commonwealth's ship, the AllSeer will come for you. They'll be forced to—"

Alex interrupted. "Fight each other. You hope they'll solve the problem for us?"

He nodded.

"And in that massacre, what is your plan? We escape,

they destroy each other, and you buy us more time?"

"Yes. Right now, I'm just trying to keep us alive. We're in no position to battle them, and we'll never be able to if we don't survive. We're not in a position of power if you haven't noticed."

The old woman smiled. She'd never been in a position of power, and she'd been in much weaker positions than this, truth be told. This was one of the first times the warrior had been in such a place. He thought she was mocking his plan, which she wasn't.

"Let's do it. Do you want to tell Thoreaux, or do you want to just run away together?"

"Are you mocking me?" he asked. "Or do you find this to be a game?"

Alex oh so slowly sat up on the little ledge and swung her legs off the side. The drathe was at her side and leaned into her gently, not enough to send her sprawling back down. She couldn't see the warrior, but she knew where he was.

"I neither mock nor think this a game. Your idea might work, or it might get us both slaughtered. I have thought of nothing else, however, so I'm willing to go along with it. My question was serious. Do you want to tell your second-in-command, or do you want to leave tonight and let them figure it out?"

It was an important decision, and one he had to make alone. She'd already shown him that he couldn't lean on her, and while it might seem cruel, she knew it was necessary. Her time in this universe was short, and one way or another, she was going to meet the gods if they existed.

He had to know he was alone. The decisions were his,

and his alone. Would he include his second in all of them, or would he put the mission above all else? Alex knew which type of leader she was. He would have to figure it out for himself and quickly.

After a long silence, Alistair shook his head in the darkness. "There is no other way to do this. If they had any ideas, any of them, they would have told me already. And if I tell them, they'll fight it, Thoreaux and Servia especially. There isn't time. If you're in, we go now, tonight."

He stood up, his massive body surprisingly limber.

"I'm in," Alex said. His decision was the right one, the one she would have made, the tough one. A leader had to think of all those beneath him, not just those closest to him.

"Will you be able to help?" Alistair asked. "Or is that part of you done?" He paused, realizing what his words might sound judgmental. "Sorry. I just don't understand you or what you can do. Your abilities are different from anything I've ever come across."

"If it's necessary," Alex whispered, "I'll be able to help. You should think of me as a last line of defense, though."

He nodded in the darkness, understanding. "Are you ready now?"

Alex called the hoverchair to her, such a small use of her mutation that it didn't weaken her. She slowly moved onto it, then turned to the Fallen Titan. "Ready."

She sensed him moving, then light filled the room.

His Whip's tentacles fell from its hilt, their red glow filling the room. The drathe was already at his side, and Alex nodded toward him. "The animal coming?"

Alistair glanced at Obs, who was looking up at him and

growling low in his throat. His message was clear. Alistair shook his head in defeat. "Yeah, I suppose he is. We'll need all the help we can get up there. Something this big will frighten at least some of the Commonwealth people. They've never heard of a drathe, I can almost guarantee that."

"Then the three of us need to get moving before too many people wake up. I take it you've let the Terram know?"

Alistair gave a little grin. "They've got a ship ready for us. One might use the word 'overjoyed' to describe them when I let them know I was leaving their rock. They about fell over themselves getting the ship prepared."

"Then, by all means," the AllMother said, "let's not disappoint."

Thoreaux was in a deep sleep, which was shocking because he hadn't slept well for the past few weeks. When he finally awoke, he knew it was much later than his usual time since the lights on the ceiling were showing a midday brightness, not the dawn of early morning.

No one had woken him up, which was odd. Alistair should have come, or if not him, certainly Servia.

Thoreaux swung his feet off the rock ledge and stood up. He stretched his arms above his head for a brief moment, then pulled a pair of pants on. He didn't bother with a shirt since his anxiety was growing.

He hadn't slept so late since arriving on this planet. *Someone*, if only Obs, should have come by to get him up.

Thoreaux went to Servia's room first.

She was still asleep, with a thin sheet covering her body.

"Servia," he called loudly from the doorway.

She blinked slowly, apparently also having been in a deep sleep. Still lying on her back, she turned her head toward him. "What time is it?"

"I don't know." Thoreaux's anxiety was growing even higher. There wasn't any way both of them should have slept this late. "But something is wrong. I just woke up too, and no one has come by all morning. Not Alistair or the AllMother, Obs, Relm—no one. Not even a Terram. Get up. We need to see what's happening."

Servia understood immediately and flipped off the rock ledge. She put on a light robe, but neither Thoreaux nor her noticed her stage of undress. The two moved quickly down the hall toward the AllMother's room without having spoken of it.

They stopped as they turned the corner.

Relm was standing in the entry to her room. Thoreaux's breath caught in his throat.

No. Gods, no. Let her be alive. Please let her be alive.

Servia spoke first. "Relm!" she called. "Is she okay?"

It was like neither of them wanted to step forward, not without the assurance that the AllMother was alive and well.

Relm turned, his face pale and a DataTrack in his hand. "She's gone. So is Pro."

He lifted the DataTrack, and Thoreaux swept forward and took it from his hand.

The letter was from Alistair.

CHAPTER FOURTEEN

Thoreaux and Servia,

I owe you two an apology more than anyone else. When the AllMother and I return, I will ask your forgiveness in person.

For now, this letter will have to do. I am sorry for not telling you about my plan, but it is the only way I see forward. I did not force the AllMother. She agreed with the plan and came of her own volition if a bit too willingly. The old woman likes adventure.

I have taken the decision out of anyone else's hands, including the Commonwealth's or the AllSeer's.

We are heading to the Commonwealth's main ship, and when we arrive, I will turn myself in.

The AllMother will alert the Myrmidons where we are.

With any luck, the two forces will destroy each other, and the AllMother and I will be back to both of you very soon.

The AllMother apologizes for the sleep she put you both in. It was necessary to ensure we were far away from the planet before you awoke.

Do not follow us under any circumstances. That's an order. If for some reason my plan fails, we are counting on you two. It will be your job to deliver our people to safety.

I haven't said this before, but I love you both. Please know I didn't make this decision lightly, and I look forward to asking for your forgiveness shortly.

Look to the sky. There should be some fireworks soon.

-Pro

CHAPTER FIFTEEN

"It is best we hide our strength from those fated to fall to us until the very last moment. Then their death will be sure."

–The AllSeer

Veena didn't trust what she saw, even though she knew it was happening.

She had sent the ultimatum to Phoenix about twenty-four standard hours ago. There had been no reply, though she knew they had received the message.

She and everyone else on this venture were more than prepared to drop through the intense atmosphere of fire to retrieve Alistair Kane, as well as kill anyone who harbored him. The planet was surrounded. There would be no escape. Either the creatures beneath the ground would give up the former Titan, or their lives would end.

DAVID BEERS & MICHAEL ANDERLE

Veena had been fine with either of those options. It was the only way back to Earth for her. Plus, she thought the Terram would be smarter than the Subversives on Pluto.

But as she watched the single corvette coming toward her dreadnought, she was not fine.

The ship had answered none of the messages sent toward it, nor had the planet. Scans of the corvette showed that it carried two people and an animal of some kind. They couldn't tell who the people were.

Its current destination was Veena's ship, and projections showed it reaching the dreadnought within an hour.

"It's him," Ares said.

Veena sat with the Titan and the woman she knew as Hel. A circular table separated them; it showed the corvette as it flew through space's darkness.

The Primus peered over the table at him. "You can't know that."

Ares waved his hand over the table, and a threat analysis appeared. "The scans show the corvette is nothing more than a transport. It's got no weapons attached to it and nothing nuclear or plasmic inside. It's Kane."

Hel was quiet. She didn't look at the table but rather kept studying the other two.

Ares appeared not to notice her gaze. "We didn't allow him an opportunity to give himself up last time. We simply attacked, and he fought back. The rest of his little group might think they can meet our forces on the battlefield, or perhaps they did before Pluto. Kane has always known, and maybe he still has some sense of responsibility. He'd rather give himself up than let two populations be destroyed."

120

Hel tapped the table with a long fingernail. "Then who's the person with him? If he's giving himself up, why would he need anyone else?"

Veena couldn't read Ares' face fully as he looked at Hel. Hate resided there, but other things as well, a mixture that wasn't readily decipherable.

The Titan didn't have an answer, so he simply stared with that weird mixture, hate bubbling to the top.

"Enough, you two," Veena commanded. "Ares might not have more than a hunch about this, but if he is wrong, who else would be in the ship? Certainly they aren't sending envoys, not after what we did to Pluto. They know perfectly well what we're here to do and what we're capable of doing." She looked at the ship and nodded. "It's him, and does it really matter who he's carrying? Do we think two people and a pet are going to somehow stop us, especially without any mass casualty weapons?"

Ares leaned back in his chair. "No, there's nothing he can do to us. My point is that it's him. We should be heading back to Earth in just a few hours. I for one am tired of this forced exile."

Hel slapped the table lightly. "Good chat. We're done here, yes?" She stood from her chair. Both Ares and Veena were her superiors, and she was extremely attuned to the hierarchy. She wouldn't leave without being dismissed, so she'd made it known that she no longer wanted to be here.

"Do you have any thoughts about this, Hel?" Veena asked. "Anything besides your desire to rush back to your dorm?"

Hel placed both hands on the back of her chair. Her fingers were long and elegant. Veena suddenly wondered how many necks those strong hands had choked the life out of.

"Do I have any thoughts?" Hel mocked. "I think whatever is in that corvette is bringing a lot of death, and I don't think we're prepared for it. I also don't think we can get prepared for it quickly enough. I think the best we can do is try to save ourselves, so that's what I'd like to do now if it's all the same to you."

Veena wanted to strike the woman, but she did her best to keep her face from showing it. "How are they bringing death? Given everything we've just discussed, I don't see the possibility."

Hel looked at her for a few seconds, silence filling the space between them. "There are things in this universe that you don't understand, Primus. It's unfortunate that you cannot scan the fourth dimension from our current place in the third, let alone the fifth, but I think if you *could* scan them, you'd find we're not alone here."

Veena was stunned. "What are you talking about?"

Hel placed her right index finger on the ship flying across the table. "If it is as our young warrior says, that Alistair Kane is on this ship, then the identity of the person next to him is quite evident; it's the AllMother. If both those things are true, then this Alistair is a clever chap, one not to be trifled with. It also means the AllSeer is near, or his minions at the very least."

She paused, and Veena knew her mask had dropped from her face.

Hel nodded, smiling. "So you both have heard of him. Now you see, yes? Where the AllMother is, his Myrmidons follow, and if Alistair Kane is bringing that old hag to this ship, you can believe the Myrmidons are close behind."

Veena understood what the dark woman was saying. There had been reports of giants on Pluto, massive men and women who made Earth's mutants look almost like children.

Hel kept smiling. "Now, if we're done here, I'd like to go prepare for the attack to come. I would recommend, my lieges, that you both do the same."

Veena shook her head. "Wait." She looked at Ares. He'd closed his mouth, and his eyes were narrow. He appeared to be considering, staring at the wall. "What do you think? Can your Titans fend off an invasion?"

Without looking over, he nodded. "We're in top shape."

Hel laughed. "You two are fools. Your best bet is not to let that Titan board if it means keeping the old woman from getting on too."

Veena raised both eyebrows. "I imagine your directive was fairly close to ours: kill or bring back Alistair Kane, regardless of the cost. Tell me how not letting him on this ship would accomplish that."

Hel looked at her shoes. She was still smiling, an animal that did not care to hide that she was different from everyone else in this room. "Yes, you're right, of course, my liege. Please forgive my cowardice. Would you grant me release to go prepare for the battle?"

Veena trusted this woman like she trusted a snake. Indeed, she'd take Ares to bed before she even shook this woman's hand, yet what could she say? *No, you'll stay at my side until we step foot back on Earth.*

That wouldn't work.

"Go on," Veena told her. The dark woman didn't look up as she took her leave, though she did lightly lay her fingers on Ares' heavily muscled shoulder as she passed.

Veena waited until the door was closed behind Hel before speaking. "I don't trust her. At all."

Ares turned slowly, and for a moment, he looked unsure of himself, like he didn't know what to do next, and his mind might short-circuit before he figured out the next step.

After a few moments, his face cleared, and he raised a finger to his lips. *Shhh.*

Veena's head jerked back as if someone had just tried to slap her. What was Ares saying? That Hel could hear them? On *her* ship?

That just wasn't possible.

Ares stood up without a word. He walked to the door, and as it opened, he looked over his shoulder, the meaning obvious: *follow me.*

Veena stood and walked out the door. Ares didn't turn around to see if she was following but kept moving as if he were alone.

Veena knew every turn and hallway of this ship, so she quickly figured out where they were going. With each step closer, Veena grew more nervous. The Primus of a fleet should never be heading in this direction on her First Ship, not unless things had gone woefully wrong, yet here she was, walking silently to an escape pod.

They finally reached the room that housed the pods. The oil-black orbs could fit a few people in each, though this far from Earth, any life inside would long be dead before returning to the homeworld.

The door to the pod room closed silently behind them, but still Ares didn't speak. Instead, he walked to one of the pods on the right and waved his hand over the entry scanner. The vacuum-sealed door opened and air rushed into the pod, creating a small breeze around Veena.

This was getting worse by the second.

Ares stepped into the pod and walked to the very back. He finally turned and motioned her inside.

Veena stepped forward, flashing her hand at the inside panel as she did. The door closed behind them, sealing them off from everyone and everything.

Panels lit up to the left and right and a voice spoke overhead, a pleasant-sounding female who was completely at odds with the reason for anyone entering this craft. "Safety Pod activated. Coordinates or would you like to rely on programming?"

Ares' eyes didn't move from Veena's as he spoke. "Safety Pod off."

"Please confirm," the female voice said. "Safety Pod off?"

"Yes."

The panels died, and the two were left alone.

"I think she can see and hear everything that happens inside the ship." The playboy was gone. The man in front of her was a warrior, hard and without mercy.

Veena shook her head. "That's impossible. I would know. My pilots would know."

"Then you would know that she can see inside the war room where we practice?"

Veena started to say something but then paused, her words dying before they were formed.

Ares nodded in the silence. "She's watching, and she's made me aware that she's watching me too."

Veena shook her head harder. That made no sense. She would know. "It's impossible. I'd be aware. No one has that kind of vision in this ship besides me."

Ares crossed his arms over his chest. "I don't care whether you believe me or not, Veena. The mere fact that I'm here instead of somewhere else on the ship should show you *I* believe it."

"How long have you thought this? Why are you just now bringing it to my attention?"

Ares raised his eyebrows. "You think I trust you, Veena? I know what you think of me, and while I don't care, it doesn't draw me closer to you. Everyone on this ship is playing their cards close, as they should, but she knows more than us, and casting my lot with her would no doubt mean death, so I'm telling you. She can see and hear everything, so anything you said in that room would be noted."

It took all of Veena's concentration to remain standing. It felt like a mutant had just sucker-punched her in the stomach. If this was true, it was traitorous. She could hardly fathom what it meant, not only from a security standpoint but an almost global one. For a Primus to not have complete control of her fleet, let alone her First Ship? Hel would have had to get permission from the Ascendant himself to be able to backdoor the security systems in such a way. No one could have done that without his express will.

"You okay?" Ares asked. "You need to sit down?"

Veena blinked hard, reached deep, and pulled up all the strength she could muster. What she felt right now could be dealt with later. She had to remain the Primus of this ship and of this fleet. "I'm fine." She took a deep breath and let it out slowly. "I'll deal with that later. Right now, let's focus on why you have me in this pod unless the reason was to tell me something you should have told the Primus immediately upon finding out."

"She might be right," Ares said, ignoring the barb. "Did you watch the videos from beneath Pluto? Before you turned the world to ash?"

Veena shook her head. She hadn't cared what took place underground, only that she hadn't acted fast enough.

"I did. I wanted to see why my Titans couldn't get to him. Even with his mutations, I thought we would be able to take him, but there were things in those halls that ran through us like water through a sieve. They were massive." His eyes went glassy like he was remembering something from long ago. "Like trees, the oaks my father grows. Large like that—things that you have to stare up at to see their full scope."

Veena's thoughts of betrayal faded as she saw something inside the Titan. The glassy eyes were remembering, but she saw something else that nearly made her shudder.

Fear.

"You said you were prepared for any other battles. You just said it, Primus."

Ares found her eyes again. "I said it in front of her. I plan on telling her nothing, not even if she needs to know. I imagine that's what she's doing to me as well. If those creatures board this ship, you'd better be ready to unload every insectoid we have. I mean all of them, Veena, and push their mindset up to Full Fury."

"What did you have yours at when you fought Kane last?" she asked. It wasn't a spiteful question, but real. Kane had beaten the insectoid, then beaten Ares as well.

"Half Measures."

Veena shook her head in confusion. "Why would you do that?"

Ares cocked his head, confused. "Is that a serious question?"

The answer came to Veena then; that it hadn't earlier showed just how different the two were. "You wanted the glory?"

"I can't tell if you're gaming me right now."

Veena could have clouted the man upside his head. "You allowed a planet to be obliterated for glory? You allowed him to escape, hoping you could somehow kill him?"

The Titan took a step back and leaned against the wall. His eyes were narrowed, but not from anger. He honestly didn't understand if she was being serious.

There wasn't time right now to go in-depth on this. It was too much to take in the ramifications of what this young man had cost the Commonwealth in his attempt at being remembered. She put her hands on her hips and looked down at the deck, trying to clear her mind of both bombshells. "Okay, right now we have to focus on the matter at hand. If you're right and he's coming, and she's right in that he's bringing the old woman, which will somehow awaken those massive warriors…"

She looked up.

"What are you proposing? Do you think we should leave but don't want to say it because it might go against your sense of glory?" She almost spat the last word.

Ares ignored the comment, having concluded that they were different people. It didn't concern him too much. "Glory or not, I don't think we can run at this point. If we do, where do we go? I don't understand this whole AllMother-AllSeer thing." His eyes flicked from the wall behind Veena to her face. "Do you?"

She shook her head, trying to sort through what the Ascendant had told them, the legends, and what she herself knew. "Not enough to matter. They exist; that's clear enough. They've got to be pretty powerful to have existed for as long as they have." Veena shrugged. "I don't understand how she'll contact them, and I don't know anything about the AllSeer's forces. Maybe the Ascendant doesn't either."

Ares nodded, pursing his lips. "So then, neither of us really knows anything except that those creatures are ancient and that they're tanks. Plus, Hel thinks we're fragged already." He was looking at the wall behind her again.

It was odd how quickly this man changed. He went from arrogance to pettiness that would ruin a world, to a strategist. The strategist was where his mind currently resided.

"We can leave, but we can't go back to Earth," he said. "More, depending on how far we fall back, it could cause a mutiny if those under you realize we're running because we don't think we can win." He shook his head, still not paying attention to her. "Running isn't going to work because if Kane is doing what Hel says and setting us up to battle these beasts, we're going to have to face them at some point."

His eyes came to her again, and he asked, "Why does this AllSeer want the AllMother?"

His mind was quick, and Veena understood why he'd been Rex. Despite his personality problems, the Titan had talent. He had immediately grasped the core issue.

Veena had no answer for him. "I don't know, but why does it matter?"

"Maybe it doesn't. Not for what we need, at least. In the end, though, knowing that might help us. If you don't care, it might just help me." He pointed at the door behind her. "If it doesn't matter right now, then we have to figure out how to defend against what's coming. For the sake of argument, let's say that each of those beasts can handle two of our Titans."

"Even with Mech gear on?" Veena asked.

Ares sighed. "Do you know what 'for the sake of argument' means?"

Veena wanted to slap him. From genius to jackass in moments. "Continue."

"On this ship, we have two hundred and fifty Titans. That's not many. My forces are spread out over the fleet—"

Veena interrupted. "You're assuming they're going to board the ship. That we can't fend them off?"

Ares shook his head in disbelief. "I can't decide if you're kidding or dense. Did you see any of those giants landing on Pluto? No. That means whatever they travel with, it's cloaked and with something we can't see through. So yes, I think them boarding is a real possibility."

Veena felt like she was a step behind this man every time they spoke.

No, she thought. He's been sitting on this information

for a long time. It's the first time you've been introduced to it.

Veena closed her eyes, and in the silence, let her mind think through the options. She believed the Titan. Whatever else he might be, he was someone who looked after his own hide, and at this moment, his hide was attached to hers.

Trust him to save himself, she thought.

Veena opened her eyes. "Right now, I need to focus on their ships, or whatever the hell they're going to bring to battle. You need to focus on your Titans." She took a deep breath before she said the next few words, wanting to make sure she meant them. "You've got complete control over them, Ares. You do whatever you think will win this coming battle, as long as it doesn't conflict with the Fleet's strategy. Do you understand that?"

The chain of command here was clear. Veena was in charge of everything and everyone in this Fleet, but she needed to trust this man, and he her.

Ares nodded. "What about Hel?"

"Nothing at the moment. Right now, we prepare for battle."

That wasn't true.

Veena would be damned before she let someone else have control over her ship that she wasn't aware of. She contacted her capo, and of course, the woman knew nothing about Hel's extra credentials. She instructed her to prepare for the arrival of the corvette and to prepare the ship for battle, then she turned her comm to one way so words could only flow to her.

Veena moved quickly through the dreadnought and took the final elevator to Hel's room.

The door was open. Veena stepped to the edge of it.

"Come in," Hel called, though Veena couldn't see her.

She reached for the StarBeam at her waist but didn't pull it out. *How has it gone this far?* she wondered. *That I'm scared of those under my command?*

Veena stepped into the room. She immediately saw Hel to her right, sitting with her legs crossed and a martini in her hand.

A MechSuit was on her right, folded down all the way to the boots, ready for her to step in and go to war. Veena saw the Whip attached to her hip.

"Your hand on the beam makes me think I should put this drink down and grab my weapon."

Hel took a sip. The Whip glowed orange, though its tentacles hadn't dropped out yet. It was sensing her anger, not apprehension. None of that resided in this creature.

Veena didn't take her hand off the weapon. "Can you view every room on this ship?"

Hel dropped her eyes to the drink as if an answer waited in it. "You don't know who I am, do you? I'm only ten years older than you, Veena, but it's like my legacy was wiped from Earth's collective memory." She looked up, her eyes as cold as space. "Yes, I can see every room on this ship. I can see every single room in this fleet, little girl. I watched as that Titan led you to an escape pod, knowing that would be the only place my communication would be cut off."

She took another sip, a small one.

"Why do you come here to ask me these stupid questions, girl? You are no threat to me, and neither is that Titan, who wants to be the greatest of his kind so he can get accolades from the little people he thinks himself so much better than. You all are rats in a cage, raging against metal that will never let you out. So why are you here?"

The insults rolled through Veena's mind like a light wind. This bitch's arrogance didn't matter one bit to her, especially not right now. "Did the Ascendant give you the access to see through my ships?"

"It doesn't concern you." She sounded almost bored as she spoke. The Whip had turned off. "Is there anything else?"

"You realize I can have you jailed? That you'll see nothing but a single room until we return to Earth, and then I'll have you put on trial?"

Hel swirled the drink in her glass. "You can try, little girl, but many will die before any of that happens, and I guarantee you will be one of them." Another small sip. She swallowed without a grimace. "Now, do you want to keep measuring our non-existent dicks, or do you want to try to stop what's coming? It doesn't matter to me. I plan on surviving regardless of your decisions, which, if you'll allow me to say so, haven't been strong so far."

Veena didn't pause. "Can you stop him? The AllSeer?"

Hel's eyebrow rose and a smirk appeared on her face. "Girl, the AllSeer is not here. He will venture from his cave when the AllMother is in his minions' possession and not a moment before that. The correct question is, can I stop the Myrmidons?"

"Can you?"

She finished her drink and set the glass gently on the table next to her, then stood without answering. She turned so that her back was to Veena. "There is no stopping them. They are a cancer without a cure. They will spread across this universe until their insane leader possesses everything, and even then, perhaps he will not stop. That isn't the question you want to ask, though. Not truly. What you want to know is, can I slow them down? Or trick them? Yes." She nodded, her back still to Veena. "You'll need to listen to me, though, girl. You and that Titan of yours. Otherwise, you're both going to die."

Later, Veena would realize the truth of Hel's words.

She also would wish she'd shot her in the back and killed her then and there.

CHAPTER SIXTEEN

"Most of humanity considers life short. To me, it has been long. Most times, too long."

–The AllMother

The AllMother stared at the massive ship.

Alistair watched her from the corner of his eye. The closer they grew to the dreadnought, the quieter she'd become. Now she was silent.

The screen in front of Alistair said they would arrive in thirty standard minutes. They were in the grip of the tractor beam now. A couple of kilometers away, two war corvettes flew on either side of their ship.

There was no way out. Only by going forward could they escape the hell to come.

"Are you okay?" he whispered.

"I fear we may be going to our deaths," she answered.

"How many times have you feared that before?" he asked.

She laughed then. "That's a good point, young man. Sometimes it's wise to remember what we've already been through in order to understand what we can survive."

"Are they watching us? The Myrmidons?"

The AllMother shook her head. "Not yet. I've managed to keep us hidden from them, though it grows tiresome."

Alistair leaned back against the headrest. "We've got a few minutes yet. Would you tell me about one of those other times you feared death?"

The AllMother looked at him and raised an eyebrow. "Right now?"

He shrugged without looking at her. "Why not?"

"Okay." She turned back to the front. "But you will return the favor when we get out of this mess you've put us in."

"Deal."

Alistair closed his eyes. He felt Obs nuzzle his hand, and both listened to the old woman's story.

THE WRITTEN HISTORY OF THE GREAT INSURRECTION

I doubt that there will be another entry written quite like this one. This book is about the present and future. However, I feel it necessary to record this story. It was passed from the AllMother to Prometheus. I am putting it down here as it was told to me. It is important because almost no one is around anymore to verify its authenticity.

Soon, there will be no one at all.

The story is written in full, and I hope it will provide another example of the sheer depravity mankind is capable of to those in the future.

The AllMother was twenty-three years old when she first learned of her father's wishes.

She and her brother were in the same room, staring at the same man, but their reactions couldn't have been more different. The AllMother, Alexandria, blinked three times. Even years later, she would remember that. She had blinked three times, thinking that if she blinked enough, perhaps the words might make sense. That somehow she could blink away the nonsense this man was spewing.

Her brother, the one who would one day be known as the AllSeer but who was simply Alexander back then, had said, "As my father wishes."

"I need to speak to our father," Alex said to the man in front of her. She knew his name, but at that point, his words made him a stranger, and a dangerous stranger at that because he sounded insane.

"He asked me to deliver the news to you," the man responded. "Your father is very—"

Alex stood up. "If you say another word to me, I will kill you where you stand. Guard your tongue carefully in the next few seconds, scientist."

The man's eyes widened, and he took a step back. He opened his mouth to say something, but then his brain snapped on and his mouth shut with an audible click.

She knew what he had been about to say. *Your father is very busy.*

Maybe so, but Alex would make sure the man found time. She looked at her brother. He was staring at her, his face its usual mask of calm.

In the early part of her life, Alex had thought that was his personality. She was fire and he was ice. She wouldn't find out until much later the rage that resided beneath that mask.

"Is that really all you have to say?" she asked. "Not another word?"

"Our father knows what's best."

Alexander stood, his height far surpassing his twin

sister's, even though she was tall for a woman. He looked past her at the doctor who was currently trying to melt into the wall. "Do you have anything else for us?"

The doctor shook his head, not wanting to speak.

"Thank you for your service, Doctor," her brother said. He walked past Alex without saying anything and left the room.

Alex turned to the doctor. "When does he want this done? Speak."

"My or-or-orders are to have the procedures finished within six standard months."

Alex departed from the room, leaving the doctor behind. She knew where her brother was going, but she'd find no comfort there. She wouldn't find comfort with her father either, and she wouldn't be allowed to speak with him yet. She'd turn to her mother first. Could she possibly know about this abomination?

Alex made her way to her mother's quarters, moving past the servants and through the labyrinth of rooms and hallways. She knew where her mother waited.

The woman was in her bed, though it was nearing noon. Alex hated to see it, which was why she rarely visited her mother anymore—the great woman who had been brought to this state. A lush who preferred the comfort of a bed to the satisfaction of action.

"Mother," Alex called from the doorway.

Her mother rolled from her side to her back, blinking slowly as she withdrew from slumber and entered the world. "What is it, Alexandria? You know I don't like to be woken up this early."

Alex sighed and entered the room. She went to the foot

of the bed. "It's tough getting up before dusk, but sometimes duty calls us. I need to know if you've spoken to Father about this…I'm not even sure what to call it. Abomination?"

Her mother pulled herself up to rest against the headboard. "What are you talking about? You know your father doesn't share his plans with me, or with anyone, for that matter."

"I'd hoped that if the plans involved your offspring, he might make an exception. I guess that would mean you'd need to get out of bed first, but here we are, all the same." Alex had to consciously push her anger down. The Imperial Ascendant and his family were supposed to be the models for all citizens. Instead, this woman slept her life away, hating a husband she refused to leave. "He's going to clone us, Mother. Alexander and me."

That grabbed her mother. She sat up fully, the sleep erased from her face. "What?"

"That's what one of his doctors just told us. He wasn't even there to deliver the message, just sent a lackey. But yes, within six months, the two of us are to be cloned."

Her mother stared at Alex, blinking like an uncomprehending animal.

"It would be helpful if you would say something."

Her mother started to speak, then stopped. Her mouth opened and closed a few times, her tongue clicking on the roof. "You should talk to your father. He hasn't told me anything about it. I'm not sure what you want me to say."

Had Alex thought she might find an ally here? Was that why she'd come? Or had she at least hoped for some righteous indignation at her mother's progeny being used for the nascent technology? "That's your only advice? To speak to him? Have you heard what happened during the last cloning experiment?"

Her mother shook her head. "And I don't want to. I hate being bothered with such disgusting things. It's not healthy for the mind, Alexandria."

"Nor the body," Alex continued. "Both the clone and the subject ended up acting as if they'd had a lobotomy. A perfectly fine twenty-five-year-old man was drooling on himself and asking his mother for ice cream. I might add that she'd been dead for ten years. And the clone? It was his twin, and it had the same memories and wanted the ice cream too. That's what is about to happen to your son and daughter."

Her mother shut her eyes tight, crow's feet forming at the sides. She shook her head quickly. "I told you I didn't want to hear such nastiness. Get out of here, Alexandria. I just woke up and don't want to hear anymore. Go talk to your father. I don't even know if the things you're saying are true."

She stared at her mother for a few seconds, wondering how someone who'd been so strong was now so weak. But she knew how. Aurelius de Finita had broken her. "Mother," Alex said, "if something does happen to Alexander and me during this insanity, do you think Father will choose you to have children with again? We both know his lineage must go on. He will *never* not have progeny. You will be cast aside. Perhaps it is important to remember that before you go back to sleep."

Alex left the room then, not bothering to shut the door

behind her. A servant quickly fluttered to it, making sure her mother remained in her self-imposed cage.

Alex went to her brother next. Maybe he'd had time to process the lunacy being thrust upon them. To research the other subjects this ridiculous science had destroyed.

It was easy to find him in his war yard. He spent most of his days here, and sometimes his nights, constantly practicing with his Whip, preparing for a war that would never happen. She thought he might hate the world for that. He'd missed his chance at true greatness because he hadn't been born before the war where their father rose to Imperial Ascendant.

The sun was descending on the horizon, casting orange and yellow rays across the world. The war yard was littered with the metal bones of the fallen 'legions' Alexander had destroyed in the past month. These legions were robot soldiers whose design and construction he oversaw. They were cleared off the premises regularly, but no matter how quickly servants came to collect the metal fragments, more replaced them.

Her brother was obsessed with combat.

He twirled his orange Whip at his side, his tall body casting a deep shadow across the yard. An alien-looking robot wobbled in front of him. Its head was missing, but it hadn't got the message to die.

Without turning around, Alexander spoke. "Are you here to whine more about Father's decision?"

"I'm here to ask why you're so willing to go along with it, or have you been out here killing scrap for so many months in a row that you haven't read what's happening with these experiments?"

Her brother retracted the Whip and hooked it on his belt. He turned then, sweat dripping down his shirtless torso. He was breathing heavily, meaning this last robot must have been an improvement in the design. "I've read the reports."

"And you don't care? Have you read about the underlying technology?"

Alexander grabbed the ponytail holder keeping his long brown hair in check and pulled it off, letting his hair fall to his shoulders. He finally met his sister's gaze. "Do you think I'm just a mindless grunt? Don't you remember we took the same classes? None of your scores were better than mine, so why do you think that would change now?"

Alex wanted to slap him but managed to hold her anger inside. "They aren't replicating small cells. They're replicating the entire person. Whatever the gods put in us, Alexander, they're taking that and duplicating it."

"Yes, they're going back to the original naming instead of the derivative 'clone.' They're calling it *klon*, and they're managing to replicate the molecular memory, not just the structure. Our cells may die off and replicate themselves regularly, but they each carry a memory. Father's scientists are now able to duplicate that process, creating a human who isn't a clone but the exact same creature." He raised an eyebrow. "Is there anything else you'd like to lecture me about?"

"The cells are retarded, Alexander. They might be the same down to their memory, but the memory is destroyed. The subject isn't the same person on either side of the cloning. The cells—

"Re-replicate, or reprogram the original host. I know."

He knows, Alex thought, not sure why. "Have you spoken to Father about this? Did you talk to him before we were told today?"

Alexander unhooked his Whip again. He turned it on and the weapon's tentacles wrapped tightly around each other, turning into a single blade. He ground the laser into the cement beneath his feet, and smoke rose into the air. He stared at the damage. "It was my idea, Alexandria."

She gritted her teeth, her jaw flexing. Her hands turned to fists. "Why? And if you want to lose your soul along with your mind, why would you take me with you?"

Her brother slowly dragged the laser eastward. "Because we're not just going to be cloned, Alexandria. We're going to be mutated as well. Modified. You've heard of this, I assume?"

Alex's breath caught in her throat. She was aware of modifications. They were new as well, something else her father's regime was exploring now that energy was apparently limitless.

But this...

"Tell me why, Alexander. Don't tell me any more about what you proposed. I want to know why."

He started walking without speaking. He dragged the laser behind him, and after about ten paces, he took a right. "Father won the war for the world. There will be more wars though, Alexandria. Many of them. Already there are small uprisings on Mars. I know Father hasn't told you about portal travel yet, but it's almost here. Within a year or two, we will be able to move from one part of the universe to another in the blink of an eye."

He turned right again.

"Father is the master of Earth, and I believe he will be master of our Solar System. I don't wish to challenge him in that realm, but even he understands that one man cannot rule a universe, no matter how powerful he is."

Another right, so that he was heading toward his starting place.

"Someone—or some*ones*—will need to bring order to the universe, Alexandria." Right before he reached the first black mark, he turned right again, forming a line inside the square. "It will be us. We will rule the universe. The reason the current clones fail is that they aren't modified. They are simply human, and right now, we can't figure out a way to get around that. Our technology isn't strong enough, and the human cell is too weak to copy everything correctly."

Another right, the resulting line shorter than the one it ran parallel to.

"Once we are modified, though, our cells will be able to copy. There will be two of us."

Alex thought she was hearing madness. Perhaps for the first time in her life, she was hearing true, unabated insanity. "Why do we need to copy, Alexander? Do you realize how crazy you sound?"

He stopped drawing and looked at her. "Perhaps I fibbed a bit. That was Father's desire. He wants our originals to remain here with him. He says it's because he loves us, but I think the true answer is a lot simpler than that. If he sends us out to rule, keeping a copy of us here will give him a better idea of what we're thinking. He's not the most trusting man."

He retracted his Whip once more. His chest was still now, his breath even. "I wanted to be the one to tell you,

Alexandria. Despite what you think of me, you are the only thing in this world I care about. I want to go on this journey with you. There's no reason to fight it. It won't do any good. The decision has been made."

Just like that, Alex realized her life would never be the same. Those who were supposed to care, who were supposed to love her, were so obsessed with their desires that she had become a tool to achieve them.

Alex got her audience with her father.

She'd received the message to meet him at the docks.

Alex arrived an hour after the message, ignoring the triumph of mankind that was all around her. Ships coming and going, blasting off from Earth and heading farther and farther into space. It was truly the dreams of almost countless generations, but when she reached her father, she couldn't have cared less about it.

Anger whirled inside Alex. It'd been a little over half a day since she spoke with her brother, and she'd concluded that there were only two ways out of this: she would have to fight or flee.

Unless she could somehow convince her father here and now how bad an idea this was.

"They tell me you've been wandering the palace like a madwoman," her father said as she approached. He was a tall man, though not as wide or thick as his son. He was in his sixties. He had not had children until his reign was solidified.

Alex used to think of him as a hero, which was how the

rest of the world saw him and the way her brother saw him to some extent.

Now she just wondered why he'd had children. The only reason she could come up with was to have his genes go on.

"That's one way to put it, I suppose," she responded. "Another might be that I was just told I'd be undergoing an untested medical procedure and then given one that will make me an invalid."

Her father didn't glance at her but kept staring at the DataTrack in his hand. "You sound like your mother. That's not a compliment."

Alex stepped closer to her father. She knew what she was about to say had not been told to him in many years. Outright refusal of someone who conquered Earth and then space? "I won't do it."

Aurelius made no sudden movements and showed no emotion. His eyes squinted at the DataTrack, and after a moment, he raised his hand and motioned for the next page. "Is that so?" he asked her.

"It's unconscionable, what you're asking of me. Just because Alexander is willing, it doesn't mean I am. I won't sacrifice myself for you or this quest of yours."

"Enough," her father replied. "Come to my quarters this evening. I'll hear you then."

Alex found herself wanting to say, "No, you'll hear me now," but her anger knew its limits. She walked away without another word, and her father didn't glance at her as she did. Tonight she would make him see the truth.

Had Alex known what would happen that evening, perhaps everything that followed would have changed.

She often wondered about that later on.

Would there have ever been an AllMother? Or her Subversives, as the Commonwealth termed them?

She thought there probably would not. Had she known, the universe would have gone down a different path, and later she would find peace in that. If humans knew the hardships we would go through, we would cower and never leave our caves, but we would never change the universe either.

Her father's "quarters," as he called them, was the Throne Room—a simplistic name his enemies gave it before he conquered each of them. They'd said it mockingly. *This self-appointed king and his little throne room.*

They soon found out her father wanted to be much more than a king, and he adopted the throne room moniker.

The doors opened before Alex, and she stepped inside. It had been years since she was called to this room, and she'd had no desire to come on her own. She didn't like it, though she wasn't quite sure why.

The throne sat in the middle of the room. It was a simple thing, unostentatious, though it was raised off the floor to allow him to look down on those who stood before him. He wasn't in it now, though. Rather, he was standing off to the left, his hands folded behind his back.

He didn't say anything until the doors closed behind her. "You wished for an audience, daughter. Here I am, and you have my undivided attention."

That was when Alex first realized something was

wrong. This room always appeared empty when one first entered it. That was the way her father had designed it. However, it was never empty since his Praetorian Guard remained at the edges of the circular room. They weren't here now. It was only her and her father.

Alex's heart beat loudly in her ears, the enormity of such a departure causing it to race. Could she hide it? You never showed weakness in front of this man, especially not after what she'd told him at the docks. She turned from facing the throne to facing him. "I don't want to do what you're asking me."

It was there, the subtle difference, and she knew it immediately.

So did he.

"Didn't you say something different at the docks?" Aurelius asked. "I believe you said you *won't* do it. I could be mistaken, obviously, since my hearing isn't what it once was, but I could have sworn that was what you said. Am I wrong?"

Sweat popped out across Alex's palms. She wanted to wipe them on her pants but knew that to do so would hamper her cause more. She forced them to remain at her sides. "No, you're correct, Father. I said I won't do it."

Her father nodded and then looked at the floor. "That perplexes me, the change in wording." He raised his hand as if to stop her from interrupting him, though Alex hadn't opened her mouth. "No, no. I understand I'm a peculiar man, but I asked myself why you would use such strong language in public." He looked up, and as he did, he spread his hands wide to indicate the room. "Yet such meek language in private?"

Alex opened her mouth to speak, but it was as if her father had mastered the art of teleportation. One moment he was across the room, and the next, he was at her throat.

He lifted her into the air with one arm. Her legs kicked uselessly at his midsection as if it were made of iron. His face was that of a rabid dog, his eyes full of rage.

As the oxygen was cut off, a calm thought moved through her head. This is what they all saw—every single person who had fallen to his hand.

"Do you think yourself so great, my daughter, that you can deny me what I want? Do you think I'm so weak that you can tell me how to run the Commonwealth just because you come from my loins?" He held her, his arm showing no signs of weakness. "Do you think you're stronger than me?"

Aurelius de Finita tossed his daughter away. He threw her as no man should be able to, into the air and at least four meters. Alex hit the floor on her back. Any oxygen left inside her was expelled, and she gasped for breath that wouldn't come.

"Perhaps my weakness," her father said from across the room, "was that I didn't teach you this lesson earlier. Only the strong rule, Alexandria, so show me how strong you are. Show me that you won't do as I say. Don't tell me."

Alex heard the words, though they sounded far away. Not mere meters, but kilometers. Finally, her lungs relaxed, and life-saving air flowed in. She rolled over on her side, coughing, her throat already swelling. Alex faintly heard his footsteps coming toward her.

She pushed up with her left arm, trying to get to her feet.

The toe of her father's boot collided with her ribs. The crack was audible, and Alex flipped over onto her back again.

Alex looked up into Aurelius' face. She couldn't speak.

"Is this all you can do, Alexandria? Are these my genes?" His voice was calm, and his expression was the same one he'd shown at the docks.

Alex tried again. She put both hands on the ground even as her ribs broke out in fresh pulses of pain. She made it to a sitting position.

Her father chuckled, though he made no movements. Alex didn't stop her slow rise. Once sitting, she turned, put one knee down, and got a foot under her.

"You will bend before me as everyone else has. I won't even give you the option to die, child. You will do as I say because the safety of this Commonwealth is above what a single human wants."

She was almost to her feet when he grabbed her by the hair. He lifted her again, this time tossing her like a doll against the wall. Alex hit it headfirst and felt her shoulder dislocate when it collided next. Bright sparks floated across her vision even as darkness swam around the edges: broken ribs, dislocated shoulder, and probably a concussion.

Alex was going under, and she knew it.

Her father walked slowly toward her.

She pushed up once again.

"Alexandria, it's no use. You've been bested. Just bow and let this be over." There was no kindness in his voice, nothing fatherly about it. No, these were the facts as Aurelius de Finita saw them.

But not as his daughter did.

Alex shoved with her leg, trying to reach her feet. She would fight back until she couldn't. Her left hand touched the wall, balancing her. The blackness in her vision swirled and her head felt like it might explode, yet she reached her feet, balancing herself with her left hand, the arm that still worked.

Alex faced her father, who minutes before, she'd known as a hard man but not a cruel one. Not like this, and yet here they were, staring at one another. Blood dripped from her nose and lips. Her neck was still swelling, now bright red, and turning purple from her father's strength.

"I always wondered about those men who fought me twenty years ago. Were they brave, or were they fools? Certainly, near the end, they knew they couldn't defeat me, yet some of them rose just as you do. So now I look at my daughter, and I wonder whether she's brave or a fool. You know the truth, though? In the end, it doesn't fucking matter."

His fist came down like an asteroid falling from the heavens and Alex fell to the floor, unable to rise again.

There was time to think and read, the only two things Alex could do. Her wounds were attended to, her shoulder fixed, and the fracture in her face set. She was allowed to see no one, and she didn't know if anyone tried to see her.

She didn't know how many days passed. Her twenty-four-hour clock disappeared between sleeping after her beating and the lack of windows in the room. It wasn't an awful room. Her father hadn't shoved her in a cell deep under the ground. Her bed allowed for comfortable sleep. Her food was warm and nutritious.

And in that room, she remained day after day, with only her thoughts to keep her company. It was there that the first inklings of what would become a revolution grew, during those uncounted nights and days where Alex started to consider what her father really was. A leader? A dictator? A monster?

She didn't know what she'd do if she did leave. Truly, she didn't think she would be leaving in any real sense. When her father decided to modify her, she would probably die, and if she didn't die then, she would come out an invalid when they decided to clone her.

Alex didn't know at the time, but they came for her at dawn.

Her father stood in front of his Praetorian Guard. They held no weapons, though Alex knew they had them.

"Hello, Alexandria," her father said from the open door.

Alex was sitting in a chair at the room's single desk with a book open before her. She looked over her shoulder at the man who had nearly beaten her to death, the man who had also given her life.

It's time, she thought. She said nothing.

"Will you come easily, or are you going to fight me again?"

Alex had wondered what she would do when the moment came. Would she fight, or would she simply acquiesce to his will? Were all those other men brave or fools?

She realized as she stared at her father that he'd been

right. It didn't fucking matter what they were because in the end, they'd done as he wanted. So would she. Even if she fought, she wouldn't be given the option to die. She'd only be given pain.

"I'll go easily." Alex stood from her chair, letting the book close.

"Very good," her father said. "Then let's get moving."

"How many days has it been?" she asked. "How long have I been here?"

"They tell me thirty, but I'm not sure. You know how busy I get."

Alex didn't step forward. "The doctor told us it would take six months before everything was ready."

Aurelius shrugged. "The doctor says what I tell him to. I thought six months would give you time to adjust to the idea, and when you didn't, I pushed up my plans, so today is the day. Are there any more questions?"

There was one, something she'd wondered since she woke up with a new jaw and shoulder. "Do you love anyone? Me? Alexander? Mother? Or is love beyond you?"

Her father cocked his head slightly. It was the first time he'd shown any sign of surprise, anything besides that rage when he'd lifted her by the throat. He was quiet for a moment before straightening his head again. "I've loved you the best I know how. If it wasn't enough, the blame lies on me, Alexandria. You've been a good daughter, perhaps the only one who ever grew close to me that my personality didn't destroy. Now, is that all?"

It was the truest thing he'd ever told her. She shook her head. There was nothing else except to go forward and die.

She walked toward the door, and her father turned and

started down the hall. Half his Praetorians followed. The other half waited until she entered the hallway, then went with her.

Alex would never remember how long the walk was. At the time, it'd seemed only seconds to her, as if she'd stepped out of one room, only to fall into another.

It was cold, this new room. Much colder than the place she'd been kept for the past month. Her arm hair stood on end, and goosebumps rose under her skin. Alex forced herself not to rub her hands over her arms. She didn't want to show weakness, despite having come along as meekly as a lamb.

Alex saw the tank. She'd heard of them, just as she'd heard about the little metal spider-like creatures that would fill it. They would pitter-patter over her flesh, modifying her in ways she couldn't understand. Her father stood a few steps in front of her with his back to her.

"Where is my brother?" she asked. "Has his process already started?"

"You don't need to concern yourself with that," the Ascendant responded. "Concern yourself only with making it through your process."

She walked past the Praetorians and her father to the glass tank that would hold her very soon. She placed her palm on it. "Why are you modifying us first, before the cloning?"

"You know the risks. If we clone and it doesn't work, your original self will be harmed irrevocably. The modifications are supposed to fortify you against those risks. Thus, we do this first, then the cloning."

To Alex, the tank looked cold, a medical device that

neither knew nor cared about the human it would operate on.

There were things Alex wanted to say, but they all centered around a single question: you're willing to risk my life for your continued domination?

But she knew the answer. It stood in front of her, this glass monument to his unsated desire for conquest.

A shiver ran through Alex, one she couldn't stop. That shiver turned into another, and then another. She stood there with a palm against the glass, shaking as if she were having a seizure.

Because she would die soon, either in this glass tank or in the next one, when they copied her cells. For Alexandria de Finita, death had come.

"Get her out of my sight," her father said from behind her, disgusted by her shivering and the underlying fear that caused it.

His Guard did as they were instructed. They pulled her away from the tank. She said nothing and made no sound, only continued to shake as she was dragged to what would surely be her death.

CHAPTER SEVENTEEN

"I never served the Commonwealth. I always served myself. If I'd been worse at that, I'd be dead. Fortunately for me, I'm pretty good at it."

–Hel vi Thraxus

"I didn't die," the AllMother said, "and even now, I'm not sure if it was my father's genius or his luck that made such a thing possible. He had a fair amount of both throughout his life."

Alistair was stunned, and at a time when being stunned probably wasn't the best idea. His logical self couldn't believe what he'd just heard. He'd been told of her mythical age, a person born at the beginning of the Commonwealth's rule still alive today.

It wasn't possible, yet Alistair didn't think he could deny it.

He didn't look at her as he spoke. "That's the truth?"

"It's what I remember," she answered. "Truth is a difficult thing to capture. Memories are much easier."

Alistair stared at the Commonwealth dreadnought. It was perhaps three kilometers away, and in mere minutes, they would be inside.

You've met someone who should be considered a universal treasure, he thought. Someone death can't touch, despite its ability to grab everyone else. Can you protect her?

There wasn't any choice. Somehow that story had changed things for Alistair. His desire to protect her had always been there, inspired by her importance to this insurrection.

Now, to him, she was much more.

"Stop," she whispered. "Stop all that thinking about me. I know I'm old."

He glanced at her, and she shook her head. "I'm not reading your mind, Kane. I'm looking at your face. Your concentration needs to be on that ship in front of us, not how I got here."

Turning his head back toward the ship, Alistair closed his eyes. She was right, and he shoved away any thoughts besides those of the coming battle. He opened his eyes and reached down to feel Obs still at his feet. "Have you alerted the Myrmidons?"

"In a manner, yes," she replied. "I don't want them to understand why they're perceiving me, so they'll see it as more like an accidental beacon than a message."

"You can do that? Disguise your purpose?"

The AllMother raised an eyebrow. "Those creatures

called Myrmidons are gross caricatures of my bloodline. They're a few steps above apes on the evolutionary ladder. I might not be able to drive them all the way into a star, but I could get them close."

Alistair chuckled at the arrogance in her voice, though it died quickly.

The bay doors were opening in front of them.

No light shone out. Only darkness was there to greet them.

"How far away are the apes?" he asked.

"You'll have to keep us alive for a bit, but they're on the way, my liege."

He turned to her, not liking the last two words. She gave him a wink and pointed at the front again. "Focus, Titan."

"Then stop talking, Crone," he shot back as he looked once more into the bay.

Their small ship went from the coldness of space into the coldness of the enemy's embrace.

Prometheus rose in the back of Alistair's mind, the killer whose pulse would not rise above ninety regardless of the danger in front of him.

He felt the ship sit down inside the bay, the tractor beam's job finished. The darkness inside this space was complete; not even his modified eyes could see anything.

"Hoods up," he told the AllMother, his hood unfolding from the SkinSuit's neck and enveloping his head.

The old woman did as she was asked without saying a word.

The NightEyes automatically detected the zero-light environment and began flashing barely detectable rays of light, amplifying them and allowing the users to see the outside world.

"That's less than comforting," the AllMother said from his side.

Prometheus remained silent as he stared out the ship's windows. His mind quickly calculated the number of enemies he could see. There were two hundred Titans in front of him, probably a third as many behind.

There was no way to win this fight, not with only him and Obs. He wouldn't try to utilize the AllMother. She was too frail, and there were too many soldiers.

What would he do?

The Titans in front of the ship began moving, creating a passage between them. Someone was coming to the front. Prometheus remained seated, though he'd unhooked his Whip. The Commonwealth now had control of this ship, and they would open the doors when they were ready.

"Obs, stay with me. Do not attack unless I do."

The drathe was standing, his hair standing on end as he stared out the front window.

Ares stepped beyond the first row of Titans. He and the rest of his men wore MechSuits. His was the deep red of spilled blood, a shade darker than Prometheus' Whip.

"Open it," he demanded. Prometheus heard him inside the ship since the Commonwealth had opened the ventilation. This was a show meant to display how weak he and the AllMother were.

Which was fine. Soon they would see a new kind of power, one very different from their own.

The ship's door opened, dropping in its ramp-like fashion. Prometheus turned to the old woman. "I can't protect you from them all, and if we don't fight, I think they'll let us live. If they wanted us dead, we would be."

The AllMother shook her head. "You might be our savior, but you're like most men. You hear nothing a woman says. I've been dealing with the likes of these since they existed. I'll survive your protégé and his minions, or I wouldn't have come on this trip. Come now, young man, and pray that I need not save you again. I'm not sure your legendary status would survive it."

He smiled beneath his SkinSuit. The old woman was as feisty as anyone he'd ever met. She was already walking down the ramp as he and Obs hustled to catch up. He still held his Whip, but he knew it was about to be taken from him.

The AllMother stopped at the bottom of the ramp. She was slightly taller than the Titans in front of her, though shorter than Prometheus when he reached the floor. Ares stood in front of them both. "The Whip, Kane."

Everything inside him wanted to refuse the demand. His Whip was like his right hand, and to give away the weapon was akin to cutting off a limb. Yet, to get out of a trap that would mean its life, a bear would gnaw off its own paw, and Prometheus was in the same situation.

He raised the Whip to Ares, weapon side facing him, but his finger millimeters from being in a place to loose the tentacles. "I promise you, I'll be getting this back."

Obs let out a deep growl.

Ares didn't reach for the weapon; one of his underlings took it. Prometheus marked the man's MechSuit color. He didn't know him.

Ares lowered the voice on his suit's external comm so very few could hear what he said. "Are you going to keep making this easy, or do we need to cut you down here?"

"You have my Whip, don't you?" Alistair responded. "Or are you so scared of me that you still worry I can defeat you?"

Ares looked at the drathe. "You brought a stupid dog with you? What in the hell has happened to you, Kane? Is it going to be a problem?"

Alistair shook his head.

Ares' external comm rose in volume. "Take him."

Titans grabbed Alistair roughly and pulled him back a few steps. Alistair offered no resistance. Obs barked menacingly but didn't lunge at anyone. Ares looked at the AllMother, his heads up display visible outside of his suit. "My best guess is you're the Subversive leader known as the AllMother. Is that correct?"

Alistair watched as her hood retracted into her neckline, revealing the lined face of an old woman with the red eyes of the modified. "And you are?"

"Take her," Ares demanded.

"That's unnecessary," the old woman said. Her voice was crystal scratching ice.

The Titans shuffled forward, but Alistair's voice broke through. "I wouldn't, Ares. She'll do as you ask. There's no need to lay hands on her." He'd never heard her voice sound like that, not even when she faced down the Myrmidons back on Pluto. He didn't know if she would survive another use of her mutation, but he thought she was about to use it all the same.

Ares raised a hand, and the Titans stopped moving. "Don't touch her as long as she listens. Freya, you're in charge of her." He took a step closer to the old woman, his MechSuit making him nearly as tall as her. He tilted his head up slightly, his HUD disappearing back inside his helmet. "If you don't listen, she'll kill you, old lady. I know who you really are, but that doesn't mean I believe the rumors. It doesn't mean I won't have you killed, either."

"You should remember that I'm here because I want to be. He and I both are."

Ares stared at her for a few more seconds, his face invisible behind his MechSuit. "Take her to the holding room."

Freya stepped away from the crowd. "Come gently, and there won't be any problems."

"Lead the way, good lady," the AllMother replied.

Alistair watched as a group of five took her through the bay, then she disappeared from his sight. When the fighting began, finding her would be his first job. Hopefully, she'd be able to find him a lot easier.

Alistair turned toward Ares, the Titans behind him still holding his arms roughly. He was taller than everyone, something he'd never realized. When Titans showed up dressed in their MechSuits, they dominated whatever room they inhabited, yet here in front of him, they seemed small. Their numbers were just too vast.

"Follow me," Ares commanded the Titans, starting across the bay.

They pushed Alistair forward roughly, though he

DAVID BEERS & MICHAEL ANDERLE

offered no resistance. Obs stayed as close as he could, his head low to the ground and a steady rumble coming from his chest. Alistair's mind kept track of each turn they made, every floor they ascended or descended in elevators. The modifications done to him had affected his body, and they'd affected his brain as well. He could find his way back to the bay easily; he just hoped his ship would still be there and usable.

The other Titans had filtered away, leaving the two with Alistair, two in front of them, and one behind. Ares was at the front, well-protected from an attack. Eventually, they reached the holding room, and the door automatically opened as Ares stepped toward it. Alistair was roughly thrown in, hitting one knee before stopping his slide. Obs was at his side in moments. He whipped around and snarled at those standing at the door.

"Leave us," Ares commanded the other Titans. He waited until the room was empty, then retracted his helmet. His youth had not faded; he still looked like he had the day Alistair first met him. It carried with it a certain arrogance, but Alistair had come to understand the truth of the man. Deep insecurity drove him, the fear that he would never be his father or live up to his family's expectations.

How did his defeat by me affect that insecurity? Alistair wondered.

"You're going to tell me your plan with that woman," Ares said. "Is it the AllSeer and his minions? Are they coming?"

Alistair was careful not to show surprise. How could Ares know? How could the Commonwealth? He said nothing.

"This silent game won't work, Alistair. I'll have my men pull your limbs off and keep you alive to watch in the next ten minutes if you don't tell me what I want to know."

Alistair was still on one knee, staring up at his former protégé. "You've seen them, I take it? Was that when you floated above Pluto while your men died down below?" He smiled. "They're massive, aren't they? They make me look like one of the Lowmen on Earth, huh?"

Ares took a step closer. Obs bared his teeth, but the Titan paid him no mind. "Are they coming, Alistair?"

Alistair slowly rose to his feet, backing up a step as he did. He was brave but not stupid, and without a Whip in such a confined space, the MechSuit would probably destroy him. "You already know the answer. The old woman was right; we came of our own accord, but we're not here alone. Those huge creatures you saw creating mayhem on Pluto are headed here, and there's nothing you can do about it. Neither can I, and neither can she. As hell-bent as you were on finding me, that's what they are on finding her. Guess who told them where she'd be? The old woman did."

"Have you gone mad?" Ares asked. He raised his arm, fingers spread, stopping it a few millimeters from Alistair's throat, and spoke through clenched teeth. "You forsake the code you took and do this to your body, then you join the group you swore to destroy, leaving your wife on Earth to think you've died. Now you've brought death here, and you tell me there is no way to stop it."

At the mention of his wife, Alistair had to hold the other part of him back, the one known as Prometheus. The warrior nearly exploded forward, but it wasn't yet time. If he ever wanted to see Luna again, he had to follow the plan.

Instead of jumping toward the Titan, Alistair reached down and touched his drathe.

"You're Primus now, Titan," he told Ares, looking past the outstretched hand at the shorter man's eyes. "Figure out a way to win."

Ares grabbed Alistair's throat and squeezed, the Mech arm assisting him as he lifted Alistair off the deck. "Hope I do, old friend, for if I don't, I promise I will make time for you before the beasts get to me."

He tossed Alistair against the wall, and the former Titan fell to the deck, landing on his side. Spit flew from Obs' mouth as he barked savagely, but he followed his master's orders.

Ares left the room, and the door sealed behind him. He was doing as Alistair would have in his position: preparing for battle. Now Alistair could only wait. When the destruction began, he would act.

Or so he thought.

The former Titan sat with his back against the wall, his eyes closed. He felt something unlike anything he'd ever felt in his life. He could hardly describe it to himself, let alone to someone else.

Alistair was trying to silence his mind. If he could get past the thoughts racing through his head, he might have a chance at focusing only on this difference. This new thing.

Then the door opened, dashing the difference he felt as well as any chance of clearing his mind.

Obs jumped to his feet, teeth bared.

A woman stood at the door. He couldn't tell if she was older than him or not, but a Whip rested on her waist. She was tall for a woman, though short by Alistair's standards.

He didn't rise to his feet, and the woman didn't reach for her Whip. The door closed behind her and she leaned against it, crossing her arms over her chest. "You're the one we've come for? The one all this trouble is about?"

Alistair studied the woman carefully. She was lean and muscular, her face tight but showing some lines. Her hair was short and her eyes did not narrow, as if there were nothing to be concerned about here. Nothing to worry about. Just another prisoner in another ship.

"Who are you?" Alistair asked.

"I'm sure you know my name, just as I know yours."

Alistair looked at her face with more focus. He couldn't place her, not even with his improved mind. "I've never seen you before."

"That's not true, Titan," the woman said with her arms still crossed. "You saw me a long, long time ago. It was one of your first hundred operations, I'd imagine. Within your first five years of being a Titan. Were you Primus yet?"

Alistair clicked through mission after mission but still couldn't place this woman.

"I suppose it doesn't matter," she continued as if she had not asked a question. "Either you were, or you would be soon. You were the one who captured me, at least the first time."

Alistair blinked. He heard the woman's words, but he couldn't believe them. It was almost like hearing what the AllMother had said hours before. Very few women had been high-value targets for the Titans for whatever reason, but there was one who rose greater than the rest, and she hadn't been a part of the Subversives.

Her name was Hel vi Thraxus.

The only non-Titan to be awarded a Whip and one of the only targets who had to be brought in alive.

Alistair rose to his feet, and Obs stayed next to his leg. The Commonwealth called her out of prison when they needed her, though her prison was probably different from any other. He'd faced her in hand to hand combat years ago. He hadn't been Primus yet but would be shortly, partly because of how he'd handled their encounter.

To fight this woman and live while not killing her had helped create his legend. His myth.

"Hel?" he asked.

"One and the same. *Salve*, Alistair Kane. Do you still go by Odin, or did they strip that from you when they stripped your legacy?"

"*Salve*," he responded, using the formal term for hello. He felt awe at standing in front of this woman. She should have died multiple times over, yet she stood in front of him without a scar in sight. "They pulled you out of prison to find me?"

She smiled at him. "Few remember me, but I see you do. They don't call it a prison anymore. They call it my retirement now; it's easier when I'm supposed to be allowed outside. Fewer of the propaganda ministry's services needed."

Alistair narrowed his eyes, trying to understand what was going on. Of everything he thought he'd see here, she was the last thing. Truthfully, he hadn't thought about her but once or twice since capturing her.

The word "formidable" didn't describe what she'd been like.

"They let you go to find me?" he found himself asking again, still not quite able to believe it.

"Burning an entire planet to ash didn't show you how bad the Commonwealth wanted you dead? But bringing an old woman out of retirement does?" She was toying with him, but Alistair didn't care.

This woman was dangerous.

"Why are you here?" he asked. He suddenly felt naked in a way he hadn't around Ares. Without his Whip, this would be a tough fight, even with his modifications and Obs.

"I'm here to ensure that you either die or are captured." She smiled. "Or did you mean, why am I here in this room with you?"

He nodded.

"The two idiots who think they're in charge of this expedition have no idea what's coming for them. For us, I suppose. You do. You're bringing them here, in their never-ending quest to possess the holy woman the Subversives follow. I often wondered how much the Commonwealth let their brutes know. Did you have any knowledge of the Myrmidons? The AllSeer? This thousand-year war?"

Alistair shook his head, wanting to say he still didn't get it. He kept silent, though. She didn't need to know he was simply trying to survive.

"I thought not. The Ascendants like to keep everyone in the dark. It makes us better tools." Uncrossing her arms, she waved away her previous comments. "I'm here," she continued, "because right now, I need you to stay alive. We can't outrun the Myrmidons, and we might not be able to kill them either. Certainly, we can't kill them all, but we can perhaps kill enough to make them reconsider grabbing the old hag. I don't believe in the myths or the fate the AllSeer preaches from his dark throne. All the same, right now I've got to stub their toe a bit, and I'm going to need your help. We fought before they added all this fabulous muscle to you, so I know you're capable."

"What about your mission to kill or capture me?"

Another devilish smile. "We can deal with that after, right, darlin'?"

He trusted her as much as he trusted Ares, yet getting out of here now beat the hell out of trying to get out later when the ship was on fire. It didn't matter how many of the Myrmidons he killed; more would come. This woman was insane if she thought she could "stub their toe." Escape was the only option, and this would put him closer to the AllMother.

Luna's voice filled his head. *Always running, my love, but right now you're running away from me. Don't you want to come home?*

I'm trying, he shot back.

"I thought you understood my plan? We're here so the Myrmidons will come. We're here so they'll destroy the Commonwealth ships."

"The issue with that plan, Kane, is that they're going to destroy you too. Right now you're locked in this room, but my orders were to come here and take you to the brig. You'll be Clipped in the brig, meaning you won't be able to do anything other than blink." She smiled. "So, dear, once they destroy us, you're not going to be able to do much running. Understand?"

Obs growled again, and Alistair stroked his head. He understood perfectly, but trust her? Not hardly.

Still smiling, Hel pulled a Clip out of her back pocket. "Your choice. You can help me hurt them and take your chances at getting out during the ensuing chaos."

His eyes narrowed and he remained silent.

"Remember, Titan, I'm here to save my hide. Ares might not think we need you or that beast at your feet to survive this, but I'm not as foolish. I need to use you to survive this, and I'll kill you afterward."

He wasn't being naïve. The woman was probably lying, but a weapon in his hand and freedom on the ship was better than being locked up here.

"I need my Whip," he told Hel. "And if you even look at the drathe wrong, I'll cut you down."

She reached behind her back and put the Clip away before bringing her hand back to the front. She was holding the Whip, and the hilt pulsed red. It sensed its master and his apprehension. "This?" she asked.

He nodded, keeping his eyes on the weapon. Twice now he'd been separated from it in the last six months, which was more times than in the previous twenty years.

She tossed it to him, and he caught it in midair. For a half of a second, he considered letting it loose and spilling her blood all over the room.

He didn't know why he decided against it.

Perhaps it was seeing someone he'd long thought dead. Perhaps it was respect for her ability to fight. Perhaps it boiled down to the simplicity of her bringing him his Whip. Perhaps it was kindness.

All the same, he would come to regret the decision. Later he would wish he had killed her and saved so many other lives.

The three of them were heading to the AllMother. The corridors were empty, which was to be mostly expected if the dreadnought was preparing for battle.

"Have you spotted them yet?" Alistair asked.

He walked slightly behind her and to the right. She seemed to trust him there since she never looked over her shoulder or checked on him in any way that he could discern.

"We have one ship still in the fourth dimension. They spotted an aberration two hours ago, but of course, they couldn't tell who or what it was. That's them, though, the AllSeer and his Myrmidons." She sounded as if she was talking about a past holiday she'd taken and all the fun she'd had.

"What's your plan?" Alistair asked. "When Ares discovers I'm gone, I don't think it'll take him long to figure out it was you."

"Worry about your schemes, Titan, and I'll worry about mine. For now, it's enough that both our schemes involve retrieving the old woman."

Alistair was beginning to regret his decision to join her. He remembered the briefing he'd been given as a young man, right before they went to catch his first non-Subversive.

The word "assassin" wasn't totally accurate, but it fit Hel vi Thraxus. She was a personal weapon of the Imperial Ascendant, plucked from the Academy when she was nineteen years old for that purpose. The rumors were that her parents had refused to allow her entry, so she'd killed them. Most likely those were just rumors, but even so, they showed the cruelty of the woman.

The weapon had lost its usefulness at some point, though that was shrouded in secrecy. The Ascendant would never let out how one of his tools had gotten the better of him. All the same, the Titans had come for her.

"Do not," his Primus had said, "under any circumstance get into a one-on-one standoff with this woman. I do not care how strong or fast you think you are; she will cut you down as if it were your first day at the Academy. That goes for you too, Odin."

Someone had shoved an elbow in his rib at that, but Alistair had taken the warning seriously.

All these years later, he was wondering if she hadn't somehow planned for the two of them to meet in that building. Had she maneuvered him into their one-on-one fight?

"Did you put us in that room together twenty years ago?" Alistair asked.

Now she did glance over her shoulder, that trustless smile across her face. "What would give you that idea?"

"Answer the question."

She turned back to the hall in front of her. They were coming to a fork. She slowed without saying anything, putting her back to the wall. She glanced down the right side of the fork and motioned for him to do the same on the other side.

He stepped up and peered down the left fork. "We're clear. Now answer the question."

She stared at him from a meter away and cocked her head to the side. "Did you think you got to that room by accident all those years ago? Are you just now figuring out that someone might have had a hand in it?"

He shook his head. "Why? It doesn't make any sense. Why would you want to face off against me?"

"Maybe I did, or maybe someone else wanted to see us do it, Titan. Was I complicit?" She shrugged. "Maybe. But ask yourself this question. If I wanted you in a room alone back then, what about now? Do you think you were in that room, unguarded, by accident? Do you think all of our forces are focusing on a battle instead of you two by chance? Or do you think perhaps there's an underlying reason for it?"

The questions were endless, but there wasn't time for any of them. Perhaps he shouldn't have asked the first one.

The only thing he knew was that he couldn't trust her. Even these answers were probably designed for some plan that ended with a Whip decapitating him.

"Let's go, my boy." Hel started down the left side of the passage. He followed her, keeping a small distance. His senses were attuned to everything around him, and he could hear nothing other than their footsteps.

She was right; the entire ship had forgotten about their captives. They were in survival mode, their attention turned toward an enemy they shouldn't know was heading their way. Except she had warned them.

What game do you play? Even with a Whip in his hand, he was trusting this less and less.

Hel came to a stop and a door opened in the wall. She stepped through, motioning for him to follow. He went inside, and the door quickly shut behind him.

The AllMother stood in front of him. Her lip was puffy and dried blood was crusted across her nose.

Alistair's eyes narrowed. "What happened?"

"Whoever they sent didn't like my answers," the old woman answered. Her voice sounded strong, which Alistair knew meant a hell of a lot more than her face. Her spirit was intact, and that was what mattered right now. "I know you," the old woman said as she looked at Hel.

"I like the sound of that." Hel smiled while raising and lowering her eyebrows quickly. "There are very few who remember my reputation. I can only assume you think as highly of me as I do."

"I doubt that." The AllMother looked at Alistair. "What are we doing?"

"Truthfully, I'm not sure. Hel, what's next?"

She ignored his question and kept her eyes on the old woman. "Is what they say about you true? Are you the only one of your kind?"

"I never concerned myself with what they say, and as to my kind, are we not human?"

Hel smiled, her eyes narrowing with it this time. "I understand why the Titans struck you. However, you've summoned the Myrmidons, so something is different about you. Can you tell where they are?"

Now the AllMother smiled. She turned her head toward the ceiling. "They're here."

CHAPTER EIGHTEEN

"Is there any difference between fate and faith?"

–the AllMother

"I honestly don't give a flying fuck if he wants to go it alone. We're not letting him. If he wants to apologize when he gets back, I think we should apologize too, for ignoring this insanity." Thoreaux looked at the group in front of him. Rage filled him, and he didn't care who knew it.

They were still underground, still in a strange land, still wondering if they were going to live through the night. Only now their two leaders had left on some insane mission, one that would surely end with at least one dead, if not both.

Servia was seated across from him with her legs crossed, looking much calmer.

Thank the gods for it, Thoreaux thought. Despite his

rage, he understood that someone had to remain level-headed to balance him.

Relm and Faitrin were here too. Thoreaux didn't know the pilot well, but Alistair trusted her, so he was fine with it.

Servia's voice was soft when she spoke. "If you want to go after him, you need a plan. Flying toward a battle with nothing but anger as your guide isn't going to end well. You know that."

Thoreaux looked at Faitrin. "If we can get another ship, can you get us there?"

The pilot nodded. "For sure. Should be able to sync with these like any other. I've talked to some Terram pilots. Everything works the same as far as that goes."

"Relm, what do you think?" Thoreaux asked.

The warrior leaned forward and placed his elbows on his knees. He rubbed his hands through his short hair, which had been raggedly cut with a knife. "I agree with Servia. What will we do if we go up there? Those creatures aren't anything to mess with lightly, and neither is the Commonwealth." He looked up, dropping his hands. "If you say we go, broth, then we go, but I think we need a plan besides show up guns blazing." He leaned back and shrugged.

They all knew the truth. There wasn't any way to plan what would happen once they got up there. That was what made Prometheus so dangerous. He planned the beginnings of attacks, things that had very little chance of success, and when he arrived, it was Improv City. That was what he was doing right now, and so far, his superior skills had kept him alive. But Thoreaux wasn't Prometheus, and everyone here knew it, including him.

"I don't have a plan," he said. "Other than to do my best to bring them both home. I understand their powers better than most. I've been next to the AllMother since I was a boy, and I've fought with Prometheus. They're formidable, but they're overmatched." He shook his head. "I don't have a plan, and I don't think one can be made on such sparse intel. I'm going to go. I'd like you to come with me."

Faitrin's eyes narrowed, and an almost imperceptible smile grew on her face. "I might have an idea, but we have to quit talking. Time is short and growing shorter each moment, so you'll need to listen." She found Thoreaux's eyes, the hint of a smile still on her lips. "Very, very carefully."

CHAPTER NINETEEN

"Trust is for the weak. The strong don't need to trust anyone because they have the power."

–Aurelius de Finita, First Imperial Ascendant

Alistair felt vibrations beneath his feet. He didn't know if it was the dreadnought's powerful cannons firing or the Myrmidons and their weapons as they boarded the ship. The AllMother had been right, her psychic mind able to tell when the enemy dropped from the fourth dimension into the third.

Hel ran in front of the group, leading the way to the dreadnought's upper levels. Alistair was between the AllMother and Hel, with Obs bringing up the rear.

"*WHERE ARE WE GOING?*" he shouted to the front. The woman was keeping a brisk pace, which was fine with

Alistair's superior lungs, but he didn't know how easily the AllMother could keep up.

"*TO STUB THEIR TOE!*" she screamed with what sounded like glee.

She's mad, Alistair thought. If Hel knew who they would soon battle and still felt happiness, something wasn't right.

They reached an elevator at the end of a hall. It was circular, transparent, and stood out from the wall. Alistair didn't like that. It meant that when they reached the next level, everyone would be able to see them. Hel got on first, with the other three in tow. The transparent wall shot up from the floor, and Hel reached out to touch it. Alistair caught her hand. Her head snapped toward him, and rage filled her eyes. How long had it been since someone had touched her in a way she didn't want?

Alistair didn't let her hand go, and Obs growled low in his throat. "Where are we headed, Hel? The three of us won't chase you through this ship."

The AllMother stepped back to the wall. She was silent as she peered at the tall woman.

"We are going to the outskirts of the battle," Hel forced out through a clenched jaw. "From there, we'll assist by fighting our way in instead of fighting our way out like everyone else is now doing."

Alistair kept her hand in his. She didn't struggle, but his grip was hard, and his right hand rested on his silent Whip. "Why aren't there any Myrmidons down here on these levels?"

"Oh, you foolish man." She cocked her head in that way she had as if she wondered how someone as dumb as he was had lived for so long. "Why do you think I've been running so long?"

She raised her left arm in a smooth line, her left hand typing on the transparent wall. Alistair didn't know what code she typed in, but the wall reacted.

The transparency disappeared, and violence replaced it. She was showing him video footage from the ship. Monsters with dual laser blades were somewhere in these white halls. Blood trailed behind them, and men screamed while fleeing. There was no pretense of bravery, no semblance of battle. It was a massacre. Body parts halved. The humans still alive weren't Titans, weren't even pilots, but the lowest of those who made a ship of this size run. They were the help, the custodians, the engineers, those who were invisible until needed.

No one had thought about them, so down here they remained. Now they would die.

Alistair stepped out of the elevator. The wall sensed him and flashed down. He'd released Hel's hand, but she grabbed his wrist, her grip tighter than his had been. He turned back to look at her while Obs stepped forward, growling.

"I know you think I'm insane," she began. "But as I watch you leave to save janitors, I wonder if you aren't the one who's out of his head." She looked down the hall, nodding. "You will surely die if you go in that direction, and I will not go with you. Perhaps the hag behind me will, and perhaps she's capable, but neither of you will come out of that corridor alive."

Alistair glanced at the AllMother. He wasn't concerned with the woman's grip on his arm. She wasn't threatening

DAVID BEERS & MICHAEL ANDERLE

violence, but something else—sense maybe. He gritted his teeth and turned once more to the hallway, then nodded. She was right. He hadn't come here to save Commonwealth servants, and he'd have to stomach watching them die.

He stepped back onto the elevator. Hel shook her head. "That's why you're being hunted. All these damned sensitivities. The gods did you no favors with that." The wall rose around them, and she raised her hand again but paused midway up and looked at him with a sly grin. "Is it okay if we continue, Master?"

Alistair didn't look at her. She typed in more codes, and the elevator started rising. Obs' teeth were still bared as he stared at the woman.

Three levels up, it stopped. Alistair's Whip came to life, and its red tentacles dropped to the floor.

The room in front of him was wrecked, and had he not faced Myrmidon technology before, he wouldn't understand. A ship sat in what appeared to be a server room. The lights were flickering, while sparks sprayed across the room from torn wires. Alistair could see five dead people from where he stood, two Titans, three server engineers. The Titans were in MechSuits, and one of them lay with one arm removed, the other cut in half. The Myrmidon ship's door remained open, though it appeared everyone had emptied out.

There was no hole in the dreadnought. No space vacuum to suck everything out. It was as if the ship had simply appeared here, and Alistair understood it had. Somehow. The technology that had allowed his ship to enter the Myrmidons' had done the same here. And the warriors.

"Can they feel you?" Alistair whispered inside the elevator.

"No, dear," the AllMother responded.

Another smile from Hel. "So, not all of the rumors are false. You do have *some* psychic ability. That could come in handy." She stepped forward, and the ship's door opened. Hel didn't turn around as she said, "Hope you're ready, Titan."

The words were barely out of her mouth when the monster stepped from the ship. His feet were as big as the woman's shins. The battle armor he wore contained the peering red eye, but never could this thing be mistaken for anything other than a Myrmidon.

A creature nearly without equal.

His dual saber whipped out. Hel darted left, though she didn't avoid it completely. It seared her right shoulder, and smoke and the smell of burning flesh filled Alistair's nostrils.

The Myrmidon grunted at the miss and took a giant step forward. Hel swung her Whip, and the Myrmidon's saber swiped at it as if it were a broomstick. The green tentacles flew to the left, with Hel barely hanging on. The Myrmidon was too strong.

The saber flashed down again, trying to halve Hel. She rolled beneath the ship, the saber hit the metal deck, and sparks flew into the air.

"A LITTLE GODSDAMN HELP!" Hel shouted from her new location.

Alistair had paused on the elevator. Not out of fear, but

simple awe. After seeing them so many times, it was still hard to believe a creature of that mass could move with such speed.

Prometheus came forward, shoving Alistair aside. The god-like warrior was here.

The Myrmidon turned toward him, and if he'd heard of Prometheus, he showed no sign. He simply raised his dual saber and pointed one edge at Prometheus. He squeezed the middle and one side of the saber shot through the air, a laser arrow aimed at the former Titan's head.

He moved his head slightly to the right, and the saber barely missed him. He didn't dare turn to check on the AllMother, but she was smart and yelled, "*I'M FINE!*"

Obs bounded out of the elevator and lashed out at the Myrmidon.

The creature swung, catching Obs hindquarters and sending him sprawling. The drathe hopped back to his feet quickly, growling and slobbering, but kept his distance.

"Stay back, Obs. You'll know when to attack," Prometheus directed.

The Myrmidon ignored the animal and walked forward, swinging his remaining saber in wide arcs. His arm length kept Prometheus at bay.

He danced back, parrying with his Whip, then sliced forward, hopped to the side, and spun away, drawing the monster farther from the ship. He squatted slightly, then launched onto one of the fallen servers, giving him the higher ground.

Beneath his heavy helmet, the Myrmidon's face showed sheer anger, like an Earth-bear that couldn't get something it wanted. He kicked out, and the server gave way.

Prometheus started to topple, but his reflexes were faster. He leaped over the top of the Myrmidon's saber, hit the floor in a somersault, and ended up at the edge of the ship.

Hel was two meters to his right, her Whip firmly in her hand.

Prometheus sighed and shook his head. "Glad you found your way out."

"Save your quips for after we kill the bastard," she shot back.

He climbed to his feet. "Obs, it's time."

The three fell upon the enemy. The Myrmidon showed no fear, but he never had a chance. They went at it as if they'd fought together for their entire lives. She took the forms that most complimented his, and within thirty seconds, the formidable warrior was on the floor, blood pumping from his throat. The drathe growled at him, keeping one paw on his chest.

Alistair stared down at the Myrmidon, wondering if the AllSeer was looking out.

He felt someone lightly touch his shoulder.

"Don't look in there," the AllMother said from behind him. "Don't look at the devil. He might see deeper inside you than you'd like."

The devil. A term from before the Commonwealth, back when humanity followed religion as if they were on a leash. He hadn't heard the word in a long time, but he knew what it meant. The devil was evil incarnate.

He turned away from the dying Myrmidon and looked at Hel. "Nice job."

"You're not so bad yourself, Titan, but there's more work to do. Come."

CHAPTER TWENTY

"I banished them because I had to. You'll never under-stand the strength I created in them. My son and daughter can break worlds."

–Aurelius de Finita, First Imperial Ascendant.
Private conversation.

"There isn't time," Thoreaux whispered.

They were two hours from the battle, yet they could see it happening right in front of them. They'd magnified their screens ten times over, and he saw the strange Myrmidon ships floating around dreadnoughts that should have ruled the entire universe.

On this night, they didn't.

The Myrmidon ships weren't firing ordinary missiles or nukes. It was something completely different from anything Thoreaux had ever imagined. Not even in his previous encounters with these strange men had he ever seen anything like this.

They weren't shooting explosives from their ships, nothing that burned. Rather, it appeared to be some sort of organic material, as if it were alive.

Tiny pellets flew from the Myrmidon ships, thousands of them, and when they landed on the dreadnought, they splattered against it, causing no damage the eye could see. Yet, within minutes, a green fungus-like substance was spawning from the destroyed pellets.

From there, it grew.

Thoreaux didn't like the word that came to mind, but he could think of nothing else. It seemed to be eating.

And the Myrmidons' defenses?

Thoreaux honestly understood those less well. They appeared to utilize the magic Prometheus had told him about. The Commonwealth's projectiles exploded before they reached the Myrmidon ships as if there were trip wires laid out in space.

None of it made any sense to Thoreaux, but right now, he didn't care. The battle was happening, and they were still a few hours away.

He was with Relm, the two of them alone in a corvette that was going at its top speed.

"It'll work, broth," Relm said from his side. "It has to. We'll be in time."

Thoreaux had been standing up, peering at the screen in front of him. He sat down as Relm tried to calm him. "You trust her? Faitrin?"

Relm scratched the stubble on his chin and nodded as his lips turned downward. "Yeah, I do. I understand why you may not, but she and I went to an occupied planet, and she could have given us up at any moment. Best I can tell, such a thing never crossed her mind." Still nodding, he finished, "You can trust her. If she says she'll do something, she's going to do it."

"Well, we put all our lives in her hands. Our movement as well." Thoreaux was grim as he stared at the screen in front of him. "I hope you're right to trust her. I hope I am too."

Servia found that she liked the pilot. Faitrin felt like a kindred spirit, someone who looked out at this fucked up universe, and instead of getting angry, saw mirth in it all. Indeed, to Servia, that was the only appropriate response to everything she'd seen since she was old enough to remember.

Well, laughter, and what she was feeling at this exact moment: abject terror.

Humanity had not lost the ability to fly ships, though, for some reason that Servia would never understand, they'd put up a lot of barriers to doing it. Thoreaux and Relm were piloting their ship, which was to say it ran by itself unless something unexpected happened. For true flight, though, one needed a pilot, someone whose brain had been modified to connect with the central AI running through every ship in existence. Those people had instan-

DAVID BEERS & MICHAEL ANDERLE

taneous communication and reaction time, with only the space of synapses slowing transmissions down.

In one sense, Servia was lucky to have that right now. Thoreaux and Relm were flying with only the AI to guide them, while Faitrin sat next to her, eyes grayed over and perfectly harmonized with their shuttle. That was the only thing that made her feel good about being here; everything else told her she was about to die.

"Are we going to make it?" she asked.

Faitrin didn't glance at her but stared straight ahead as if she were alone on the ship. "It's going to be tight."

"What's the AI telling you?" Servia asked.

"Based on current activity, everyone will be dead or dying in two hours. It will take us two and a half to get there."

"That's grand, isn't it?" Servia slumped in her seat.

Faitrin turned to look at her then. It looked odd, no matter how many times you saw a harmonized pilot. Her eyes were grayed over like dirty snow was falling across them. It appeared as if she saw nothing, but she smiled. "Take it easy, Servia. I've been in tighter spots than this. I was Plutoborn and made it to Earth, and from there, I rose high enough to betray a Primus. You don't do all that without a little gumption. If I were you, though, I would head to the back and strap in. This is going to get rough."

Servia nodded as the pilot turned back to the screens in front of her.

Faitrin's confidence was reassuring, but it wasn't contagious. Servia couldn't shake the feeling that everyone involved was in way over their heads. That for once, Alistair had taken on more than he could handle, and the rest of them weren't strong enough to help carry the weight he'd hoisted onto his shoulders.

She listened to her pilot and headed to the back of the ship, then strapped in and leaned back, closing her eyes. There would be no sleep, but maybe she could ignore reality for a brief time.

CHAPTER TWENTY-ONE

"We lie so that we don't get caught telling the truth."

- He vi Thraxus

Prometheus didn't need Hel to lead anymore. He only had to follow the carnage. The ship was suffering power outages in major parts of it, the lights either flickering or out. They'd been walking the halls for ten minutes and so far had seen no one alive, just the dead. A lot of Titans, a few Myrmidons.

"The Commonwealth never stood a chance," he whispered as he stepped over a Titan still in his MechSuit. He hadn't seen Ares yet, and part of him thought the sight was improbable. He might be young and insecure, but his physical abilities had been better than Alistair's before the modifications.

Yet, who could stop these creatures?

Hel was a bit farther ahead, with the AllMother in the rear. The chance of attack from behind was small. Hel looked over her shoulder. "Oh, the Commonwealth has more tricks up its sleeve than you realize, Titan. Perhaps just not here in deep space. When the AllSeer comes closer to Earth, you'll see that his strength isn't as great as it seems out here."

"That's enough," the AllMother said from behind. Her voice was strong, despite the age of her body. Alistair stopped and looked over his shoulder at her. The AllMother was peering past him at Hel. "You can end your game. I see through it."

Alistair reflexively took a step toward the AllMother, looking forward as he did. The hair on Obs' back stood on end.

Hel had turned to face them. She was smiling, her Whip unfurled at her waist. "Yet we are so close to the final destination, Mother." She nodded at Alistair. "I do not like my chances against him alone, though I wouldn't put them at zero. How about we go a bit farther, then we can end this charade in style?"

Alistair didn't understand. The Commonwealth was dead, in front of and behind him. There was no way there would be an ambush. He'd only kept going because Hel was right; it wasn't a genius idea to let the Commonwealth be wiped out while they escaped in a corvette. The Myrmidons would simply give chase and catch them all quickly. The plan had been to have the two wipe each other out, but...

I trusted too easily. Too eager to get this over.

"Back up," Alistair told the AllMother without taking his eyes from Hel.

The AllMother did as she was told, and Alistair

backpedaled a few steps as well. He found the last dead Titan they'd passed, his helmet open. Alistair hadn't stared at the dead, only glanced briefly to see if he recognized any of them.

And have I? he asked himself.

Not a single fucking one.

Now he saw why. This was no Titan. This was a janitor who had been thrown in a MechSuit. Where was his Whip, and how the hell had Alistair not noticed that detail before?

Because as smart as I am, I wanted to believe we would get out of here, so I ignored the evidence that said we wouldn't.

He looked up. Hel was still smiling. "If you come with me now, I'll make sure she lives. If you fight me, you may kill me, Titan, but I promise you I'll kill her first, and you won't escape. I am who I am, not because of the things you see, but because of the things you don't. So tell me, does the old woman live or die? Either way, you're a ward of the Commonwealth now."

Oh, you godsdamn fool, Alistair told himself. *You rushed into battle, thinking yourself strong enough to defeat the universe, and now everything you've struggled for is in the hands of this creature disguised as a woman.*

He looked at the AllMother. Her eyes were on Hel, a mixture of intense hatred and curiosity on her face. "How did you block me from seeing it until now?"

Hel laughed, which sounded like the light pitter-patter of rain on grass. "Do you think the Commonwealth would create something like you, lose you in the wild for a thousand years, and not create defenses to stop you? Are you both so arrogant as to think the true power rests with you?

I know that your brother, that AllSeer, does. I mean, his self-given name alone oozes arrogance, but you two are the same? The only real question I have is how you broke through our psychic blocks. Perhaps you're stronger than we gave you credit for." Her eyes focused on Alistair, her pithy attitude turning to a laser-like focus. "What's it going to be, former Titan? You going to put on a Clip, or will I kill her and then force one on you?"

He didn't need to look at the AllMother. She spoke as soon as Hel finished. "It doesn't matter to me, Prometheus. I can die here or live another thousand years. My choice was right with you, so you choose."

There wasn't a choice. He knew the woman wasn't lying, though he didn't understand what was happening outside this small hallway. He retracted his Whip and hooked it on his belt. " First, tell me what will happen to her."

"She's a ward of the Commonwealth as well. You both will be treated as terrorists, though the Commonwealth has a long history of treating Subversives much better than they ever treated us." She smiled at that because both of them had killed countless Subversives. Without looking away, Hel reached behind her to her belt and pulled out two Clips. She tossed one to Alistair, who caught it with his right hand. Hel's Whip followed quickly, stretching out so that the laser tentacles nearly touched Alistair's chest. "Put it on her. Then we'll do yours."

Alistair turned to the AllMother. "I'm sorry."

She smiled at him. "Don't be. This is only the beginning. Come, let's see how deep this rabbit hole goes."

Alistair had never heard that phrase before, but the

time for questions had passed. He grasped the edges of the Clip and gently pulled, and the black stick began changing shape immediately. The blackness faded, light blue replacing it, and it took the form of a half-circle.

The AllMother gave a slight nod, and Alistair placed the Clip on her forehead.

He turned back to Hel. "I'm going to kill you. Not now, not in this hallway, but it's my hand you'll die by."

"Oh, sweetheart," the woman said. "Do you know how many silly, silly men have told me that before?" She moved forward, but Obs barked menacingly enough to make her pause.

"I'll put this on, but if I do, the drathe comes with me," Alistair told her.

"Ha!" Hel laughed. "Do you think I'm going to cart a beast around with me?"

"I don't think you have much choice. One word from me and the drathe will be at your throat. You can't stop us both. Even if we don't make it off this ship, you're going to die."

Hel's face grew quizzical. "You're just going to trust me? Suppose I say yes and the Clip goes on, then I kill the beast?"

Alistair smiled and looked down at Obs. The animal was still growling. "You've never come across one of these before, have you? They're linguaphiles. He understands everything we're saying. If at any point you go against our deal, he'll do everything in his power to rip your throat out. If you think you can kill him, go ahead and try."

Hel was staring at the animal. "And if you tell him to behave, he'll listen? Even once you're Clipped?"

"He'll listen to everything I tell him."

Hel's head jerked up; she looked annoyed. "I don't have time for any of this. Sure, whatever you want me to say. I won't hurt him."

Obs looked at Alistair, awaiting instruction. "I want you to follow me, Obs, and don't harm anyone. If they look like they might hurt me or the AllMother or you, I want you to take out as many as you can. Understand?"

The drathe wagged his tail and laid on the floor. He wasn't exactly calm, but he was not aggressive either. Alistair knew he shouldn't trust this woman, but he didn't have any other choice. Given his position, it was the only option he had.

"Oh, I like this," Hel said. "You having to trust me with a human and an animal." She started forward again, her Whip retracting with each step but also growing closer to Alistair's chest. It was mere millimeters from burning a hole into him when she stopped. She'd already extended her Clip and held it in her left hand. "Put this on, and let's quit with the theatrics. I tire of them."

Alistair thought of the letter he'd left and how foolish it had been. He hadn't trusted those closest to him and had left them in the dark, then given them a letter telling them what he was going to do. All so that he could end up here, placing a Clip on his head.

The AllMother stood next to him, as still as a statue.

Alistair accepted the Clip. He said nothing but brought it up to his forehead, and then he moved no more.

CHAPTER TWENTY-TWO

"The irony is that I created a perfect society, and the person who wants to bring it down."

–Aurelius de Finita, First Imperial Ascendant

Being harmonized with a ship was very hard to describe to someone who couldn't do it. Few people asked pilots to describe it because for a long time, they'd been told it was impossible. Faitrin didn't agree with that. She thought the best way to explain it was describing a relationship that had lasted for forty or more years. There were the petty arguments that didn't matter but constantly happened, the kind long-married people might engage in. There were the periods of silence because neither needed to speak, both knowing what the other person was thinking.

All of these were things outsiders could see, but the undercurrent of the relationship was love, and not the kind written about in books or the fairytales of old. It was a love in which each knew what the other would do in any given situation. It was a love that tied one to the other in sickness and in health. It was an underlying current that couldn't be seen by outsiders, except in the brief moments where he puts more potatoes on her plate before she asked for them.

He simply knew she wanted more.

For Faitrin, that was what being harmonized with a ship was like. The petty arguments, the long periods of silence, and knowing what the other thought before they thought it.

That was what happened when the pod launched.

The ship's AI began to speak, but she cut it off.

I've got it. What is it?

Well, madam, I just saw the damned thing.

Faitrin liked this AI. She hadn't seen one like it before, but it was feisty and spoke with an accent, which she'd also never experienced. Some AIs were droll.

The pod had launched from the main dreadnought. It was, without a doubt, the fastest ship she'd ever seen in the third dimension.

Are the Myrmidons turning toward it? she asked.

Now *you want my help*, the AI answered. There was a brief pause, then it said, *I think they're unsure about it as well. It's traveling at a tenth the speed of light. I'm not aware of a human ship that can travel that fast.*

Neither am I, Faitrin responded. *Can you reach Thoreaux?*

If I must. I'm not a fan of his attitude.

You must, she said. *Connect me to him now.*

There was the equivalent of a sigh from the AI, then a few moments of silence.

You're on with His Majesty, the AI said.

Faitrin kept speaking mentally, with the other ship's AI relaying the message. *Thoreaux, did you see that ship, the pod?*

It was Thoreaux's voice she heard in her head. *Yeah. What the hell is it?*

I don't know. I've never seen anything like it. We've got a choice right now. We can continue with the original plan, or we can modify it and find out what that is.

I don't understand. Why would we modify the plan? That could be anything.

The AI knew what she was thinking without her having to ask, but another reason she liked this one was because of its raw power. The Terram certainly understood technology.

Given target values and the likelihood of the dreadnought's destruction, I put it at an eighty-three percent chance that Alistair Kane and the AllMother are in the pod.

It was an instantaneous statistic. Faitrin continued speaking. *Look, my AI is calculating that it's a four-fifths chance that they're in the pod. That dreadnought is about to be a floating rock. Even if we continue this plan, it's not going to work as we wanted. There's going to be nothing left up there.*

So, what do you say we do? Thoreaux asked. *Remember, this choice could be the last one you ever make.*

Fuck it, she told him. *Let's get that pod.*

The AI overrode any response. *While I find you a crass lass, I do like your style, madam.*

Relm saw the torture on Thoreaux' face.

They'd both heard Faitrin's voice, and they both understood the decision that needed to be made. Faitrin said that Alistair and the AllMother were most likely in that escape pod.

But if they weren't? Well, there wouldn't be any other chances.

Thoreaux didn't look at Relm as he thought. Faitrin had just given them her opinion on the matter in her positive and crass manner. Thoreaux didn't share her sunny optimism, though. He had the dark cold of Pluto in his very bones, and looking at him now, Relm was glad he didn't have to make this choice.

After a few moments that felt like an eternity to Relm, Thoreaux spoke. His voice was low, and each word seemed to hold weight, perhaps the same weight that he felt now. "Let's go after the pod. Figure out how we're going to catch it."

Faitrin's voice came over the comm. "Yessir."

"She has disconnected, sir," the AI told Thoreaux.

His response was simple and emotionless. "She's going to give you new vectors. Follow them."

"Yes, sir."

He grew silent as the ship turned toward the pod. Relm reached forward and touched his monitors, wanting to look at the Myrmidon and Commonwealth fleets. The Myrmidons still weren't going after the pod. "That's going to be the death of them," he said absently.

"What is?" Thoreaux asked.

"They can't operate as fast as the Commonwealth or us. Look at them. They aren't allowed to move without the AllSeer's permission. That's gotta be what's holding them in place, even though they have ships to spare. Nothing is done without his permission, and it's slowing them down."

"You might be on to something there," Thoreaux said, sounding interested.

"Every once in a while my brain kicks in, broth." He leaned back in his chair and looked at the monitors. Thoreaux leaned forward on his side and zoomed in on the pod. It was still streaking across space at a nearly unbelievable rate.

They were silent for a few minutes, still waiting for Faitrin to tell them how the hell they were going to catch up to it.

Relm spoke softly. "You made the choice by trusting her, Thoreaux. She's not going to let us down. That I'm sure about. Now we just need to make sure we don't let Pro or the AllMother down."

Thoreaux nodded without looking over. Relm couldn't decide if he believed him, but the die had been cast, and there was nothing to do but wait.

CHAPTER TWENTY-THREE

"The greatest Titan ever? It wasn't Alistair Kane, regard-less of the legend he built."

−Alexander de Finita, Imperial Ascendant, after being questioned by a reporter about Alistair Kane's legacy

The plan had been simple and ruthless; Alistair realized that now. He was trapped inside a body that wasn't his to command. He thought about everything he'd gone through, just to be so stupid in those final moments. It took everything in him not to keep chastising himself because it would do no good. He owed it to the AllMother and everyone back on Phoenix to try to salvage what he'd destroyed. It would take every bit of his concentration if it was even possible.

The Commonwealth had played their hand flawlessly.

The cost would have been great no matter what they did, but Alistair now thought it was Hel who'd planned it all. She had to be the one who understood the Myrmidons' strength and knew they would lose vast numbers of people as well as ships. She'd chosen which people and which ships.

Alistair didn't know how many of the lower-value workers had been placed on the dreadnought, but he imagined the numbers were high. Once they'd understood which dreadnought Alistair and the AllMother were headed to, they must have immediately started the exchange of Titans and high-value crew for the lower-value ones. And what would the Myrmidons care, even if they had known? The AllMother had told them where she'd be; that was all that mattered. Whether janitors or Titans guarded the dreadnought was inconsequential.

Thus, the trap had been set. Once the Myrmidons landed on the dreadnought, they worked toward the center of the ship and the bridge. Hel had led Alistair and the AllMother behind them, and it was only at the last moment that the AllMother had been able to break through their blocks.

The Myrmidons had missed it in their bloodlust, the pod and those hiding near it— probably the only warriors on the ship. Perhaps some pilots had been slaughtered, but they were expendable to a degree. The dreadnought would be lost, but the targets they wanted would be captured, which was all the Imperial Ascendant appeared to care about: getting Alistair at any cost.

And so, with Clips on, Hel had led the three of them to this pod, where Ares, along with a handful of Titans, were waiting in hiding. The entire show before had been just that, a show. Those people scattered through the ship wearing the MechSuits were dead janitors and engineers.

Had they known they would be slaughtered? Or had they been lied to?

A question came to Alistair that he didn't want to answer: had he done something similar to people without his knowledge? Had he led people to their slaughter due to an order from the Ascendant?

Like the previous chastisement, he shoved it away. It would do no good right now to consider such things.

When one is Clipped, one can still see and hear everything around them. They just have no control over their body. Rather, they are controlled by voice recognition and codes that are preprogrammed into the Clip. Hel was authorized to give them orders, and so was Ares.

The group had stepped into the escape pod. Obs remained at Alistair's side, quiet except when one of the Titans feigned that he might do something. The drathe had risen to his full height and opened his mouth wide, letting out a vicious growl. The Titan had backed off.

The pod took off from the ship, and Ares stared at Alistair from across the small room they both inhabited. Hel glanced at him from time to time, that wicked smile on her face. Alistair could move nothing but the involuntary movements of his body like blinking and breathing. There was no smile on Ares' face, and Alistair couldn't say what the man was thinking, but his stare never wavered.

Alistair felt the move from the third dimension to the fourth. His body handled the intensity that event created easily. He couldn't look at the AllMother or check on her much frailer form. He could only see Ares and Hel, both of them showing immediate signs of distress before calming. Their bodies shook almost imperceptibly, but Alistair could see it. They weren't built for this dimension and now he was, or even the fifth.

Maybe I can use that, he thought, putting it away for later.

He couldn't know for sure, but he thought they were heading to another dreadnought. The Commonwealth would have been smart about their attack on Phoenix, or at least they should have been. Putting all their ships forward would create an overwhelming risk, even if the chances were small that an attack would occur, so they were most likely heading to the reserve fleet. Were the Myrmidons giving chase, and if so, would this pod exist one minute, and the next only be small fragments and dust floating through the darkness?

Something else it wasn't good to think about.

They would either die or arrive at the dreadnought soon enough. Alistair couldn't close his eyes, but he managed to retreat into a state that wasn't quite sleep but was its twin.

The dreams of the modified came then. It was a very strange one this time.

CHAPTER TWENTY-FOUR

"The greatest Titan? You'd have to ask a Titan that question, but I think you might get a different answer than Alistair Kane."

–Alexander de Finita, Imperial Ascendant, after being questioned by a reporter about Alistair Kane's legacy

He was with Luna, but he didn't know when. The rest of his dreams with her had been in the past, though sometimes he was able to change it. He didn't remember this place, though. It wasn't anywhere they had ever visited.

She stood in the distance, facing him. The ground between and around them was black. He forced himself to look away from his wife and look down at his feet. He stood on ash. His head jerked up, and he looked into the distance. The sun was faint, its halo barely making it this far out.

They stood on the remains of Pluto, the ash world that had once housed thousands and thousands.

"You stand on their remains, Allie."

Luna was suddenly next to him. How she had crossed the distance was up to the mysteries of Alistair's changed mind.

"I didn't want them to die," he sputtered. He desperately wanted to defend himself to this woman, the love of his life. "I never wanted any of this."

She had always been shorter than him, but now she was much shorter. Still, she stared at him with the same fearlessness she'd always shown. His height, his differences, didn't matter. "Are you going to carry that forever, my dear?"

"What?" he asked, not understanding.

"The guilt." Her beautiful green eyes narrowed. "Do you plan on carrying it forever, like some sort of bag you're afraid to put down?"

Alistair stepped back, confused. He spread his arms and looked into the distance. The wind blew, picking up ash and tossing it around. There was more ash underneath, and ash where it fell. "All this is because of me. All these people died because of my choices. Look at me, Luna. Do you think I grew this tall just because I was on Pluto for a few weeks? You know what I am. I'm a fucking mutant."

He knew it was only a dream, a delusion the modifications helped create. His psyche was more powerful now than it had been, yet, he couldn't help it. He couldn't help but say the things he felt, acting them out on the version of his wife his mind created.

Luna took a step forward, closing the gap between them. "You're my husband, Allie, and you're carrying around things you have no business with. Tell me, Alistair Kane, did you give the order to nuke this planet?"

He said nothing.

"Did you fly dreadnoughts across the Solar System to kill people you've never met?"

He didn't answer.

"Did you make a mistake when you let those parents go? That's the real question, isn't it?"

Alistair opened his mouth to say yes. Of course, it had been his fault because he should have Clipped or killed them, just like he'd done thousands of times before. They were Subversives, enemies of the Commonwealth, and thus his enemies.

Yet the word caught inside his mouth. He could not say it, not for that reason, at least. Saying it was a mistake now would be to disavow Thoreaux and Servia and the AllMother. Perhaps even Obs. Everyone who depended on him, and dare he say, loved him.

He couldn't do that. At least not for that reason.

Alistair found the words. "It was a mistake because it took me away from you."

His wife didn't slow. "Maybe that's true, and maybe it isn't. But was it a mistake because of what happened here? Because of the dead you now stand on?"

He wanted to say no, but something inside refused to give.

"You can't let it go," she told him. "You want to carry this guilt, and that's not something I understand, Allie. It's not the man I married. It's not the man I love." She gently placed her hand on his elbow. "The physical change?" she said, grinning mischievously, "Let's just say I think we can have some fun with these new muscles running up and down your arms." She gave his bicep a light squeeze, then the smile dropped. "The changes that matter aren't physical. They're what's in your heart. You took up arms against the Commonwealth, but you still haven't shed what they made you believe."

She took her hand off his arm and crooked her index finger, beckoning him down to her. He bent down, and Luna brought her lips to his ear. "My love, you cannot destroy something you let rule your heart. It would be like the hand killing the body without the mind's approval." She turned her head slightly and kissed him. "I love you. Set that bag down; it's not yours. Or, if you must carry it, bring it to its rightful owner."

CHAPTER TWENTY-FIVE

"The greatest to come out of the Academy is a name not mentioned often. I will not mention it here."

–Marcus de Reespen, Current Primus Academy Director

Luna Kane once had a different name: Luna de Valerius. Her lineage was long, her family a strong, proud one. When she'd decided to take the name Kane and marry someone not of a superior house, her father had been shocked. Not just surprised, shocked. Yet he'd been a fair man, and after he had time to think the idea over, he'd asked his daughter only one question.

"Do you love him, Luna?"

"I do."

"If he's wounded beyond repair as a Titan, will you love him then?"

"If he's burned so badly I cannot recognize his face for the rest of our lives, I'll love him, Father."

He'd looked at her hard then, and after a few moments, had given her a nod. "You have my blessing since you love him like that."

Luna Kane had. She'd loved him in his stubbornness, in his righteousness, in his faults. She'd loved a man and looked at him as a complete creature, not as a romanticized version. Not as Primus. Not as the most famed Titan to ever hold a Whip. She'd loved him as Alistair, and when he'd disappeared, that love hadn't stopped. If anything, his absence made her love him more.

"My heart breaks to tell you this, ma'am, but your husband is dead."

The words still sounded in her ears as if they had just been spoken. Your. Husband. Is. Dead.

She hadn't believed it when the man from Control stood in front of her, his hat in both hands. She'd simply said, "Thank you," and shut the door. She didn't know what had happened to that man, whether he'd stood on her porch, confused or jumped into his transport and flown off. She hadn't cared, either. It took an hour before the words finally hit her, then Luna Kane had collapsed in her bedroom. She'd curled into a ball and sobbed.

She'd screamed.

When she couldn't cry any more tears, she still didn't believe the words. She turned on the holo and watched the news. Indeed, they were reporting her husband's death as well, and she cried some more, yet once again, when she ran out of tears and screams, she didn't believe it.

It wasn't Control that came for her next. It was an emissary from the Commonwealth. They were going to give her husband an honorary Commonwealth funeral, and they wanted her to attend. They would not make a big deal out of her presence if she didn't want them to, or she could speak in front of the entire world. She'd done the only thing she could think of at the time: bargained for more time. She told them she didn't know what she would do.

Her father had holoed, and the only words he had were, "I'm sorry, and I'm here. For anything."

Her mother had holoed as well, and the two of them had wept together. The words were minimal. Neither had anything to say. Luna had no siblings, so when those holos were done, she was alone.

When the Commonwealth came to speak to her again, she sent them away without an answer. Luna hadn't cared in the slightest what they did at that funeral. Her husband's body had been destroyed in the firefight, according to official sources. She would never get it back, and the ceremony of launching the warrior into space was just that: a ceremony because there weren't any remains.

Luna didn't believe it. Then the Communication Ministry started their machine, ginning up people for war or something like it—the total destruction of a planet and anyone who lived there, which included tens of thousands of people.

The headlines were severe: *Insurrection beginning on Pluto.*

Refusal to come to the bargaining table.

Weapons of mass destruction available to Subversives.

They went on and on, but the final message was received. The only way to retain peace was to kill.

So they did it. The Imperial Ascendant and all the forces he could muster sent dreadnoughts to a planet and burnt the thing until nothing would ever exist on it again. Luna was stunned but not stupid. There had been no nuclear blast on Earth, so to say her husband's body no longer existed didn't make a whole lot of sense. They should have at least had a skeleton.

And the unprecedented genocide of Pluto?

She didn't know what was happening, but she knew it was more than she'd been told.

So when the Imperial Ascendant himself sent word that he was requesting an audience with Luna Kane, the woman did not send away the messenger without an answer. Rather, she said it would be her honor.

A transport came for her and flew her thousands of kilometers, treating her as if she were part of the Imperial Family—the Ascendant's daughter herself. She'd flown alone, which she'd preferred. She slept and dreamed. She dreamed a lot now, much more than before Alistair had disappeared. Weird dreams, different. She didn't cry on the transport, though. For Luna, the tears were gone because she didn't believe her husband was dead.

Or at least, she didn't believe what she was being told.

The transport arrived at the Imperial Residence, and Luna was met by two servants. A host of others took her bags, but the two servants who welcomed her told her that they were at her beck and call. Whatever she needed at any hour, she had only to let them know. She asked for a room and some time to rest before meeting the Ascendant.

"Of course," the woman told her.

"Your meeting is scheduled for tomorrow. He'd like to

have dinner with you tomorrow as well if that fits your purposes," the man told her. They sounded pleasant enough, though everyone involved here knew that her purposes were his purposes.

"Do either of you have any idea why he wants to meet? I haven't been told."

"No, ma'am," the woman answered as they walked through the Residence's front doors. "Our liege will send word soon, I am sure of that."

Luna took in the sights of the Imperial Residence without showing any emotion. The Praetorians were visible, yet they blended into the background, a presence that could go unnoticed if one wanted to ignore it. Luna didn't. She wanted to know the reality of her situation.

The servants led her to a room, a short walk that didn't show her much of the castle-like existence the Imperial Family lived in. She was able to see no one but servants and guards, most likely because that was how those in charge wanted it.

Her room was immaculate, but what else would one expect when staying in a world conqueror's domain? Or at least his family home. Dinner came, and even though it might have been the best food she'd ever placed in her mouth, Luna found it tough to eat. She only finished a quarter of the plate. To say why except that her husband was missing and had been proclaimed dead would have been hard to do. The male servant asked her if it was to her liking, and Luna blamed her lack of appetite on nerves. After all, she would be meeting humanity's idol the next day.

There were a few other brief interruptions, but in the

end, Luna was left alone to sleep. There were holovids and an endless body of books to read on the DataTracks throughout the room. She turned on a holovid, but focus was hard to achieve. After a while, she laid down in the bed and tried to sleep. There was no message about what this meeting concerned; Luna would have been frightened, except that her love was gone and someone was lying about it.

She found sleep, and she dreamed once again.

The weird ones.

The next morning she met the Imperial Ascendant, Alexander de Finita, the second of that name in his lineage. According to official doctrine, the first had died during horrible experiments a thousand years before.

A small, intimate table sat in front of floor to ceiling windows that stretched from one end of the room to the other. There were no other tables and only one other person in the room.

"My liege," the servant who had brought her said, "this is Luna Kane."

The man sitting at the table stood. He was tall, even taller than Alistair had been. His hair was gray and parted on the side. His face was thin and lined from a level of stress that Luna realized very few humans had ever experienced. He was old, though how old, who knew? He seemed to be in his mid-fifties, though it was factually impossible. He wore the purple color of his family, a single-piece suit that stretched from his neck to his ankles. It covered his arms to his wrists as well.

"Thank you," he told the servant. His voice was strong and confident and rang out across the vast room like that of a man who had been listened to his whole life and expected to be listened to until he drew his last breath.

The servant gave a short bow and exited the room. The doors closed behind him, which was when Luna first saw the Praetorian Guard. They were situated around the room, wearing the MechSuits Alistair used to wear. He'd tried to explain the difference between Praetorian Guards and Titans once since the rivalry ran deep between the two groups.

"They're fine with standing around their whole lives. Most of them will never see a day of action."

And yet, before them now, alone with this powerful man, she knew how small she was. She wasn't afraid, but she should be. Nothing about this was right. Nothing about this had been right since Alistair disappeared.

"Thank you, good lady, for coming to see me. I know the trip was long, and I know life has been hard of late." He took a step to the side and gestured at the table. "Will you sit with me? And if you are hungry, would you dine with me?"

"It would be my honor, my liege. I am at your service." She bowed as the servant had done and as she had been taught to do since she was a schoolgirl, whenever the Imperial Ascendant appeared on any sort of holovid. Luna wore the black of a widow, a dress that was neither overly conservative nor showed too much. She approached the table slowly. The

Imperial Ascendant moved easily behind her chair and pulled it out for her. "Thank you, my liege." She sat down and allowed him to help her scoot the chair beneath the table.

He crossed to the other side and sat down. Not a moment passed between him sitting and the servants bringing food. They appeared as if out of nowhere, one bringing drinks and the other an appetizer. It was a plate of shrimp and not the lab-grown kind most of the population now ate. These were from the ocean, sticking out of ice in a perfect shade of pink.

A glass of water and a pink alcoholic beverage were placed before her. The Ascendant had water and a drink that appeared a bit stronger. It was clear, a vodka tonic perhaps.

Allie used to drink those. Did the Ascendant know that, or was this a mere coincidence?

He remained still as the servants left the room, then took a sip of the alcohol and nodded at hers. "That's my wife's favorite. I thought you might like it."

Luna had done these things before, the galas and balls with dignitaries. Marrying a Primus carried such obligations, and she'd been better at it than Alistair. "A woman as wise as her, I am sure I will."

He smiled, but whether it was kind, she couldn't say. The categorization of his smile was as elusive as his age.

The Ascendant took a shrimp, put it in his mouth, and ate it in one bite. He looked out the window as he chewed, and Luna was grateful he didn't offer her one. She thought she might vomit. Sipping the pink drink was more than her stomach could handle at the moment.

"I grew up with these views," he said. "I don't think I even see them anymore."

Luna looked out the window. She hadn't grown up with sights like this, but her family had been wealthy, and she'd seen similar vistas for much of her life. They were much different from the relatively small place she and Alistair had chosen. Despite the heights to which his job had taken him, he said he preferred being on the ground as much as possible. "It is truly breathtaking if one lets themself fall into it."

The Ascendant scratched his shaved chin. "Maybe one day I will find that again." He took another shrimp and ate it whole, discarding the tail delicately on the small plate before him. "You have flown a long way, and I know you asked only once what this was about, yesterday on your arrival. Are you still curious?"

"Of course, my liege. I would not be so rude as to ask you why I am here when I'm sure you'll tell me in your own time."

He looked at her then, perhaps for the first time, and smiled. This one could be categorized: amusement. "You have been trained well, haven't you? Was it your family or the events you and your late husband had to attend?"

Late husband. Even from his mouth, Luna didn't believe it. "It began with my family, but Alistair's talents allowed me to put it into action."

"And honest," he mused. He glanced at the shrimp. "I would offer you one, but I assume you'll eat when you're ready. Sometimes people have difficulty eating around me. I sympathize, even if I can't empathize."

The third shrimp disappeared into his mouth.

"Why did you not attend your husband's funeral? Why did you send no message back?"

He turned so that they faced each other. There was no escaping his gaze.

Luna didn't want to answer right away. She turned and looked out the window, leaning slightly on the arm of her chair. Buildings stretched past the clouds and transports flew through them, everything mapped out on an aerial grid. The Ascendant said nothing as she stared out.

She was not sure if she should lie to him. Would he know, or was her training good enough?

Why not tell the truth? Alistair asked her inside her mind. He had always asked the tough questions in life, the ones she couldn't get around, and he asked them plainly, in a way that couldn't be avoided. She heard his voice as if he were at the table with them.

Luna looked at the Ascendant. To not look at him while speaking would be extremely disrespectful. "Because unless his body was on Pluto when he died, there's no reason you shouldn't have been able to recover it. Was he on Pluto, my liege?"

The Imperial Ascendant pursed his lips, and after a moment, a hint of a smile poked out. "Tell me that wasn't what they said. That they couldn't find his body?"

"Technically, my liege, the message was that his body had been destroyed."

His lips turned down, though there was still humor on his face. "I'll have to look into that. I wasn't aware. So you didn't attend your husband's funeral because you think you were lied to, or because you think he's still alive?"

Luna slid the chair back and crossed one leg over the

other. "Both. But I do not think you were involved, my liege. I understand that the mass of information you must deal with at any given moment is beyond anything I could possibly understand. I imagine you leave many details to others beneath you. However, I only had one piece of information, and it didn't ring true."

The Ascendant nodded. "Did your husband ever say anything about his death when he was still alive? What you should expect?"

"Once or twice, but I didn't allow him to talk about such things too often. He was Primus, and his abilities were renowned. Plus, whatever was to happen, I trusted the Commonwealth to do what was right if that time ever came. Despite his profession, my liege, I never truly believed that it would."

"And now you believe the Commonwealth has lied to you?"

His voice was stern, his smile gone. This was the face of a man who expected answers when he asked questions.

"I believe my husband is most likely alive. One lies for gain, and I can't see what the Commonwealth would gain from the fiction. I imagine if the truth was not put forth, it was to protect me from something harsher than death. I do know things like that exist."

Luna walked a tightrope now. She didn't know what might happen if she slipped. The fog was too heavy to say. Perhaps there was a net waiting to catch her, or maybe she would fall and hit the ground.

Or maybe she'd make it across.

The Ascendant appeared to be considering her answer.

"I do not know if that is the truth or your training in

the realm of politics, but the answer is the right one. How about for both our sakes, we assume it's the truth?"

Luna bowed her head slightly. "I would never lie to my liege."

"Then let's operate on that belief from now on, shall we?"

Luna didn't detect any extra motion from the Ascendant, but the servants were suddenly back, more this time. They carried away the appetizers and put another course in front of them. The food smelled wonderful, but again, Luna could find no appetite. She still didn't understand what was happening here.

The Ascendant took a bite, and she forced herself to as well.

"Your husband is alive," the Ascendant said once he finished swallowing.

Luna showed nothing on her face, or at least as close to it as she could muster. Inside, she soared. It was hard to find words because though she hadn't believed he was dead, she'd never really believed someone would tell her the truth.

Your husband is alive.

She opened her mouth, hoping a sound might come out, but she couldn't force anything.

"I called you here to tell you that, Luna," the Ascendant said. "I called you here because I want to be truthful with you about what happened, and if you're willing, I'd like you to help us get him back."

She blinked, her face still a mask, though her voice had betrayed her. After a few more moments, she managed to say, "Bring him back?"

From where or who hadn't occurred to her. He was alive. Alistair. That was all that mattered. Her husband, her mate, lived.

"This is going to be very hard for you to hear, Luna, but it's extremely important that you listen to every word. I won't ask for any decision from you tonight or even tomorrow, but very soon, I'll need to know what you'll do. Time is of the utmost importance. Are you ready to hear it now, or would you like some time to digest what I just told you?"

Luna needed no extra time, not when it came to Alistair. She nodded. "I'm ready."

Alexander de Finita had nearly finished his duties for the day, though the hour had grown late. It was nearing one in the morning Standard Time, and he was just now heading to the Room of Ascendants. He was tired, and no matter what he seemed to do, his Fathers continually told him the odds were worsening for him. He didn't know exactly how this latest gambit, the game with the wife, was going to affect things yet.

Supposedly, it would help the Commonwealth's chances, but that depended on what the woman decided. The Fathers couldn't know everything, despite what they might say. The behavior of an individual was outside their realm of knowledge, or at least that was what Alexander told himself. Yet, they thought they knew what was going to happen with this damned Titan.

He was the coming destruction of the human race,

pretty much, but Alexander still wasn't sure he believed it. Yet he knew his duty and would follow it through until he could no longer draw breath.

He rose to the Room of Ascendants. The orb sat where it always did, appearing to be dead. Alexander knew that was never the case. His Fathers never slept. They watched over the human species the same as the gods, but if the gods did exist, they could never be as arrogant as his ancestors.

Alexander bowed. The orb came to life, a light showing in the center of it. As it spoke, the light formed a line circling the orb. "Did you talk to the wife?"

From one knee, Alexander looked up. "It's been done."

"And her answer?"

"She needs time," Alexander answered.

The line on the orb reverted to a single dot for a few moments, then shot out once more. "Time is what we don't have, Alexander. The situation is growing more crucial with each passing second."

"We have him in our possession," the Ascendant stressed. "Him and the individual of my lineage. The newest reports show the other old one is not even in pursuit. We have lost only one dreadnought, and soon the entire fleet will portal back to Earth. Have you processed all the information yet?"

"All of the information has been received and processed," the orb said.

"Then please, Fathers, in your infinite wisdom, tell me why our chances are still decreasing. I do not understand."

"You still believe we don't understand humanity. You think that because we've been uploaded into a server, somehow the lives we lived and the programming we were given isn't enough to do what we've done almost since the beginning. Are we wrong in that?"

Alexander didn't move. "No, you're correct. I don't understand how we can be in possession of the man you think will end everything we've built, yet you still think we're losing."

The voice sounded like a group of speakers, yet when they spoke, it was as one. "You know about the American Revolution, correct? The Russian Revolution? Everything going back to the Third War?"

"Of course." Alexander's schooling encompassed every major and most of the minor events in history.

"Ideas move people, Alexander," the orb continued. "There was a saying long ago—perhaps you know it—that no force on Earth can stop an idea whose time has come. These Subversives believe they've found a demi-god in this Fallen Titan. They will stop at nothing to save him. And him? Do you understand that his psychological profile is the worst possible one in terms of stopping him? His single goal in life is to get to the woman you're saying needs more time. He will gladly die as long as the killing blow comes while he's taking one more step toward her."

It was the first time the Imperial Ascendent had ever felt scolded in this room. As a child, of course, his father had been harsh to him, but since he'd become Imperial Ascendant? It was unthinkable.

"Right now, Imperial Ascendant," the orb nearly spat, "the chance that some sort of rescue mission has been launched is nearly one hundred percent. While you sit here saying you've won, understand the seriousness of this matter. We cannot say if this is an idea whose time has come, but we can say that the Subversives believe it is."

The orb paused as if it were catching its breath. Alexander needed to retreat to his mental citadel because his rage was growing, but he knew his duty, and he remained bowed.

"The closest thing to the gods humanity has ever achieved runs through your veins. That blood created you, Alexander. We are growing tired of stressing to you how dangerously close you are to losing everything your fore-bears created: the greatest period of peace for humanity ever, the ability to travel to the ends of the universe, life expectancies that dwarf anything previous generations could have hoped for. If this Titan returns, it will all be lost. The human species will retreat into a dark age unlike anything previous. Demockracy and the will of the mob will rule."

Again the orb quieted, and the line retreated to the single dot. Long moments passed, and when it spoke again, the voice sounded tired. "Perhaps you are too weak, Alexander. Perhaps our bloodline has grown too thin. We hope that's not the case, but regardless, it is you whom fate has put in this position. If you are going to come back here to deliver non-news or excuses, don't, Alexander. Even now, we can sense the anger growing in you. You are upset that someone would speak to you as we have, much like a spoiled child being upset by being scolded. All of this we do not care about, as long as it doesn't affect what must happen. Save humanity, Alexander. You are our last hope."

The orb went silent, and the light disappeared. They were through talking. They had informed him of their calculations, what must happen with the wife, and the new information that some sort of rescue team was coming for Alistair Kane.

Maybe the Fathers were right.

Alexander stood and turned his back on the orb. He still felt the anger within him, but they were right. That was a childish emotion, and he needed to discard it quickly.

Probably the Fathers were right. A rescue team *was* coming for Kane. Alexander needed to make sure they were prepared, though he thought Hel would be expecting some sort of rescue attempt.

There were always more things that needed to be done, but if his Fathers genuinely thought he was weaker than they had been, they were wrong. Alexander de Finita had held this world together singlehandedly for his whole life.

Yet perhaps his arrogance had gotten to him a bit. Bringing the Titan back to Earth was a greater risk than he should take. They should just kill him now, or as soon as Hel got the message. The AllMother too—a stupid name if ever there was one.

Alexander gave a slight nod, having made up his mind. "This will be over before the sun rises."

He didn't turn around or wait for the orb to respond. He stepped onto the elevator and left.

CHAPTER TWENTY-SIX

Should we bring the other one out?
He's too old. His time has passed.
*It might be necessary. He's a mutant. He isn't aging like
the unmodified.*

—A brief conversation among the Fathers inside
their orb, loosely translated

The AllMother had been Clipped once before, right after
her modification, when her father had decided he'd gone
too far. Back then, she'd thought she would never escape
and her life was over.

It had been for one of them, one of *her*, since she had a
clone at that point. Not a twin, but a replica of her that
remembered everything the same as she did and most
likely thought the same thoughts. The AllMother had
never met the woman. She'd left Earth before she'd had a

chance, and sitting here now with a Clip on her head, she oddly wondered if she might see this sister of sorts.

Long ago, when she was first Clipped, the AllMother had thought she would die. Now, in this small pod, staring straight ahead and with men ready to take her life at any moment, she had no fear of death, or rather, she didn't think it was possible. There were things about her gifts that no one knew. At least, no one on this ship did.

The Commonwealth had surprised her with their block. She hadn't expected their technology to be so focused on her, especially not given how little they seemed to care about the Subversives' actions. She had suspected it briefly on first entering the dreadnought but said nothing. That had been her mistake and one she couldn't take back, but she wasn't sure yet how costly it would be.

She thought Thoreaux and Servia were coming. Her connection to them was strong because of how long she'd been around them. Neither this Clip nor any blocks they had constructed could keep those two from the AllMother's mind.

That was something she didn't think those inside this pod knew. The Clip did keep her from stretching far or seeing very clearly, but even so, the thoughts around her couldn't be completely blocked.

The only head she didn't attempt to enter was Alistair's. She didn't need to; she had chosen well and knew he would do what was necessary to free them.

Thoreaux and Servia were coming, and perhaps others. She didn't know for sure, but it was a possibility. The AllMother could only look forward, but she could see from the corners of her eyes. There were powers she hadn't shown, and she was wondering if it was time.

It wasn't. The woman who had led them to this treachery was dangerous, perhaps more so than the Titans. She'd seen her fight the Myrmidons, but the AllMother now knew she'd been holding back. Testing Alistair. Seeing what he was made of.

The time for her secrets would come, but it wasn't here yet.

Hours had passed on the pod, with Veena cut off from the outside world. The pod lacked whatever psychic blocking shit her dreadnought had been equipped with, yet another lie or a half-truth that had been hidden from her. Veena wasn't happy, but right now, there was nothing she could do about it. In fact, there might never be anything she could do about it, and this hours-long escape was allowing her to slowly accept it.

It's almost over, she told herself. *All of this madness, for good.*

Of course, Veena had known about the pod. It had been in development for the past five years, and she wasn't too surprised that Hel knew about it as well. It was meant for a Primus to escape in if all else had failed on his or her ship.

The plan had been Hel's, but it seemed to have worked perfectly.

The dreadnought was pulling the ship into its bay, and Veena would shortly have access to everything she'd missed.

She'd spent some time studying the Fallen Titan from where she sat. His mutation seemingly went well beyond the red in his eyes. He was big on the scale she imagined the Myrmidons were; she hadn't seen any, due to Hel's plan. He looked like a killing machine. She could think of no other way to put it, and all of Ares' practice with his droids would have done nothing. Veena wasn't sure a MechSuit could stop this monster.

Yet here he is, as meek as an Earth-lamb. You hate Hel, but perhaps you should respect her a bit.

She felt the dreadnought's greater gravity take over, the pod's disappearing beneath it.

Thank the gods, they'd finally arrived. The pod door opened, and Veena was the first to stand. Her capo Helenus de Maxine was waiting for her at the bottom. Veena stopped walking at the top of the ramp, the capo's face giving her pause. "What is it?"

"We're waiting for a transmission from Earth," her capo informed her.

"Control?" Veena asked. Control would be better than the alternative.

Helenus shook her head. She knew better than to say more.

"Let's go to my quarters." Veena looked over her shoulder at Ares. "Take them to the brig. I'll meet with you shortly."

The Titan gave no pushback, and Veena was thankful for that.

Hel spoke up from the very back of the pod, her tone teasing. "Will you meet with me too, Primus?"

Veena ignored the comment and left the pod behind her.

"Your quarters are ready, my Primus," Helenus said as she led the way. "Earth made contact a little over one standard hour ago."

"How long will it take for the message to be fully received?" Messaging inside Earth's Solar System was nearly instantaneous, but even the Commonwealth hadn't mastered interstellar messaging. They could send messages through the fifth dimension, but that could still take days. The only thing that was near-instantaneous was the initial contact, due to the extremely small bits transferred.

"We're looking at twenty-four more standard hours."

"And what of the Myrmidons? Do we have any idea if they're following?" Veena asked.

"No. What would you like us to do?"

They'd reached the Primus' quarters. The door scanned Veena and opened for her, shutting after the capo entered. The room adjusted to Veena's preferences: paintings appeared on the wall, holographic knickknacks on surfaces, and the music she liked played softly in the background. It allowed the Primus to feel at home on any ship she entered. The AI had also been replaced from what her capo preferred to Veena's the moment her signature was detected.

Veena felt herself relax a bit as the room adjusted. It wouldn't last, she knew, but for a moment, she felt like there wasn't a death sentence on her head.

She stood with her back to her capo and let her SkinSuit peel off her. When one signed up for the Commonwealth's

Interplanetary Fleet, one had to be comfortable with the bare human body, or one wouldn't make it long. Veena didn't answer her capo right away but stepped into the shower. It was a small box without any doors. Water was thrust from above. A small mixture of soap was added at the beginning, and it poured at a rate where scrubbing was unnecessary.

The choice here was a simple one. Interstellar communication was not possible when ships were moving. The distance was too great and the point of contact too small. They couldn't have received the contact message if the dreadnought had been moving. Now, they could either head back toward Earth or wait for the rest of the message from the Ascendant.

If they missed it? That wasn't something Veena wanted to consider.

The water stopped and air was pushed down immediately after, drying her off in a few seconds.

She stepped out of the shower and grabbed the clean uniform to the right. She spoke as she stepped into the pants. "We're going to have to wait. I don't like it. This is..." She wanted to finish the sentence with "idiocy," but who knew what was being monitored at this point? They had the fucking target in possession, but would now wait for another message? "Is there any part we can decipher yet?"

"No, Primus." Helenus was solemn, standing with her hands at her sides. She understood as well as Veena, and though she'd piloted this dreadnought the entire time, the two knew each other well enough to understand that all was not right.

"We wait, then," Veena decided as if there were any choice in the matter. Missing the message could do real damage. Veena couldn't say one way or the other at this moment. "I want scouts dropped into the third dimension as well as patrolling the fourth at a range of one thousand kilometers. If anything is coming our way, I want to know about it in advance. We've got a fifth-dimensional scout on this dreadnought, right?"

"We do."

"Get it launched immediately. If the Myrmidons are coming from a higher dimension, I want to know."

The capo nodded, and though she didn't say anything, she didn't leave.

"What else, Helenus?" Veena asked. She was tired. She needed a stimpack, but she couldn't get that until she summoned a medic, which wouldn't happen until Helenus left.

"This woman, Hel." Helenus paused, though her voice didn't quaver. She wasn't fearful of asking the question but wanted to make sure the words were right.

Veena interrupted her. "You're smart enough to figure that out on your own. Let's not discuss it further."

"Yes, my Primus," Helenus nodded. "Permission to leave?"

"Permission granted."

The capo left, and Veena called the medic. The holovid appeared in the middle of the room. "What is the problem, Primus?"

"I need energy. What do you have?"

The holovid was a complicated AI meant to give the Primus what she demanded. There were, of course, human medics aboard the ship, but Veena wouldn't use them unless something major was needed.

"Check your wall mount," the holovid said.

Veena heard something drop into the tiny mount.

"Will there be anything else?"

"No, thank you."

"My pleasure." The holovid disappeared as quickly as it had come. Veena walked to the wall mount and took out the stimpack, then placed it under her left arm. It didn't work immediately, but it was still quick. She could go another twenty-four hours on stimpacks before the negatives began to build up.

She didn't want to see Ares. She certainly didn't want to see Hel. Right now, what Veena needed was to understand the old woman's capabilities. The psychic blocks had allowed for a miraculous escape, but she needed to understand her more deeply.

Using the comm on her suit, she contacted Ares and Hel. She didn't want to speak to Hel alone, and Ares was the closest person she had to a partner in this besides Helenus.

"Both of you meet me at the brig."

"Here now," Ares responded immediately.

"When would you like me there, Your Highness?"

"Now," Veena responded, ignoring the barb. She left her quarters and moved through the dreadnought as quickly as possible. Those passing her saluted in the Commonwealth fashion, right hand touching the left shoulder, followed by a crisp movement down to the side again. Veena didn't slow. She would come to know this crew if time permitted, but they had mere hours to protect themselves from enemies onboard and outside.

She reached the brig in ten minutes. Ares and Hel were already there. The brig was a state-of-the-art prison that had been installed on each of the dreadnoughts, including the one they'd lost to the Myrmidons. It was on the bottom half of the ship, centered to reduce the possibility of escape. The brig was built around an elevator, with three rooms on each of ten levels. It allowed those inspecting it to move easily from cell to cell, and the cell blocks could be rearranged as necessary to put prisoners closer to or farther from each other.

Three Commonwealth soldiers stood guard at the top of the elevator.

"I placed one at the bottom and one three levels down from us," Ares commented. "The old woman is at the top. I figured if something happened, I wanted it to be harder for Kane to climb out."

Veena didn't know if she liked the Titan yet, but she trusted him more. When her alternative was the woman in front of her, there wasn't much choice. "I don't suppose there's any reason to keep the message from anyone. You need to know, Ares, and she'll get it regardless. For right now, we're in a holding position. It'll take twenty-four standard hours for the message to get here, and until then, we can't move." Her eyes fell on Hel. "I need to know exactly what this woman is capable of, no mights or maybes. We have to sit here for twenty-four hours, and I need all the information I can get."

The circular hole beneath them glowed with white light all the way down. Hel turned her eyes, though she couldn't see past the first row of cells. For once, her voice wasn't full of wrath-based mirth. "I'm not a hundred percent sure.

I only know the myths. The Ascendant didn't tell you more than those?"

Hel was older than Veena, and Veena was older than Ares. Veena had never heard the myths and had only known of the AllMother as the Subversive leader. "We never heard myths until the Ascendant told us who we were chasing. Am I wrong, Ares?"

The Titan, still dressed in his MechSuit with the helmet retracted, shook his head. "Never heard about any of this shit, or the AllSeer."

Hel nodded without looking up. "We're all fine with what they feed us, as long as we feel full. Even if it's shit they're shoveling into our mouths because we've never tasted anything else."

Veena wanted to tell her to shut up and get to the point, but this was the first time the woman had sounded anywhere near sincere, so she held her tongue.

The assassin sighed. "Telepathy and telekinesis, from what I understand. She can talk using only her mind, as well as rummage through others' heads, and move things without using her hands."

"Anything else?" Veena asked.

Hel looked up. "Do you want there to be more, or do you think that's enough to deal with right now?"

"I want to know the truth."

"And you have it, Primus," Hel snapped. "As I know it."

"The psychic blocks," Ares interrupted. "Explain what's going on there."

"Do you ever wonder how you go through life questioning so little?" Hel asked, and without waiting for an answer, continued, "The Imperial Ascendant knew the

AllMother was alive, as was her brother. He began working on a way to block her abilities the moment she escaped. The psychic blocks are how they stop what she can do."

Veena realized they hadn't tested something. "Does it stop the telekinesis or just the telepathy?"

"I believe the blocks stop anything she can do, but I didn't create them, so I don't know."

"And the Clip; it's endowed with these blocks?" Veena asked.

"Would appear so," Hel answered.

Veena nodded. She didn't think she'd get much more out of Hel, and certainly no answers about her ability to see throughout the entire dreadnought. "Ares, the Clip will hold Kane, right? There's no need to worry?"

"It'll hold. He won't go anywhere as long as that Clip isn't removed."

"Okay. Keep that damn animal locked up in a separate cell." Veena placed her hands on her hips and glanced down the white tunnel. "I've got scouts looking everywhere. All dimensions. We can't leave without the message."

"Yes, it would be awful, wouldn't it, to disobey the Ascendant?" Hel mocked.

Again, Veena ignored her. "We have three dreadnoughts in the fourth dimension, plus scouts, war corvettes, and a few other ancillary items. Despite all that, if the Myrmidons attack again, we won't have much in the way of stopping power."

Then the idea hit her.

This ship needed to wait for the message, but not the others. "What's the risk of transferring them again, Ares?"

He raised his eyebrows. "Higher than leaving them in the brig."

"It's only this ship Earth is targeting for the message," she continued. "If we move them, the rest can continue the journey home. The risk of losing them to an attack drops."

Ares started to say something, then went quiet.

Hel spoke up as she took a step closer to the hole. "It's not a bad idea—unless the Ascendant wants us to keep these two aboard this ship."

Veena didn't need to be told why. "If a rescue mission is on the way, moving them off this ship in a pod or corvette could be disastrous. The question is, how would they know? There's no way they could have been notified. It's only been twelve hours since our escape."

Hel was staring down the hole now, her feet inches from stepping into it. "There are things that you don't yet know about the Ascendant or the Commonwealth. The old man has ways of knowing things. Let me talk to the AllMother, and I'll find out if a rescue mission is coming."

Veena looked at Ares, but he was staring at Hel. Veena was confused. Should she stick to the original plan and jettison these two toward a portal as quickly as possible, or wait for the message?

Hel looked up, then unhooked her Whip from her belt and tossed it to Ares, who caught it with ease. "You'll know if I'm not myself when I come back up. If I'm not me, kill me. Whatever happens, don't let the old bitch back up, though."

Ares raised both eyebrows and chuckled briefly as he realized what she was saying. "You're going to risk your life for the Commonwealth?"

"Our lives will be worth less than nothing if we don't make the right choice here. There's no way in all the gods' heavens that I will let her get hold of me. The Whip is just an insurance policy. Enough talking. I'll have what's going on out of her shortly, one way or another."

Ares looked at Veena. She knew what the assassin meant. She would brutalize the prisoner until the old woman told her what she wanted to know. Was there a rescue attempt coming?

"No." Veena's lips compressed to a thin line, and she shook her head. "We're not torturing anyone for information. If you say the Ascendant has ways of knowing things, we have to believe they sent that message to hold us here. We wait."

Hel's eyes narrowed, and she took a step toward the Primus. Veena thought the woman might strike her, but she didn't move back. "Is there something you'd like to take up now, Hel?"

Ares' Whip unfurled and hung an inch above the deck. With his free hand, he hooked the other Whip on his MechSuit. His helmet rolled out from his neck, then the comm-driven voice spoke from the hood. "Yes. Is there?"

The assassin looked at the two. Her face had morphed to something nearly non-human and animalistic—the true creature behind the human mask. "You two will be the death of yourselves. You realize that, right? Neither of you is going to make it to old age, surrounded by loved ones, thinking about a life fully lived. No, you're each going to die gasping for breath as blood streams out beside you. Just don't say I didn't warn you or try to help. Don't you dare say that."

Hel turned her gaze to Ares. "I want that back before the message arrives, Titan, or your death will come even quicker than you think."

With that, the woman stalked out of the brig, leaving the two Commonwealth representatives to themselves.

Ares retracted his helmet. "Was that the smart choice, denying her something like that?"

Veena looked after the woman. "It was the right one."

There were things Hel wanted to say but didn't. For one, she wanted to tell the two fools who thought they were in charge that it could very well be that the Imperial Ascendant and his globe full of the dead had decided the best thing to do now that the Titan was captured was to wait here while another dreadnought received word to fire on this one.

In fact, if Hel was the Imperial Ascendant and wanted the former Titan dead, that was exactly what she'd do. However, she kept her mouth shut on that front because there was a small chance that everything that happened on these ships would get back to the Imperial Ascendant.

Unfortunately, these two people were blind in their faith in the Commonwealth. They would never figure out that possibility on their own, which left Hel in a very dangerous predicament. The message's timing was peculiar to say the least, and there were no good alternatives.

She needed to see the old woman, and the old woman had to tell her what was coming.

Hel walked into the brig. The light from the hole shone

up into the darkness surrounding it. It was fancy, but not something Hel would have used if she was designing this. Then again, she didn't plan on holding many prisoners, so maybe it would work. She stepped to the edge of the hole and scanned her hand above the elevator. It read her signature and rose from its holding place.

Hel stepped in. "The old one."

The system's AI understood the age differences of the prisoners and immediately began its descent. A third of the way down, it stopped and spun to the left, putting Hel in front of the old woman once more.

Ares had allowed her to sit, though Hel would have made her stand until her legs gave out. She still had the Clip hovering over her forehead. The AllMother stared straight forward as if Hel wasn't there.

"Open the cell and let me in," she told the AI.

The two enclosures opened, and a ramp unfolded from the elevator to the cell.

Hel stepped off and into the old woman's cage. The elevator and ramp remained where it was, which was what Hel wanted. If either of those two idiots tried to come stop her, she wanted to know the moment the elevator went back up.

Hel stepped up to the old woman and reached for the Clip, pausing just before she grasped it. "I'm going to take this off, and if you do anything I find the slightest bit offensive, you'll be dead before your body hits the floor."

She stared into the woman's vacant eyes, unable to tell if the AllMother understood a word she said. After a moment, Hel put her hand on the Clip and removed it.

The old woman gave a slight gasp as the vacancy in her

eyes disappeared. They slowly moved from staring forward to Hel.

"Did you understand what I just told you?" Hel asked. She'd been Clipped before and everything had kept going mentally for her, but she wanted to make sure the two were on the same page.

The old woman nodded, one hand reaching up to rub her throat. Her voice was weak as she spoke. "I understood."

"Good." Hel nodded. "I have no reason to hurt you right now. Truthfully, your life has nothing to do with mine. My mandate doesn't involve you. I'm sure you can tell there are no blockers on you right now."

Another nod from the geriatric woman.

"What I want to know is simple, and then I'm going back up. Whatever happens to you happens, but I promise it won't be at my hand so long as you tell me the truth." She squatted so that the two were eye level with each other. "Is there a rescue team coming for you?"

The AllMother said nothing, nor did she move. She simply stared at Hel, her eyes a cold blue that looked more Plutoborn than Earthborn.

"Don't act like you don't know or can't tell," Hel instructed. "I'll break you where you sit."

"You have met my brother's minions, haven't you? Before the little charade you played earlier with Alistair. You know their power, yes?"

Hel placed her hand on the old woman's wrist and put pressure on the frail bones. Not enough to cause pain, but enough to make it known that pain could come. "That doesn't answer my question."

The AllMother glanced at her wrist. "My brother believes in fate. He believes the universe's arc is toward his will, and there's no way to avoid it." She gazed into Hel's eyes. "I never believed in such notions until now. I say all that to tell you there's no need to threaten me with violence. There's nothing you or anyone else can do to stop what's in motion. I know there is fate now and that we all serve at its pleasure. Yes, there's a rescue team coming for me and the man below us. They'll come whether you kiss me or kill me, assassin. They'll come, and you won't be able to touch them."

"How large?"

The AllMother smiled. "A handful, no more."

Hel had been called crazy countless times in her life. Mad. Insane. A psychopath. She didn't know if those words were accurate, only that she was different from others she met. Looking into this old woman's eyes, she felt the same about her. This AllMother was different. Crazy, even, because she believed everything she said. Even if Hel killed her right now, she believed fate would carry her side to victory.

Hel stood up, still holding the Clip in her right hand. "Anyone ever told you that you're out of your mind?"

"They usually saved that for my brother, but I suppose now that we both believe in the same mysterious hand guiding the universe, it fits."

"The gods would say that's blasphemy."

The old woman shrugged. "Maybe it's the gods' hands guiding us. It doesn't matter. It all comes down to the same result."

Hel raised the Clip to the old woman's forehead, though

she didn't put it on immediately. "I like you. I hope you make it out of this alive, though I don't think that's in fate's plan."

"Me either," the AllMother responded. "And that's okay, too."

Hel placed the Clip back on.

Hel found the Fleet's Primus quickly. Nothing on these dreadnoughts could hide from her, regardless of what the Primus wanted.

She met Veena on the bridge. Clearly Veena was taking some sort of stimulant since no one could go so hard for so long. Physically, she didn't appear to be on anything, though Hel wouldn't expect any less from a Primus.

"Can I help you, Hel?" Veena asked without looking at the woman. She was focused on the screens in front of her pilots. Hel was no pilot or Fleet commander, but she understood at a base level that everyone in this room was watching the scouts who'd been sent out.

Hel was a bitch but she wasn't stupid, and she knew better than to insult a Primus in front of her entire command. It wouldn't help her end goal. "Primus, I'd like to speak to you away from the bridge, if possible. Do you have a moment?"

Veena still didn't look at her but gave a short nod. She led the way, and Hel followed. The capo would take charge, though Hel didn't care if one of the pilots did. All they were doing was sitting in space, waiting for a message.

Veena led them to a small meeting room off a hall that

connected to the bridge. The door shut behind them, and Veena turned to face Hel, who remained at the door. "To be honest, I've seen enough of you over the past twenty-four hours to satisfy me for the rest of my life. What could you possibly want right now?"

"I didn't hurt her," Hel said. "I didn't have to. She told me what I wanted to know."

The Primus grew solemn, her voice low. "I could have you thrown in the brig right next to her for disobeying me. You're stretching, assassin, and I promise, you're growing very, very thin. Keep stretching, and I'll finish pulling you apart."

Hel didn't care about her threats. Survival was the name of the game right now. "There's a rescue team coming, and if I were to bet, that is what the message is about. I wasn't sure at first, but they don't want us to leave. We only had one pod like the one we used; they'd catch us if we got into another one. Even the fastest pod is going to come up short against a corvette. So we hold here, let them board, and take off once they do."

Veena opened her mouth to say something, but Hel saw that she understood the wisdom in her plan.

After a few moments, the Primus spoke. "How big is the rescue party?"

"She said it was a handful. Five, maybe ten. Maybe less."

"You believe her?" Veena asked.

Hel nodded. "She's a lunatic. She's not lying because she believes ten of them can defeat us."

The Primus turned her back to Hel and stepped to the opposite wall. She waved her hand across the white paint, and the wall turned transparent. Veena quickly brought up the scouts and the data they were relaying. "We're still not seeing any pursuit from the Myrmidons. I don't understand why, but right now, never mind. Regardless of what the old woman thinks, ten people won't even be able to search the entire ship before we reach a portal." She nodded, and Hel thought it was to herself, acclimating to the new plan. "Why waste effort trying to kill them from afar? Just let them board, then have our Titans hunt them down."

She turned.

"It could work."

Hel crossed her arms over her chest. "It will work. Even if they're cloaked, we don't have to defeat them as they arrive, and once they're on board, we take off. If the Myrmidons give chase, it'll be close, but we have a chance."

"Our scouting parties still don't see anyone coming, and we're using de-cloakers," Veena responded while slowly turning back to look at the wall. Hel didn't know who she was talking to, but it didn't matter. The woman was a genius by any standard humans had created. She would figure this all out in due time.

"I'll leave you to the details, Primus," Hel said.

Veena's head whipped over her shoulder. "Disobey me again and you won't make it home, assassin. However deadly you may think you are, understand I didn't make it through the Academy or rise this high without knowing how to defeat my enemies."

Hel smiled and gave a slight nod. It was a mere acknowledgment that the threat had been accepted. She had other matters to attend to at the moment.

CHAPTER TWENTY-SEVEN

"Do not cry for the dead. They certainly do not cry for you."

–The AllSeer

Thoreaux had Faitrin explain why the Commonwealth's scouts hadn't been able to see them. Only a pilot on this side of the stealth device would have been able to understand it.

"The coding is different. The Commonwealth has kept within its own solar system for so long, the underlying coding has morphed more than any sort of evolution could cause. They can't decode the Terram's stealth technology. I'm not sure if the Terram can de-cloak the Commonwealth, but I'd guess yes, given that the original coding came from them."

Thoreaux understood that. He'd ordered Faitrin's ship

to come to his, and now the two flew close enough to view each other. The old plan had been scrapped, and how often did that happen? In holovids or the tales of old, the plan was always the same, and the heroes stuck to it. Now? With Prometheus in charge? Plans were like water, constantly changing shape and direction.

The AllMother was a peacetime leader. Perhaps this was what happened in war.

Thoreaux looked out the corvette's window at Faitrin's ship. "Can you tell me why all the scouts have disappeared? I'm sure that doesn't have anything to do with coding."

The AI relayed her voice. "Don't ever let anyone call you dumb, Thoreaux. Your intelligence knows no bounds. No, coding didn't make them disappear. I don't have any insight here except..."

Her voice trailed off, but Thoreaux knew the answer. The Commonwealth was inviting them in. If they couldn't find them in the black of space, why not simply allow the group of four under the bright killing lights inside their dreadnought?

"Servia," Thoreaux said, "what do you think? Is it a trap?"

There was a brief pause, then Servia's voice filled his ship. "Yes. It is. They want us to come aboard. It's not a complex plan. Once we're aboard, there's nowhere for us to go. They have Mother and Prometheus, and then they'll have his lieutenants."

Thoreaux gritted his teeth and turned his head forward. These were the odds placed before Prometheus every single time, and every single time he'd pushed forward. Now the odds had finally won out, or it appeared that way unless Thoreaux did something about it.

He nodded to himself. Without those two, what insurrection did they have? Little to nothing.

"Go to the fifth dimension. We'll get on board that dreadnought, and we'll either free them or die trying."

The woman in front of Alistair only looked human. To call her a serpent would be giving her too much credit. She was less than animal and closer to a virus than anything he'd seen before. She wore a person mask, but beneath was something alien.

The Clip remained on Alistair's forehead. He sat where he'd been sitting since arriving. Perhaps at some point they'd let him empty his bladder, but most likely, he'd have to piss himself.

Not in front of this creature, though.

Hel vi Thraxus.

"They're coming for you," she said. The elevator that had brought her to the very bottom of this prison remained behind her, the ramp out in front of it. If he could somehow remove this Clip, he could kill her and rain hell down on this entire ship.

Instead, he could only stare forward, not even able to focus his eyes on one thing. In the background, he could see Obs pacing in a cell, his eyes focused on Alistair.

"The little band of misfits you've joined up with has somehow decided that trying to rescue you and the wench above is in their best interests." She shook her head and stepped farther into the cell. "I don't understand people's willingness to die."

She reached up with her right hand and touched his shoulder, lightly letting her fingertips dance across his muscles. "I'm going to let them come in, Titan. I'm going to welcome them all into my arms, then I'm going to lock them up here with you. I don't know how many are coming, but I know that some are."

The woman stepped onto the platform he sat on and dropped down behind him, then wrapped her legs around his waist. She placed arms around his chest and pulled her breasts against his back. "I know more than the others on this ship. I know a lot of things that might interest you, Titan." The last word was whispered in his ear, her breath hot against his skin. "For instance, I know the Ascendant will contact your wife, or may already have. I know he's going to use her in more ways than one."

The creature's tongue crept out and lightly flicked his earlobe.

Alistair could only blink and breathe as he listened to this thing rattle off lies.

"My hope, Titan, is that we can get you back in time to see it. As you've changed, I do not doubt that the Ascendant plans on changing her as well."

Anger rose in him, anger that he could neither suppress nor loose on this gods-forsaken creature.

He felt her tongue lick his ear in earnest. As if he could ever be sexually interested in something like her.

She remained seated for a few moments, then popped up as quickly as she'd sat down and stood in front of him again. "If I take that Clip off, I know you'll try to kill me. Your eyes are as glazed as the dead right now, but rage rests inside that broad chest of yours, doesn't it? The masters of this ship might not like me torturing your friends in front of you, but I'm not sure I care too much about that. It would make me happy, Titan, to torture them in front of you. That drathe too, and even with the portal and dimensional travel, we have some time to kill. A good bit of it, actually."

She squatted so that they were at eye level. "I'll bring them down to visit soon. We have a lot of rooms in this little prison, and I'll keep them there like refrigerated meat until I'm ready to dissect them in front of you. Yes?" She smiled. "You don't have to answer."

Hel stood and went back into the elevator. The bitch had his Whip hooked to her belt, almost teasing him. As the ramp retracted and the elevator closed, she waved at him, her fingers wiggling as if the two had been flirting. Obs had stopped pacing and was now staring at Hel.

She would die at Alistair's hand.

I swear it on my wife. I'll stand above you as you take your last breath.

Faitrin's eyes were still grayed over as she piloted the corvette.

They were a few kilometers out from the dreadnought, barely any distance. Faitrin could have laid across the space separating her from Thoreaux's ship.

No one in either party had any delusions about what

was happening. They were flying into a trap, one that wasn't even trying to remain hidden.

"Are you nervous?" Servia asked from Faitrin's side.

"How do Subversives feel about lying?" Faitrin responded. "Do you frown on it, or is it acceptable?"

Servia shrugged. "Up to the Subversive, I suppose. Lying to the AllMother doesn't make too much sense, however."

"Well, given that you're not her, I'll go ahead and say I'm not nervous at all. Excited, actually. Never flown into certain death before, and I've been thinking this life thing is overrated anyway."

Faitrin heard Servia chuckle. "You're not half-bad for a traitor."

"That's just until I screw you over," Faitrin shot back.

"True enough."

The ships had begun coasting thousands of kilometers before, slowing down for the eventual landing. Now it was here.

Faitrin's AI spoke to her. *Well, madam, would you like me to announce us, or do you think we should just let them blast us to bits out here?*

Always the pessimist, she responded. *Try to code yourself into a small dock, and do it without letting them know or leaving a signature.*

Perhaps you'd rather I just teleport the two of them out? it asked curtly, then went silent.

Faitrin waited patiently. She didn't know all the technology this dreadnought would have, but she was pretty confident her AI could get them in unnoticed, which might help.

Minutes passed, then the ship started moving, automatically communicating with Thoreaux's AI. *Your wish is my command,* the AI said.

Where's that from? Faitrin asked.

A long time ago in a land far away, the AI responded cryptically.

Faitrin let it drop as they wound their way toward the back at the bottom of the dreadnought. A tiny dock was opening, so small that Faitrin wasn't sure both ships would fit until the AI fed her the dimensions.

Very carefully, her ship set down, then Thoreaux's beside hers. There was barely enough room for everyone to step out into the bay at once.

Nice job, Faitrin told the AI.

'Twas nothing, my dear.

Faitrin liked its accent and turns of phrase. It was a welcome breath of fresh air in an otherwise stale world of AIs. *Were you able to locate the brig?*

Yes. Sending coordinates now. Let us hope your human brain can keep up with them.

It wasn't quite a download, nor an upload. The detail she received was unlike anything a non-pilot could understand, yet they fit into Faitrin's brain as succinctly as a clasp fit on a bracelet.

We're going inside. Do you know what to do? she asked.

Sleep until you return.

Right. Had Faitrin been speaking to a human, she would have rolled her eyes. *Don't let Prometheus catch you sleeping. You may never wake up.*

See you soon, darling, the AI said.

The ramp to the ship descended behind them, and both

women stood and exited. They each held StarBeams as they met the two men at the bottoms of the ramps.

"Here," Relm said, handing a MechPulse to Faitrin while Thoreaux did the same to Servia. "Put the beam away until this overheats, then slap this one on your back until the pulse overheats. Back and forth, back and forth. Got me, broth?"

Faitrin's eyes had cleared of the static-gray. "I prefer to be called 'brothess' if you don't mind."

Relm gave a small grin. "Whatever my brothess wants, my brothess gets."

The group turned to Thoreaux, weapons crossing their chests.

"Ready?" Faitrin asked.

Thoreaux stopped just before they hit the door that would grant entrance into the main ship. "Faitrin, how much can you do with the AI in this dreadnought?"

"Not a whole lot," she responded. "I've got my AI working on some things, and it's best I link with it instead of this. Pilots might be wired differently than the rest of you, but we're still not wired like a full-blown AI. If there's any chance of avoiding tripwires, my AI will do it better than me."

"Fair enough. You're sure about the brig?" he asked.

Faitrin's eyes didn't gray over to reconnect with her ship. "That's one thing it's positive about. Middle of the ship, and tunnels downward. They can't hide the blue-print until they either detect my AI or shut down all

ancillary AIs, which would shut down the whole
enterprise."

Thoreaux nodded and took one last step to the door. It
opened automatically, and he peered at both sides of the
corridor, pulse raised. "All clear."

The crew quietly entered the dreadnought and the door
shut behind them. Faitrin took the lead, with Relm in the
rear. The hallway was wide enough for Thoreaux to walk
on one side with the pulse at eye level while Faitrin did the
same on the other side.

"How far from it are we?" Thoreaux asked.

"It's a four-kilometer walk," Faitrin said without
looking at him.

Thoreaux had put their lives in this pilot's hands. There
was nothing to do but believe her because *he* sure as hell
didn't know where they were headed.

They wound through hallways and reached elevators,
some taking them up, others down, always with Faitrin
slightly in the lead. They saw no one, neither coming nor
going.

They don't care if we're here, Thoreaux thought as
sweat popped out of his forehead and was absorbed by his
SkinSuit. Or if they know, they're going to let us walk right
up to Pro and Mother. They want us to find them.

He said nothing. The people with him were smart
enough to realize the same.

Four kilometers at their pace took a long time—hours
—and not once did a single person, Titan or cleaning crew,
show themselves.

Finally, Faitrin came to a stop. She didn't look at
anyone as she spoke. "They know we're here. The AI

confirmed it almost as soon as we started walking. I didn't say anything for the same reason none of you did. It wasn't necessary. They wanted us to find what we're searching for, and according to the coordinates, they're through those two doors."

Thoreaux had lost any semblance of direction. The doors in front of him were larger than others they'd passed. "Relm, check 'em."

The soldier remained where he was. "Don't need to. They're triple-reinforced. Blasting through won't work, not with what we're carrying."

Thoreaux wasn't worried about that. He just wanted to know that whatever was behind them was what they'd come here for. To be in a trap was one thing, but to be trapped somewhere the target wasn't? That was a different thing altogether. "We won't have to blast through." He looked at the pilot. "You're sure that when I step through there, there's not going to be an ambush. That's the brig?"

"As sure as I am about anything right now," Faitrin said. Her hood had retracted into the SkinSuit, and he watched a drop of sweat roll down the side of her cheek. Her eyes were gray, but after a few seconds, they cleared. "The AI says the room is clear. No one's waiting for us."

Fuck it, Thoreaux thought. They'd come this far, and there wasn't any going back. He stood up, lowered his pulse, and walked toward the doors.

As soon as they sensed him, they opened, sliding into the walls on either side.

Thoreaux stepped into the new room. It was a dome, and pure white light spilled out of a hole in the middle into the room. The other three made their way in behind him, their guns lowered as well. The four formed a line and the doors shut.

There was silence for a long minute. Thoreaux understood what he was looking at, even if he didn't know how to get into the cells. The AllMother and Prometheus were in that hole with Clips on their foreheads.

The voice came from a single spot on the ceiling, though it boomed as if one of the gods floated above. Thoreaux turned his head up as it spoke.

"This is Primus Veena de Ragnimus. There is no way for you to leave this room, and if you attempt to either rescue those you've come for or escape, you will die. You are now prisoners of the Commonwealth, charged as traitors to the Imperial Ascendant as well as your species. Place your weapons on the ground and step ten paces forward, then lie face-down with your arms and legs spread."

Thoreaux had never heard the voice before, though he knew the name. He looked at Servia, both of them still holding their weapons. "They sent the fucking Primus of the whole fleet to get Pro?"

She smirked. "I told you he was the right choice, didn't I?"

"Sort of a ridiculous time for an 'I told you so,' isn't it?"

Servia shrugged, still smirking. "I take 'em where I can get 'em."

Relm looked up. "All broths and brothesses, my name is Relm of Go Frag Yourself. I didn't come here to put my weapons down, and I certainly didn't come here to give you guys a good look at my ass by lying on the ground, so how about this? I'm going to drop down that hole and free the people we came for. Now, Primus Shut The Fuck Up, you can send your Titans in just about that much time, and we'll dance until one side falls. How's that sound?"

Thoreaux raised his eyebrows and looked down the short line at Relm. The soldier shrugged. "How was it?"

Thoreaux nodded as he turned to look at the hole. "Better than I could do." It was certain death, but in life, when was that not the case? No one lived forever, and to be given over to the Commonwealth? To fly back on this ship with a Clip on his forehead? Thoreaux would rather be beheaded. "I'm going to get them out. Keep the bastards off me long enough to do that."

Servia faced the door they'd come in through. "You're too much the brooding type for glory, Thoreaux. However, given the circumstances, I'll give you your chance."

The other three followed her lead and spread out in a semi-circle around the door.

Thoreaux walked toward the edge of the hole, from which white lining shone up at him.

"This is your last warning," the voice said from above. "We'd like to do this with as little death as possible. It's unnecessary."

"No. It's inevitable," he whispered.

The doors behind started to open. Thoreaux looked down and saw the narrow space between the elevator and the wall.

A shot exploded behind him. He stepped off the ledge.

CHAPTER TWENTY-EIGHT

"The difference between my sister and me is that I know our father loved us. She thinks he was incapable of that emotion."

–The AllSeer

The Imperial Ascendant had given Luna twenty-four hours. She would be summoned today.

It had been the second-longest night of her life, right after the one where she'd been told her husband was dead. Sleep had come at the end of the night, but even that had been awful. Another weird dream, this one different from all the rest.

She'd woken up startled and sweating, though she had thrown the sheets and blankets off while sleeping.

Luna shoved the dream from her mind. There was no time to focus on it. She had a decision to make today, and it was beyond clear that no one in this endeavor could be trusted. Luna had considered calling her parents, but in the end, she wasn't naïve enough to think she could spare their lives if things worsened. She understood that not calling them might look suspicious as well, but that was an acceptable risk.

She'd brought almost nothing on her trip here, but the closet had been full of clothes that fit her perfectly. That wasn't surprising, though Luna found herself hating them as she put them on. They fit too well, as if an AI knew every part of her body. While logically she knew that was true, it didn't mean she wanted to wear the clothing it had picked for her.

She dressed and thought about Alistair. The thoughts that had plagued her the entire previous night refused to stop. No one could be trusted; that was clear.

Perhaps not even Alistair.

That idea nauseated her. How could her husband not be trusted? The man who had laid next to her for so many nights, who she'd made love to countless times? Even he might be an enemy now.

If Alistair is an enemy, then I have no friends, she thought. Yet if what the Ascendant had told and shown her wasn't true, Alistair would have contacted her somehow. He wouldn't have run. Luna didn't know everything about the clandestine world of the Commonwealth bureaucracy, but she knew there were ways to get messages past security.

None of that matters right now, she told herself. *He's alive somewhere, and if he is, what does that mean to you? What do you want to do with that information?*

That was the only thing she felt sure about. The rest of

it was a quagmire of questions pulling her down without a lifeline of answers.

Luna finished dressing and looked at herself in the mirror.

She wanted to say the words aloud, but she knew they would make their way back to the Ascendant's ears, so she thought them instead. *If he's alive, all I care about is seeing him again. If what the Ascendant said is true, I want to look him in the eye as he stabs me. If he's alive, please gods, let me see his face one more time.*

The summons came, and Luna followed a servant. They didn't go the way they had last time; instead, Luna found herself in a fabled room, one that had lasted a thousand years. The Throne Room.

The Ascendant sat on the throne like a king of old might have. It should have been surreal to her, but it wasn't. Somehow knowing that Alistair lived made everything else seem possible.

She knew the etiquette expected and knelt on both knees when she reached the throne.

The Ascendant spoke first. "One People. One Purpose."

"One People. One Purpose," she repeated as she looked at the stone floor beneath her.

"Rise, Daughter of the Commonwealth," the Ascendant said. Luna did as she was told and finally met the man's eyes. "Do you have an answer? Will you help us stop the coming massacre?"

In the end, Luna didn't have a choice. All the thinking, the tossing and turning, had been for nothing. She would do anything to see Alistair again. Burn down a universe. Join people who'd tried to kill her husband. It didn't matter. Seeing his face again mattered, if only one more time.

"It would be my honor to serve the Commonwealth in any way I'm needed," Luna told him.

The Ascendant stood. "I knew you would make the correct choice. You've made me, your parents, and the entire Commonwealth proud today. Come, there is much to do."

About that, the Ascendant was right. What he'd failed to mention, and what Luna would wonder about over the coming months, was how much of her soul she was willing to sell for Alistair.

The answer, it turned out, was almost all of it.

CHAPTER TWENTY-NINE

"Once you see him, you will realize that no force in this universe can stop him."

–The AllMother

Thoreaux fell with not much hope. He had two things going for him, neither strong. The first was a team above him that would try to kill whatever warriors the Commonwealth sent. The second was his SkinSuit's tech.

If either of those failed, he wouldn't be long for this universe. Even if neither of them did, he probably still wouldn't last long.

The SkinSuit covering his hands and knees emitted a polymer as he fell. He slapped his right hand and both knees against the side of the elevator, then slammed back against the wall. If this didn't work, he'd have to fucking try to crawl down like a spider.

Thoreaux raised the pulse to the glass elevator. It was the only clearance the machine would recognize. He fired the weapon with only his left hand, and it jammed his shoulder against the wall. A few things happened simultaneously next, and somehow Thoreaux managed to process them all at once.

If he hadn't, he surely would have died right then.

The impact of the pulse with his left shoulder damaged something, causing him to scream. At the same time, the glass in front of him overheated to the point of melting and blasted inward. His suit worked as it should, automatically adjusting the outside temperature to keep any burns from occurring, but he lost his grip on the elevator.

He fell as pain radiated over the left side of his torso. He desperately stretched forward, hoping to grab something. The pulse slammed onto the elevator's floor, and his right hand sought for purchase while the rest of him slipped through the space between the elevator and wall.

His right hand hit the floor, and the polymer just barely stopped him.

Thoreaux looked down. His body was dangling beneath the elevator. He couldn't tell how long a drop it was, but he knew he didn't want to make it. Above him, the sounds of pulse blasts echoed off the walls, which was a good thing. When those stopped, he would die.

Hurry, he thought. He pulled himself up, the damage in his shoulder crying out as he did. He managed to lift his body into the elevator and wanted to lie down. His chest was heaving from the effort, and the suit wasn't numbing his shoulder. *Hurry*, he told himself again.

He climbed to his feet. There were glowing pieces of

glass at the edge of the elevator, and he hoped to the gods the glass had Cut-Off tech.

He stepped over the red-hot pieces and waved his hand in front of the glass that was still standing. It took a second, but a digital panel appeared in front of him. He didn't think the thing was operating at full capacity, but it appeared to have sealed itself off from the damage. Finally, some luck.

The panel showed that three of the cells were occupied, one halfway down and two at the bottom. Right now, Thoreaux needed Prometheus. In truth, he didn't want the AllMother involved, not until things were settled above. He hit the button for the bottom cell, and after a few awful moments of nothing, the machine started moving.

He still heard firing above, though it was more sporadic.

"Hurry, godsdammit," he cursed at the elevator.

It passed the middle cell, and Thoreaux had to keep from lunging out at what he saw and firing his weapon until the transparent walls melted. The AllMother sat inside, a Clip hovering in front of her forehead. She stared straight ahead as if she were looking through him.

Thoreaux raised his hand and touched the glass. "I'm coming."

The elevator passed her. Pro was at the bottom. He had no idea who was in the third cell.

The next few seconds felt like hours. The pain in his shoulders was amplifying, and as the elevator slowed to a stop, he raised the pulse.

He blinked, seeing someone he didn't recognize.

"Let me help you with that, darling."

The glass in front of him disappeared, as did the cell's barrier. Thoreaux paused no more, firing the pulse.

The person in front of him moved like a ghost, hardly any form to her. A Whip flashed in front of his eyes and suddenly his pulse was cut in half, the front part of the barrel on the ground and smoke filtering up from the section still in his hand. Thoreaux's instincts guided him because if his mind had, he would've been halved like his weapon.

He dove forward and slid across the deck, feeling the heat of the Whip graze by his head. Pro was in front of him, Clipped just like the AllMother. Thoreaux flipped onto his back and fired the pulse. A scattershot of plasma splattered out, but the woman had anticipated that, so she'd turned sideways and skated near the cell walls to avoid it. Thoreaux shoved back with his heels, propelling himself toward the ledge Pro sat on. His leader sat unmoving, staring forward as if no one was around him.

Thoreaux's back hit the ledge and he tried to stand, raising the sawed-off pulse as he did, but he was too slow. The Whip was a blade now, and the woman thrust it forward. He felt the laser burn through his already savaged shoulder, tendon, bone, and muscle giving way to the intense heat. The laser exited the other side and burned into the ledge. He gasped, almost unable to take in air. He looked up at the creature, the thing that moved without shape, a formless nightmare.

She smiled down at him from her standing position.

"*Salve*," she said formally. She turned to look forward. "I'm going to hurt him now. Badly. And if your compatriots are still alive above us, we'll take our time tearing them apart, yes?"

Thoreaux turned his head to the left and up, desperately struggling to get a look at Pro, hoping somehow the man might be able to save him. Prometheus just stared forward. The Clip had him locked.

The woman looked back down at Thoreaux. "Ready for the real pain?"

To the gods with it all, he thought, knowing that what he did next was the last thing he would ever do.

He was slower than the creature above him, but his right hand shocked her with its speed for a moment as it moved to the StarBeam hooked to his belt. Her mouth opened slightly and her right wrist twisted a bit, causing the nerve-endings to burn in his shoulder. Thoreaux whipped up the smaller weapon, instinct guiding him again because there wasn't a chance in all the universe he could aim the damn thing.

He fired it at Pro's head.

Thoreaux expected to see blood and bone spray backward and a body slump to the deck.

Instead, the Clip fell into Pro's lap in two pieces, and the man's eyes cleared of the vacant stare.

A god arrived in the room, and his foot launched forward with the power of an exploding star. It connected with the woman's chest, and she rose into the air like a loose sheet of paper caught in a hard wind. Her hand pulled free of the Whip, and it died as the connection to her biometrics fell away and dropped to the deck, useless. Thoreaux let go of the beam and absently touched his shoulder as he watched the violence unfold in front of him.

DAVID BEERS & MICHAEL ANDERLE

Pro had moved on top of the ghost. She was frantically trying to create space between them, her feet pushing against the deck, her hands straining upward, but the god above her had no mercy. His left hand held her shirt while his right thrust down over and over. Blood smacked the deck beneath her, and the hand came down again. More blood splattered the wall as it pulled back. Again it was thrown forward.

"Yield," the woman cried. "Yield!"

The god's back swelled hugely as he bent over the woman, looking like it might fill the entire cell. Breath surged in and out of him, then his hand rose once more, the fist like a massive hammer. After a moment, he threw her into the elevator like trash.

Prometheus clenched both hands into fists. His chest heaved. Blood covered his right hand and lay across his chest and face like war paint. Thoreaux looked behind him at the woman. Her face was a battered mess, unrecognizable as the person who had stood over him smiling moments before. She groaned and gasped for air. Thoreaux thought he saw teeth scattered around Prometheus' feet.

"You okay?"

Thoreaux looked at his shoulder. There was no blood. The Whip had seared the flesh. Thoreaux nodded. "I'm okay." He nodded at the ceiling. "They're not, though. If they're still alive."

Prometheus, still looking god-like to Thoreaux, tilted his head up. The sounds of pulses and beams echoed from on high. "Let's go." He offered his hand to Thoreaux, who grabbed on with his right hand and was slowly lifted off

274

the deck. The pain in his arm screamed at him to stop the ridiculous movement, and Thoreaux groaned but managed to stay on his feet.

"Steady," Prometheus told him. "Stay behind me. Use the beam."

Thoreaux bent over and picked up the discarded Star-Beam. "What are we doing about her?"

"I'll take care of that." Prometheus moved into the elevator, then reached down and grabbed something off her belt. As he rose, red lasers unfurled from the handle of the Whip.

A giant, holding his weapon.

Maybe, Thoreaux thought. *Maybe with him, there's a chance.*

Thoreaux followed him into the elevator. Prometheus pulled up the interface panel and spun it. Obs' cell opened and the drathe jumped in, first sniffing his master, then checking on Thoreaux.

"Be ready, Obs," the god said without looking around.

As they rose past the floors, the sounds of battle grew louder. Thoreaux looked at Prometheus, who stared forward, his Whip almost touching the deck. The woman still lay on the floor between them, groaning.

They passed the AllMother, but Prometheus didn't look at her. He just said, "We'll come back."

When they were nearly at the top, Prometheus grabbed the battered woman by the hair with his free hand. She cried out, but there was no forgiveness on his face. He didn't even look at her. It was like she was nothing more than dead meat to him. "Remember, stay back and cover me. Obs, kill everything that moves and is not one of us."

He still didn't look at Thoreaux. He was a man possessed.

The top of the elevator crossed the plane of vision and Prometheus didn't shrink or duck. He didn't try to hide.

And then they were among their brethren. Plasma and lasers filled the room, but the other three had been smart about what they'd done. They were plastered against the walls of the round room in locations that gave them a shot at anyone coming through the door. An enemy had to be in the room to have a shot at one of them.

Gas poured out of vents above them, and smoke from overheated weapons and scorched metal filled the room. Thoreaux could only assume the gas was poisonous, though it was useless against the SkinSuits. "You want mine?"

Prometheus was already moving. He leaped from the elevator, Whip in one hand, screaming woman in the other. Smoke and gas vapors flowed around him, hiding him from those who wished him harm. Thoreaux couldn't see through the door from this vantage point since there was too much smoke and gas in the way. His suit's hood rolled across his head, and he rushed to the wall as fast as he could without being able to move one arm.

Servia was there, her MechPulse discarded in front of her and the StarBeam in her hand. "Is that him?"

Thoreaux nodded.

"It doesn't look like him," she said breathlessly.

"It's something else wearing his body."

Ares could hardly believe his eyes. Even with the MechSuit on and the HUD active, he was having a hard time believing what was unfolding in front of him. He stood at the back of the brig's entrance. Dead Titans lay in front of him, but not one fucking Subversive. They were holding the room with three people, and the gas from above was doing as much good as his Titans from outside. They couldn't get through the doors without being splattered with plasma or drilled by lasers.

Then the elevator rose, and Ares thought he must be dreaming. He knew the bitch was waiting down there with her Whip. It had to be her coming up, right? That had to be it.

He signaled his HUD to scan and identify. A war was still going on in front of him, but that elevator was all that mattered because if Alistair was coming up, this stand-off wouldn't be an impasse much longer.

Cannot identify scrolled across his vision, so it wasn't the bitch with her Whip.

Ares didn't need any more confirmation because he saw Alistair step out of the elevator and the red lasers that had once been a Titan named Odin's Whip. This man was much bigger, his shoulders almost as broad as if he wore a MechSuit. He was dragging the bitch by her hair, and she was screaming and hitting him uselessly.

Ares understood what that meant. He dropped his pulse to the deck and grabbed his Whip. "Any man who does not go into that room and kill Alistair Kane right now will be killed by me. *GO!*"

The soldiers heard his order and moved, none daring to challenge their Primus. They rushed into the room, and many were hit in the head immediately. They fell to the ground, their MechSuits failing under the close range of the enemy's weapons. Some of his men died and others lay immobilized, yet some broke through.

Massive metal beasts heading for one man carrying a woman.

Ares waited and watched, knowing that to go in now was too dangerous.

Alistair threw the woman face-first at the Titans, and she screamed as she flew through the air. Ares didn't care if they cut her down, but someone batted her away with a metal arm.

She collided with a wall and was silent.

The battle started in earnest. The Titans fell on the Subversives' hero while being slammed with long-range weapons. The damn beast was darting back and forth, tripping people and ripping flesh when he saw it.

Ares watched the dance as Alistair took on four at once. He moved faster than Ares had ever seen him do. It was like he'd grown into his body, when he'd only been an adolescent earlier, trying to figure out how to work with his new gifts. No longer.

He jumped and twirled, his Whip slicing and reacting with deadly speed. Two Titans fell at his feet, one with a hole through his heart and the other missing his head. The still-helmeted head rolled through the door toward Ares, and he stepped over it as he moved closer to the entry. More of his Titans were flowing through now, some trying to take out the backup against the walls. His people were being gunned down but making progress, each body falling a bit farther in than the last.

Alistair saw this and started cutting his way toward the Subversives. Titans fell in his wake, and a tunnel opened behind him as he pushed forward. His kicks demonstrated the power of a MechSuit, bending metal and denting the skulls beneath it.

His back was to Ares now. He had smartly not gotten in the way of his backup but had left them space to mow down the Titans.

It was time. Ares shortened his Whip and took off, his legs pumping. He launched past Titans, his training during the past several months apparent. The Subversives fired from their spots on the wall, but Ares focused on the only man that mattered.

He reached Alistair, and the man's back was still to him as the former Titan swung his Whip, slicing through a MechSuit and the intestines beneath. Ares' Whip lengthened as he propelled it forward, aiming for his mentor's head in a decapitation blow to end this lunacy with one strike.

The dark red Whip hit Alistair's neck, slicing through his skin and bone and sending his head to the floor.

Ares blinked, not understanding.

Alistair turned and kicked out. His foot connected with Ares' chest and threw him to the deck. Alistair had ducked as if he knew the blow was coming. He hadn't lost his head; he'd evaded the killing strike.

Now Ares was on his damn back with Alistair stalking forward. The Titans surrounding the two of them were losing their organization. The backups' fire wasn't slowing because none had been reached or hurt yet, and the monstrosity coming toward Ares was cutting his men down as if they were cornstalks. Ares shoved with one foot, which gave him two meters of space, and then flip-kicked up onto his feet. Someone swung at Alistair from the side, and again he seemed to anticipate the strike. He ducked and spun, and his Whip sliced through the would-be hero. Alistair didn't slow but kept moving forward.

Ares took his form.

Alistair came on, no form taken but fighting in a way Ares had never seen.

The two Whips slammed into one another in the air, Ares meeting Alistair's red eyes as they collided. Ares dropped and tried to sweep Alistair's legs, but the man stepped over them as if he were moving in slow motion. Ares tried to get to his feet in time, but he felt Alistair's knee strike his helmet, and the HUD flickered for a moment and then went out. Ares' head was turned to the side and he had his knees on the deck, with his left hand holding him up. Alistair stood over him, the tip of his Whip ten centimeters from Ares' temple. "Tell them to stand down. All of them."

Ares said nothing, then he heard the first sizzle of laser on metal.

"I'll kill you first, then I'll kill the rest. You know it's true."

Thoughts sped through Ares' mind. Few things mattered to the young Primus, mostly his honor and capturing the man burning a hole through his MechSuit. He'd lose his honor by stepping down, but he could do nothing to stop Alistair from dying. He could regain his honor. He could not regain his life. "Stand down," he said into the comm. "Everyone stand down."

A Titan was in motion behind Alistair, his Whip moving to slice him in half at the waist. As if he had extrasensory perception, he dropped and swung his Whip. The man's lower legs were chopped in two. He fell, screaming inside his helmet. Alistair was back at Ares' head, and he wrapped the Whip around his throat this time. "Drop your weapon and slowly stand up."

Ares looked at his Whip. Giving that up would be like giving up his right arm.

"Now you understand," Alistair said, obviously following his thoughts. "How many times I've had to give it up, and how many times I've had to get it back. Let's see if you have that kind of wherewithal."

Ares took his hand off the Whip. The lasers retracted.

"Now stand up."

Alistair's Whip remained wrapped around Ares' neck as he carefully stood up.

"Retract the helmet."

Ares did as he was told. The helmet folded into the neck, and he immediately felt Alistair's Whip wrap tighter, singeing his neck. Ares didn't wince but stood staring at his former mentor. The gas from above was starting to clear. Ares had no idea how Alistair had managed to survive with it pouring down.

Alistair's voice boomed around the room. "Every Titan is to put down their weapons, step out of their MechSuit, and get in line. This ship is being commandeered."

The large animal bounded over to Alistair's side.

Ares' eyes widened. Sure, they had lost this little battle, but what was Alistair proposing? "You've lost your mind," he said through clenched teeth.

Even as he said the words, MechSuits were folding down to their shoes. "Maybe I am; only time will tell. Thoreaux! Get the AllMother and bring her Clip!"

"Yes, sir!" one of the Subversives shouted from the wall.

"Servia, once the AllMother is up here, we're heading to the bridge. All these Titans will lead the way. I want everyone to keep their weapons poised on them." He looked at Ares. "Where's the camera?"

"Above." Ares could hardly believe any of this was happening. Moments before, Hel's plan had been working perfectly, and now they were going to force Veena to give up a dreadnought? "You're—"

Alistair cut him off, tilting his head slightly up. "We're coming to the bridge. If any of you, anyone at all, tries to fight back, every single Titan here will die, including their Primus. We have disarmed them all and we're taking their weapons, and there is nothing you can do to stop us."

Alistair met Ares' eyes but spoke to someone behind them both. "Relm, if that bitch I came up here with is still alive, grab her."

"On it, broth." The Subversive jogged across the room and knelt next to Hel. He put his hand on her throat and felt for a pulse. "She's alive!"

The elevator rose to their level and an old woman exited, followed by an injured man. She stopped after a few steps and looked around the room. "Was it necessary to kill so many?"

Alistair rolled his eyes. "I forgot to tell you to muzzle her. Let's go to the bridge."

CHAPTER THIRTY

"I am coming for you, and I am going to win."

— Prometheus

Alistair watched his former protégé walk in front of him, a line of Titans leading them both. He knew some of them by name, most of them by face. He'd worked with quite a few over the years, and many of the ones he'd killed had been friends at one point.

Ares had been silent since leaving the brig.

"How far away are we?" Alistair asked.

"A few more turns," Ares said. The Whip was still wrapped around his neck, and Alistair had no plans to take it off. He wanted to put Faitrin in the front of the group, but he didn't want to have anyone's back to one of these Titans. Even without their MechSuits, they were dangerous.

Obs was patrolling the line, growling from time to time.

"What is your plan?" Ares asked. "Let's say Veena gives us the ship. What will happen after that? Do you think you're going to be able to get back to Earth with this dreadnought?"

"I'm sorry. Did you think me asking you a question meant that you could ask me some? Because it didn't." He knew Ares was angry and that the young man was wondering what he'd done to his honor. It was always honor with Ares. His family's, his own. He'd been indoctrinated early in life and had never been able to shake it. He'd given up his honor by surrendering, and Alistair understood the young man well enough to know it burned him worse than any brand could.

He had no words for his old protégé, or none that would be heard. They lived on separate sides of the universe now, neither of them able to understand the other. Alistair doubted Ares understood anything about him anymore, and the young man who'd had so much potential now seemed more like a killer than a human to Alistair.

No, there's good in him, he thought as they walked. He's not like that creature named Hel. There's good in him, he just doesn't know what it is. He doesn't know how to access it.

Maybe that was why Alistair hadn't just killed him. Twice now, he'd had the chance, and he'd passed. The man had yielded, as had the rest of the Titans. Killing them wasn't justified. It would be straight-up murder.

The Titans up ahead slowed and stopped.

"Faitrin!" Alistair shouted to the pilot in the back. "That what we're looking for?"

"Yes, sir," came the response. "Best I can tell, that's the bridge."

"Is it?" he asked the man in front of him.

"Go on in and find out, traitor," Ares responded.

"If you think my kindness will last forever, look at your comrades up there. Think of them without legs and arms and split in half the next time you have something smart to say. Where are the cameras?"

"They're all over," Ares answered. "They see your every move. They hear everything you say. Veena is watching you right now."

"Primus!" Alistair yelled down the corridor. "We are commandeering this ship. Whatever armed forces you have in there with you will be killed. You have no way out. You can lock yourself in the bridge if you want, but you know I will find a way in. More, I'll kill these Titans and let you watch as they die while you sit safely inside. Perhaps to someone who burned a planet to ash that doesn't mean much, but let's see how much bloodletting you can stand, shall we?"

Alistair looked over his shoulder. "Relm, bring the explosives from the MechSuits to the front. Figure out how many we need for that door."

"On it, broth." The soldier passed him, talking to the Titans as he moved to the front of the line. "One of you bastards looks at me the wrong way and I'll blast you to the gods."

Alistair continued talking to his crew. "Servia, get in front of Ares here and put your MechPulse to the head of the man in front of him. When I tell you to, send him to his Maker."

Servia said nothing, only moved with a speed and efficiency that said one more dead Titan meant nothing to her.

"How long to get in, Relm?" he called to the front.

"Going to say ten minutes, bossman."

"Okay, Primus!" Alistair shouted. "In ten minutes, I'm going to be in there one way or another, but during that time, I'm going to kill one of these Titans each minute, just because you're making me wait. We'll start the countdown now."

Veena had sat next to the man as they rocketed to this dreadnought. She'd seen how large and strong he was, yet the Clip had stolen some of his majesty. She hadn't understood how dangerous he was. She wasn't sure she'd ever imagined anyone with his capabilities, but she'd seen him in action in the brig. She had looked on from the camera as this man moved like his body was a Whip, twisting and turning, cutting through anything that got in his way. And when he saw that his brethren might be hurt?

He had turned the entire battle toward them. Titans had chased him and died. And his friends? The ones who had come to rescue him? Every one of them had survived, while Hel had been tossed around like a child's doll.

Now this man and his small group sat outside her bridge, readying the explosives to blow the door. Inside the bridge, Veena had a few soldiers and a few Titans dressed in MechSuits, but what could any of them do to this man? He'd once been named Odin, god of war, and Veena now understood why they'd given him that moniker. He brought death to his enemies, and they fell before him like leaves hitting the grass in front of a huge oak.

Veena looked at the screen in front of her. He stood in the hallway, huge like a planet, demanding she open the door or he would kill the best and brightest warriors the Commonwealth had.

Ares had yielded. Both he and she knew the rules: they could not return to Earth without this man dead or Clipped.

But you didn't allow yourself to die, she thought. *I don't think you're a coward. Do you still think there's a chance to stop him, even after all this?*

"*YOU FUCKIN' BITCH, OPEN THE DOOR!*"

It was Hel, screaming at one of the cameras outside. Her voice was slurred, and her face was a mess of black and blue. She was missing teeth, and her tongue had swelled in her mouth.

"*HE'LL FUCKIN' KILL US ALL!*"

She understood because Kane had beaten her to within an inch of her life. Now she felt fear.

The minute was nearly up. Was Veena going to sit here and watch him kill the Titans, knowing that sooner or later he was going to get in?

Would she be responsible for more death? Trying to hold the bridge was futile.

"Open the doors," she commanded. "I don't want any resistance. Put your weapons down. We will fight him, but not here, and not now."

Veena started to her left. There were ways off this bridge that very few people knew about, certainly no one outside the main doors. She wasn't running from fear; she knew the only way to protect the rest of her fleet was to get the word out about what was happening.

She couldn't do it from the bridge. Truthfully, she should have done it earlier, but she hadn't been able to believe what was happening.

Behind her, Veena heard people moving to protect themselves from whatever the barbarians at the gates might do.

Veena moved silently and slipped out of the bridge through a backdoor.

"They're opening, broth!" Relm shouted from the front of the line.

"Faitrin," Alistair called to the back, "how are you holding?"

"Still seeing nothing, Pro!"

Was it going to be this easy?

But no, that wasn't true. It had not been easy to get here, even if this last part felt like it. All Alistair needed to do was focus on the wooziness inside his head. He'd breathed that gas for far too long, only sheer determination forcing him forward. He'd have to have himself looked at soon, though now wasn't the time.

The doors opened while Relm disabled the explosives hooked up. Servia stepped back from the Titan she'd held the gun to and started walking up and down the line of Titans. "Not a movement from any of you, or I'll kill you all."

The Titans looked straight ahead; Alistair knew they were all feeling the same shame as Ares. This was the most elite group of warriors the Commonwealth had, and they'd been taken down by a handful of people.

"It's open!" Relm called.

"Come, Ares. To the front we go."

Ares moved very carefully since the Whip around his neck would cut his head off at the slightest wrong movement. The two marched to the front of the line. Alistair caught the glances at him, some of hatred, some awe, some just confused. None of this was supposed to happen. Everything had been planned perfectly: fifty Titans versus a group less than ten. What could this little insurrection possibly do?

And yet, Alistair Kane, banished Titan, was walking past them with a Whip wrapped around their Primus' neck like a noose.

Relm stood with his MechPulse pointing at the pilots and the few armored Titans on the bridge. Alistair stopped when he reached the door and peered into the bridge he now owned. He wasn't sure how that was possible either, but here it was in front of him. He tilted his head toward Relm. "All of them on their knees facing the far wall. Find Clips and put them on 'em—I know the ship has plenty. I imagine the Fleet Primus has fled and is warning the rest of the fleet. I want you to send Servia after her. Thoreaux needs medical attention. He'll fight it, but get it to him. And get Faitrin up here as quickly as possible."

"On it." Relm motioned to Hel. "What do you want me to do about her?"

Alistair cast a glance her way. He'd heard her shrieking.

DAVID BEERS & MICHAEL ANDERLE

Right now she was in survival mode, but he knew the evil that lurked beneath. He wouldn't be fooled again. "Clip her. If she gives you the slightest bit of resistance, kill her."

"Don't want me to kill her now?" Relm pointed the pulse at her. "I don't see any reason to keep her around."

Alistair thought back to when the man in front of him had tried to have him killed. They'd cornered him on the edge of a building, where his only choice was to jump or die at their hands. Sure, they might have captured him, but in the end, he would have been murdered.

Alistair shook his head. "No. Clip her."

Relm shrugged. "We're going to need to figure out what to do with all these POWs."

It was a new thought—what to do when you were winning. But Alistair knew they weren't at that point yet. Not by a long shot.

He walked into the bridge, Ares still in front of him. "Where is your Primus?"

He studied the eyes carefully and saw someone glance to his right. Servia rushed that way, saying nothing.

"There are a few things I need immediately," Alistair instructed as the captured soldiers were forced to their knees near the back wall. "We brought fifteen Titans with us, plus the few that are in this room. I need Clips for all of you. Doubt my desire to kill, and you can ask where the rest of the Titans who came for me are. Next, I need a comm connected to the rest of the dreadnought." Faitrin stepped up next to him, and he nodded at her. "As far as any of you are concerned, this woman next to me is the new Primus of this ship. You'll do what she says, or you'll end up frozen in space for eternity." Looking at

Faitrin, he said, "Get us heading toward the nearest portal."

She didn't question him, and neither did anyone else.

Faitrin stepped to the nearest pilot, her eyes graying over as she did.

That part was done. Now he had to speak to the rest of the ship. A Titan was delivering Clips to Relm, his helmet retracted into his neck. Thoreaux was carrying his weight for the moment, though his shoulder would need attention soon. Alistair appreciated what he was forcing his body to do right now. They needed every hand they had.

A pilot brought him a small comm that fit in his ear. He took it with his left hand but didn't place it in immediately. He let the Whip fall away from Ares' neck. "Turn around."

His former protégé did as he was told, but what Alistair saw on his face didn't surprise him. Rage. It surpassed anything else Ares might be feeling. Rage about what had just happened, about being marched through a dread-nought for everyone to see that he'd been beaten.

You left me no choice, Alistair thought. *It was either that or die, but you don't see that do you?*

"Relm is going to Clip you," he said instead. "Go over against the wall and take your place."

"Give me a soldier's death, rather than this farce where you try to look like you're better than us. I've seen you kill, Odin." He spat the last word.

"Against the wall, Ares. I'm not going to kill you here, but if you don't listen, I will *hurt* you."

Ares stared at him for a second longer, then did as ordered. He went to the wall and knelt. Alistair let the Whip retract, then put the comm in his ear. He looked at the pilot standing a meter or so away. "Is it connected to the entire ship?"

The pilot nodded. She was frightened of the man Alistair had become, a giant with red eyes.

"I want all the ships in this fleet to hear me, as well as anyone who might be listening in. Send it to the planet you tried to capture as well. I want you to send this as a message back to the Commonwealth, too. Can you do all that?"

She nodded again, though she didn't speak. Her eyes went gray for a few seconds as she connected with the ship's systems. After a moment, her eyes cleared, and she nodded once more.

She seemed too scared to speak.

He turned away from her, knowing that his voice would be heard by the Imperial Ascendant, every person in the First Fleet, and hopefully, by the Myrmidons as well. Maybe, and most importantly, by the rest of the AllMother's children. He glanced at her, standing in the corner. Her eyes were on his, and she nodded.

"My name is Alistair Kane, and I have taken control of the Commonwealth's dreadnought. This message is to anyone who wants to challenge the AllMother or her Insurrection. I am coming for you, and I am going to win."

AUTHOR NOTES - DAVID BEERS
FEBRUARY 26, 2021

It's a tough balance for me, writing a book with soul and having enough action so that the reader doesn't simply drown themselves in tears of boredom. It's a tough balance for me to create characters that you care enough whether they actually live or die. To care about them, you must know about them, but much of what you learn isn't in the moments where Prometheus cuts someone down. Those are the moments in which everything in the past culminates to make a break or character.

I think it's a lot like life. Sure, books have a lot more of these make or break moments. I haven't been in any laser fights recently. Yet, we do have those moments, where terrible—or great—things happen to us, and how we react wasn't made in that moment, but in all the moments before.

Prometheus, or Alistair if you like, continually hits high moments—but life is always there to show him they aren't forever.

The thing I admire about him—nay, the thing I love—is

that he doesn't listen to life. His own heart and mind directs him. The good times may not last forever, but that doesn't mean he has to let the truly bad ones do so either.

Prometheus' story is nine books long, and this is only book two. Come along to the third with me. I can only promise the highs get higher, and the lows get lower, plus a little soul and a lot of action.

-db,
Atlanta, GA, 2021

Thank you for reading both the story and all the way to the back for these author notes, as well!

I find it interesting (and refreshing) to read David's author notes about 'How we react in the moment was built on how we chose to react in the past.'

Ok, that's my version of what he said, but I think I got the gist of his comment.

No character is without form and void as an author. While I might not be able to answer a simple question sometimes about a character, I have a gut feel for a character how they will react in the larger picture.

Perhaps that certainty has been built on the subconscious connection I've made between the character in question and a real individual I've known (or a character I'm aware of in a movie, for instance.)

So, ask me, "does Mark like sloppy joe sandwiches?" and I might have to think about it. However, ask me, "will Mark run towards a bomb going off a block over, or run?" and I'll probably have a faster answer.

Because I'll answer from my gut. If I don't know the answer, then (one can argue) I haven't spent enough time learning this character. Or perhaps the question and answer isn't one I've ever answered for myself, so I don't think about it for characters, either.

We want you to feel like you are amongst the characters in our stories. Living their situation mere feet away, perhaps ducking the laser beams to get a better view of the action.

Perhaps when you pull back, you realize your hair has been singed with a stray shot.

Now THAT is a level of verisimilitude I'd like to convey!

Along with that, what will make sure you enjoy Prometheus and these stories is feeling the emotions of the efforts they go through.

While you might not smell the burnt hair, perhaps you will wake up the next morning thinking back to the agony of betrayal or the joy of success when those who do bad things…

Have bad things done to them in return.

Ad Aeternitatem,

Michael Anderle

Las Vegas, Nv… and Henderson.

Ok, really I'm in Henderson, Nevada but how many people know where Henderson is?

(Minutes away from Las Vegas.)

Nemesis

She's coming and no one can stop her...

An alien Queen, Morena, was removed from power and forced into exile. Doomed to roam space forever, with no hope of return.

Until a random party brings a man named Michael to her crashed ship. For the first time in millennia, Morena sees her salvation. First, in Michael … and then Earth. The perfect place to repopulate her species. And those already here? **They can bow or die.**

As Morena begins her conquest, can Michael warn the world before it's too late? Can anyone stop the most powerful force the world has ever seen?

Earth's final Nemesis has arrived.

Don't miss this pulse-pounding science fiction series! If you love thought provoking thrill-rides, grab this book today!

The Singularity

One thousand years in the future, humans no longer rule...

In the early twenty-first century, humanity marveled at its greatest creation: Artificial Intelligence. They never foresaw the consequences of such a creation, though...

Now, in a world where humans must meet specifications to continue living, a man named Caesar emerges. Different, both in thought and talent, Caesar somehow slipped through the genetic net meant to catch those like him.

Eyes are falling on Caesar now, though, and he can no longer hide. The Artificial Intelligence wants him dead, but others want him to lead their revolution...

Can one man stand against humanity's greatest creation? A don't-miss epic science fiction novel that pits one man fighting for the future of all people!

Red Rain

What would you do if you couldn't stop killing?

John Hilt lives The American Dream. His corner office looks out on Dallas's beautiful skyline. His amazing wife and children love him. His father and sister adore him. John has it all.

Except every few years, when Harry shows back up. Harry wants John to kill people. Harry wants to watch the world burn.

Murderous thoughts take hold of John, and as flames ignite across his life, the sky doesn't send cool rain water, but blood to feed their hunger.

If you love taut, psychological thrillers, grab Red Rain today and prepare to sleep with the lights on!

The Devil's Dream

He'll raise the dead, at all costs...

Perhaps the smartest man to ever live, Matthew Brand changed the world by twenty-five years old. In his mid-thirties, he still shaped the world as he wanted, until cops gunned down his son on the street.

Brand's life changed then. He forgot about bettering Earth and started trying to resurrect his son.

Eventually, Brand's mind overpowered even death's mysteries; he discovered how to bring back the dead--he only needed living bodies to make his son's life possible again. Why not use the bodies of those who killed his son? In the largest manhunt the FBI's ever experienced, how do they stop a man who can calculate all the odds and stack them in his favor?

https://twitter.com/MichaelAnderle

https://www.instagram.com/lmbpn_publishing/

https://www.bookbub.com/authors/michael-anderle